She trembled despite her resolve. "I'm sure your idea of long term and my idea of long term are totally different."

Kenyon stepped closer. He smelled like silk, gold, and diamonds all rolled into one.

"Let's find out," he whispered near her ear. "I know you're attracted to me."

Marti turned to him then, eyes wide with surprise.

"From the second we met, I could see it in your face." He stroked her bottom lip with the pad of his thumb. "Tell me, what do you see in my face?"

She had always been able to tell when a man was attracted to her, but the look in Kenyon's eyes said much more. It said that he wanted to possess her and that any refusal she gave would be challenged. It said that as a man accustomed to getting his way, he wouldn't stop until she was naked and opening herself to his desires.

"You're wrong, Kenyon," she said, thinking of his scandalous past. "I don't find you attractive at all, and the last thing I intend to do is become number who-knows-what on your list of conquests."

He combed a hand through his long waves of hair. "Are you sure that's what I had in mind?"

"Let me ask you a question. How many serious relationships have you had?"

He stepped back. "It depends on what you mean by serious."

Marti squared her shoulders. "Have you ever had a relationship that wasn't based on sex? In other words, have you ever loved someone?"

It didn't take a rocket scientist to tell Marti that the reason she was asking that question was that she was starting to feel something beyond mere infatuation for the wealthy and handsome man. She was treading into dangerous territory now. Her heart was at stake . . .

BOOK YOUR PLACE ON OUR WEBSITE AND MAKE THE ARABESQUE ROMANCE CONNECTION!

We've created a customized website just for our very special Arabesque readers, where you can get the inside scoop on everything that's going on with Arabesque romance novels.

When you come online, you'll have the exciting opportunity to:

- View covers of upcoming books

- Learn about our future publishing schedule (listed by publication month and author)

- Find out when your favorite authors will be visiting a city near you

- Search for and order backlist books

- Check out author bios and background information

- Send e-mail to your favorite authors

- Join us in weekly chats with authors, readers and other guests

- Get writing guidelines

- AND MUCH MORE!

Visit our website at
http://www.arabesquebooks.com

TRUE DEVOTION

Kim Louise

BET Publications, LLC
http://www.bet.com
http://www.arabesquebooks.com

ARABESQUE BOOKS are published by

BET Publications, LLC
c/o BET BOOKS
One BET Plaza
1900 W Place NE
Washington, DC 20018-1211

All Kensington Titles, Imprints, and Distributed Lines are available at special quantity discounts for bulk purchases for sales promotion, premiums, fund-raising, and educational or institutional use. Special book excerpts or customized printings can also be created to fit specific needs. For details, write or phone the office of the Kensington special sales manager: Kensington Publishing Corp., 850 Third Avenue, New York, NY 10022, attn: Special Sales Department, Phone: 1-800-221-2647.

BET Books is a trademark of Black Entertainment Television, Inc. ARABESQUE, the ARABESQUE logo and the BET BOOKS logo are trademarks and registered trademarks.

First Printing: December 2002
10 9 8 7 6 5 4 3 2 1

Printed in the United States of America

ACKNOWLEDGMENTS

This book would not have been possible without Brenda Woodbury, who suggested I write a book about each one of the Allgood sisters; Michael Wilson—a gifted painter and friend; Michael and Julie Cook, who shared the story of their oldest daughter's birth with me; my critique group—Pam, Patti, Marie, and Elaine, who encourage me on a weekly basis; Ms. "R" who shared her wonderful "kiss" story on an on-line forum; and all those readers, including Word Diva, who never stopped asking, "What happened to Jacq and Davis?"

I owe you.

For the fans

Prologue

She looked to be about fifty years old, although he knew her to be much younger. Victoria Willis stepped off the number 35 bus as she had for the last twenty years. Today she carried full and bulky brown paper bags.

The three-quarter brownstone loomed four blocks away. Her steps toward it came down weighty and tired. The gray hushpuppies she wore hit the sidewalk like muffled yells.

Most signs of the day's rain had dried, leaving only small damp rings around flower basins and sewers. The faint smell of clouds heavy with moisture made him breathe harder. He walked quietly, keeping time with the woman's march home.

Her struggle to unlock the front door tempted him to rush to her side. As the contents of one bag tumbled down the stairs, he dashed out of the shadows and caught the other sack before it fell to the cold concrete.

"Thank you," she said, picking up fresh celery, tomatoes, and a bag of apples.

He smiled, unable to speak, the earnestness in her eyes rendering him temporarily mute. *What had her life been like?* he wondered. She was a cashier at Michigan Community College. She'd worked there since her son was born twenty-two years ago. On her feet all day. He hoped she would treat herself to a long foot massage.

"Have a nice day," he finally managed.

"You too," she said, going inside.

He was stepping into a limousine one block away when he heard her scream.

One

"One hundred thousand dollars!"

Bursting with news, Kathryn Runningbear sat across from her friend Marti Allgood. "Can you believe it?"

"Not for a minute. Why would anyone want to give me that kind of money?"

Kathryn stirred her hot chocolate. The white swirl of whipped cream disappeared into the brown pool.

There weren't many patrons in the café area of the bookstore, but those who were stared at Marti as if they were ready to call security.

"First of all, calm down. Artists are commissioned to do portraits all the time."

Marti pushed her plate of coffee cake away. "Kathryn, you know I'm not an artist!"

"Oh really? That painting you brought to my gallery says otherwise."

"That was a favor."

"No, darling, that was fate. Mr. Williams, *Kenyon* Williams mind you, took one look at it and bought it immediately."

"You *sold* my painting?" Marti's stomach churned in hard anguish.

"Why are you so upset? He paid ten thousand dollars for it. Cash." Kathryn took an envelope out of her purse and handed it to Marti. "Normally, there's a gallery fee of sixty percent, but since you're a friend . . ."

Marti stared into the envelope. The dark smoky aroma of fresh roasted coffee beans mingled with a whisper of vanilla and new bills. "What type of person carries around this kind of money?"

"The wealthy type."

"I want my painting back, Kathryn, and I'm not doing any portrait." Her heart was pounding now. The soft glow of the orange-red acrylic paints she'd used swirled into focus. When her mother passed away fifteen years ago, grief had sent her groping for answers, solace, and her brushes. Within days, the culmination of her feelings came to life in an abstract portrait she called "Mother's Love." The thought of her intimate feelings belonging to a stranger made her dizzy and nauseous.

"Marti, it's me, remember? We went to art school together. I was with you when you cried at Brenda's opening last year."

"I cried because her work is beautiful."

"I know. And you also cried because you wished it was you."

Marti looked away.

"God has given you a wonderful talent. Why on earth won't you use it?"

Anger and fear twisted together inside Marti's chest. A montage of memories flooded her mind like errant thoughts in spectacular Technicolor. Tarp on her apartment floor splattered with blue, red, and yellow. Collages of newspaper clippings, magazine cutouts, and construction paper. Brown and green mudlike debris clumped under her fingernails from spinning clay pots. No. She would not go through it again. "Because, Kathryn," she said, turning back, "I can't control it."

Kathryn was thoughtful. They'd been friends for over ten years. Whenever Marti was in a relationship that wasn't working out, she would express her sadness and her pain through her art. For Marti, intense feelings caused intense creativity. When she was in that zone, her work was brilliant.

"I can't just conjure up the muse. It doesn't work that way for me. I'm *not* an artist, Kathryn. I'm just someone who takes her frustrations out on canvas and clay."

"All right." Kathryn said. "But *you* tell him. You know I have a hard time saying no to men, and he seems like the type that's used to getting his way."

Kathryn drained her cup. "I wish you'd reconsider, Marti. With one hundred thousand dollars, you could quit your job, rent a studio, buy supplies, and be ready for a show in a few months."

"Are you deaf? I said no! Now do you have a number for the guy?"

"No. And I'm sure his number is unlisted. You might have to go to his mansion and ask for it back."

The corner of Marti's mouth twisted with exasperation. "Of all the . . . Do you at least have an address?"

"Don't you know who Kenyon Williams is?"

"Should I?"

"His family owns Williams Brothers."

"The suit company?"

"The suit company."

Marti sat back against the wooden chair, memories of college and concerts flooding her mind. "I remember back in the day, me and my girlfriends wouldn't even look at a brother unless he was wearing a Williams Brothers suit."

"And the ultimate combination was Williams Brothers suit and Stacey Adams shoes."

The two women laughed.

"I heard that their profits took a nosedive when hip-hop fashion took over," Kathryn said.

"Well, they must not be doing too badly if they've got a hundred thousand dollars to just give away. What did you tell him, that I was starving?"

"Of course not. I told him the truth. That you are gifted and with the right support, you would be the hottest brushstroke since Basquiat. When he asked how much support, I threw out one hundred thousand dollars. I got a check by messenger first thing the next morning."

Kathryn reached inside her purse again and retrieved the check. Marti stared in awe at her handwritten name adjacent to a boatload of zeros. She took the check and stuffed it into her pocket. "I'll return this, too."

Marti lifted her drink. A faint heat from the rising steam warmed her lips. The dry flutter of pages turning mixed with the low murmur of voices as if they were in a library and not a bookstore.

"Suit yourself," Kathryn said. "But I don't think he's going to like it."

Marti finished her tea and planted the cup on the table. Like it or not, she would get her painting back.

Two

Marti climbed down the ladder and stepped back. "Fabric Factory" blazed like a brilliant blue flare on the front of the building. She collected her paints, brushes, and ladder and headed toward her truck. Her chest swelled with pride.

She loved her job. She'd worked as a sign painter at a company called Sign Language for two years. Her position as senior designer came with the responsibility of focusing on lettering arts and the flexibility of getting out of the office and meeting customers. She'd never really outgrown activities like coloring or finger painting. This way, she hoped she never would.

Setting her supplies in the cab, she smiled at the stencils her boss had sent with her. She hardly ever used them. She preferred to do her work freehand. It took a little extra time, but the clients received her personal touch, and she liked that.

Marti went back to remove the tarp and do minor cleanup. Then she went inside and got the manager to inspect her work and sign the work order. Usually she called it quits after a morning at a client site, but she knew she had one more job to do—get back her "Mother's Love."

* * *

Driving through town, she stole a quick glance at herself in the rearview mirror. Not too bad, really. Just a few splatters here and there. She didn't care how rich Kenyon Williams was, she was presentable enough to get her painting back and return his money.

Kathryn had been right. His number was unlisted, but she'd heard about the Williams's mansion and had a pretty good idea where it might be. People said it was out by the Tallapoosa River, although no one seemed to know the exact location. And no one could describe what the mansion looked like. But they all agreed that once on the river highway, one of the off roads led to it. The big rumor was that it had four floors and an elevator. Beyond that, no one knew very much.

Marti turned on to the river road. Lush green trees and bushes jutted out, encroaching on each side. She rehearsed her speech as she took the winding path out of the city.

"Mr. Williams, I'm glad that you liked my painting, but it's not for sale. Here is the money you paid for it. Thank you very much for being understanding. I also want to return your patron's check. I won't need it since I'm not an artist and I have no desire to paint your picture. The gallery was mistaken. I apologize for any confusion."

That ought to do it, she thought. She relaxed and settled in for the ride. She was tempted to pop her brother's new CD into the player, but the radio couldn't seem to get enough of him lately. Every time she tuned in to a station, something from *One Thousand Words* was playing. She loved her brother and was happy for his success in the music business, but enough was enough. She put in Method Man instead.

While the rapper's lyrics ricocheted off the walls inside her truck, Marti slowed on the stretch of highway she believed contained the road to the Williams's mansion. She gazed at the roadside, green with large trees, bushes, and other vegetation. She could barely see beyond them. Whoever lived back in that wooded area really wanted privacy.

If she had blinked, she would have missed it. The intersection came out of nowhere. Although Marti had traveled this route before, she never noticed the off road. It was only because she looked for it so carefully that she saw it and even then, she almost drove right past.

Marti turned left, slowing considerably as her truck created a thin brown cloud behind her. She rolled up the window, so the rising dirt wouldn't get inside. The smoothness of the path surprised her. She had imagined that it would be bumpy and rough going. It was, however, darker than she thought. To see better, Marti switched on her fog lights.

Shrubs and other growth flanked her at each side. From what she could tell, the road went straight ahead for about a mile and then turned. Mr. Meth's gruff staccato chanted on about breaking up to make up, and Marti slowed to a halt. The road opened up into a quaint area complete with ranch-style house and flower garden. This can't be it, she thought, and turned around to go back the way she came.

The river route was full of dirt roads that led to houses and cottages. Some impressive, some dilapidated and hurting for a bulldozer. The roads were like small tributaries shooting off from the main artery. She found out, when she got lost, that a few of them were even connected. Marti turned off her music to concentrate on navigating the maze of dirt lanes.

Maybe there is no Williams mansion. Frustrated, she turned onto yet another dirt road. This one came with the same "No Trespassing" sign as the others.

The road wound to the right, and Marti thought she was headed even further out of the city. *Where is the end?* The road continued to curve. She approached an opening. If this wasn't it, she was going home.

At the end of the dirt road, Marti stopped her truck. She'd found it. The large, stately house sprawled across a lush acreage like some modern-day castle. It looked like something conjured from a fairy-tale. A home a giant and his family might live in. And behind it, the Tallapoosa River roared like a small ocean.

She rolled down the window and inhaled. Fresh air. She loved it. She put her truck in gear and continued up the road. Soon, dirt changed to pavement and within moments, she pulled up to the entrance.

Marti parked and got out. The massive front door opened, and an elderly black man in a Williams Brothers suit stood there looking at her.

"May I help you?" he asked.

Marti was taken aback by the man's age, not sure if he should be standing. "I hope so. I'm here to see Kenyon Williams."

"Do you have an appointment?"

"No." She felt like she had been sucked into a time warp.

The man's face crumpled into a frown, just when she thought that it couldn't get any more wrinkled. "May I ask what this is regarding?"

Marti shuffled her feet from side to side. *This was a mistake.* Did she think she was just going to waltz right up to the door of someone like Kenyon Williams and make demands? Unease created a warmness in her face.

"I . . . he bought one of my paintings. It's . . . not . . . for sale. And then there's this money for more art work . . ."

His face perked up. "Art, you say?"

"Yes . . . I mean . . . I should have made an appointment, but the number is unlisted. Can I just make an appointment now, because I can come back to . . ."

"Come in." The raisin-looking man beckoned and opened the door.

Marti stepped into the hallway. *Classic marble, just like an old movie.* She followed the man into the foyer where she was greeted by the most stunning display of art she'd ever seen. Marti had spent enough time around artists to know that what she was seeing rivaled almost any gallery she could imagine.

Sculptures by Amanda Johnson, tapestries by Lou Stovall, paintings by Lee Andrew Thomas. Not all of the artists she recognized, but she could tell that their work was of the highest quality.

"Wait here, please."

The quickening of her heart told her she'd be glad to. While the old guy went off, she supposed to get Mr. Williams's appointment book, Marti had a look around. On a wall to her right, a display of paintings called to her. They were masterpieces, side by side, an entire row of them. She followed them down the hallway, reading each artist's name and admiring his or her work. Penny Gamble Williams, Tia Prather, Gerard Sekoto.

Some of the techniques were tried and true, and variations of impressionism and primitive folk art, but some were new and intriguing, using styles that Marti would never think of using in a million years. She considered her work, compared to these geniuses, and took a sharp breath. Hanging next to these wondrous works of art was her own attempt, appearing amateurish and out of place. She rushed over to it, wanting to cover the embarrassment with her body. *And I thought he had exquisite taste.*

She rehearsed her speech yet again in her mind. The sound of water splashing startled her. She'd been so consumed by her own thoughts that she didn't notice the Olympic-size pool across the hall. Moving closer, she realized the smell of chlorine hung in the air. The humidity of warm water clung to her skin. As she looked on, a man climbed from the pool and stared in her direction.

Marti had seen handsome men. She'd seen cute and pretty men. But the specimen dripping with water before her was truly and utterly beautiful.

He stood kinglike, clearly unashamed of his nakedness. "Can I help you?"

His voice sounded like dark chocolate at twilight. It was rich and deep and did something delicious to Marti's insides.

"Uh," she said, watching closely as he pulled a towel from a rack and dried himself. "I'm trying to make an appointment."

His skin was the color of Grandma's molasses—one solid stroke of blemish-free midnight. His hair flowed down his back, an ink-black river of waves. The paintings she had just admired held no comparison to the work of art standing in front of her.

The older gentleman entered the pool area, arms draped with clothing. He eyed Marti suspiciously. "I instructed her to remain in the vestibule."

"Yes, well," Kenyon said, pulling on a pair of soft cotton shorts. "Just make sure you show her out." After handing the older man his damp towel, he walked away.

"Mr. Williams!" Marti shouted, determined to have her say. He paused, but kept his back to her.

"Andreas?"

"Yes, sir?"

"Get rid of her."

"Yes, sir!"

The gnarly man moved in her direction. Furious, Marti stormed toward the front door. "Fine. I'll just take my painting now!"

She marched around the corner, threw the envelope containing the money and the check on a nearby table, yanked her painting from the wall, and charged out of the mansion.

Three

"You did what?"

"You heard me. I grabbed my painting and left," Marti said, stepping back from her wall. She let the full effect of her art wash over her as it caught the morning light from a window. It was in her house, where it should be.

"I can't believe you just *took* it. Mr. Williams is probably upset."

"Who cares? He's a snob. Besides, he wouldn't listen to me."

"Well, all I can say is I know not to make you angry. Everything in my gallery might disappear."

Marti laughed into the phone and then heard a beep. "Hold on, Kathryn." She pushed the "Flash" button on the receiver. "Hello?"

"Hey, cow!"

Marti smiled. "Girl, have I got something to tell you. Just a second." She clicked back to Kathryn. "Can I call you back? I want to tell Jacq about my rescue mission."

"Humph. I wouldn't tell Ms. Jacq-o-lantern a thing. She doesn't seem like the type who can keep anything to herself."

"You two really should learn to get along."

"She's just too out there for my tastes. But I'll let you go."

"All right. We'll talk later." Marti clicked back to her friend Jacq. "Hey."

"What's up, girl? Who were you talking to?"

"Kathryn."

"Uga. Gag me with a docent."

"She's a good friend. Besides . . . why are you always so nosey?"

"Because one of these days, you're going to tell me it's some fine brotha spittin' game, and I'm going to want all the details!"

Jacq's mention of a fine brother placed her like a sweet wish poolside at the Williams mansion. This time everything tracked in slow motion. Like special effects on a DVD, the image of a dark-muscled man rose from the pool, dripping with water, regality, and sensuality. His voice matched the twilight hue in his skin.

"Hel-lo!"

"Sorry, girl. What?"

Jacq sucked her teeth. "I *said*, what did you want to tell me?"

Marti relayed the entire story, starting with her shock at Kenyon Williams's commission, continuing with her anger at the purchase of her painting, and ending with her adrenaline rush when she took the painting back and drove away with her work.

"He was *naked!*"

"You haven't heard a word I said." Marti flopped down in her big blue beanbag chair and lit a lemon chiffon candle.

"I heard the word naked and want to know just exactly what you mean by that. You mean naked, naked, like not a dang thing on, naked?"

"You are so silly."

"Um-hmm. Now, what's he look like?"

The yellow citrus aroma of the candle permeated

the air. Marti bent over and lit another. This one cinnamon. She liked the blend and waited for the scent to relax her. "He looks," she said, closing her eyes, "nice."

"Girl, you know what I mean. When ol' boy steers into the harbor, is he driving a tug boat or a luxury liner?"

Yes, she knew exactly what Jacq meant, and despite herself, she recalled all the details of the man's body as if she had created them on canvas herself. Her smile was wide and warm. And from what she could tell, he was the captain of a mighty fine ship. "I am not even going there with you." Her smile broadened. "But I will tell you this . . ."

"What?"

The phone rustled on the other end and Marti knew Jacq was settling in for juicy details.

"He sounds like Avery Brooks."

"Ooh, no!"

"Yeah . . . only, better."'

"Marti, ain't no voice better than brother Avery's."

You haven't heard Kenyon Williams, she thought, recalling the natural thunder in his inflection. Suddenly it occurred to her that she might have been too hasty in her actions. The baritone in his voice may have made his words sound harsher than he intended.

Oh man, she mused, opening her eyes. *Did I overreact?*

The hard knock at her apartment door made Marti jump.

"Someone's at the door. You want to hold on or should I call you back?"

"I'll wait. That may be Mr. Smooth Talk now."

"Girl, please. Hold on." Marti walked the few steps to the door, frustratingly aware of the flutter in her stomach at Jacq's comment. "Who is it?" she asked.

"Police, ma'am."

Cold fear shot through her veins as she twisted the knob and opened the door. *Please God, don't let anything be wrong with anyone in my family.* She thought of her brother overseas and on tour in Japan. She'd told him not to overdo it. Maybe he'd passed out on stage.

"Yes?" she said in a voice as weak as she felt.

"Are you Marti Allgood?"

"Yes."

"Ma'am, we're investigating a complaint."

She blinked and shifted her weight. "A complaint?"

"Yes, ma'am. Mr. Kenyon Williams filed a report that you entered his home and took his property—a painting."

"You must be kidding." Now the weakness she felt spun into amusement.

Marti threw her head back and laughed. "Okay, fellas. Thanks for the joke. You can tell Mr. Williams or Ms. Runningbear, whichever sent you, that I had a good laugh."

The officers frowned. "We'll need to ask you some questions."

"You're serious."

"Yes, ma'am."

Marti's body tingled with apprehension. A sick feeling took up residence in her lower abdomen. "All right."

"The officer closest to her flipped open a metal pad holder. "Were you at Kenyon Williams's house yesterday?"

"Yes. I went there to . . ."

"And did you take a painting from the wall?" the other officer asked.

After Marti explained what happened, the other officer pulled a set of steel handcuffs from his belt. The metal glinted a bright and cold silver in his hand. "I'm afraid we're going to take you into custody. And bring the painting, ma'am. We'll need to take it in as evidence."

"Can I at least hang up my phone?" They nodded. She sighed and grabbed the receiver.

"That no good so-and-so called the cops on me."

"What!"

"Yeah. Mr. *Smooth Talk* is having me arrested.

"You want me to call your sisters?"

"No! I'll be all right. It's *my* painting. They can't keep me in jail for taking my own painting."

As Marti hung up the phone and removed her mother's portrait from its place on her wall, another vision of Kenyon Williams entered her mind. This time it was just his face, with her fresh handprint glowing an angry red against the side of it.

Marti stared up at the beige steel ceiling, unable to believe her predicament. The fact that she'd been handcuffed, read her Miranda rights, and booked would now become a permanent memory. And then to be lying in jail cell . . .

She turned over and faced the wall. More cold steel.

While you are detained here, you are expected to follow all rules and regulations, respect the authority of the staff, and treat other detainees with respect.

Are you talking any medications?

Are you on any dietary restrictions?

When she heard that one, she'd protested. "I'll be seeing a judge tomorrow to straighten out this mess."

"No, ma'am, you won't."

"What? Why!"

"Because tomorrow is Saturday. Judges don't hold court on weekends. You'll have to wait until Monday morning."

Marti had been sick to her stomach ever since.

"First time?" the woman sitting on the stainless steel toilet had asked when Marti arrived. After riding in the back seat of a cruiser and being fingerprinted, she thought nothing else could shock her. She was wrong.

"Yes," Marti replied, turning her head away from the sight as the holding cell door clanked shut behind her.

Even though her glimpse was brief, she could tell that the woman doing her business in the open held a different world-view than most folks. Her hair was an explosion of color, orange, purple, dark blue, and gold. Her heavy and exaggerated makeup gave her a permanent look of surprise. And her dress was sewn together from at least nine different patterns and fabrics.

"*Yo soy Abuelita*, little grandmother." She extended a brown hand, giving Marti's arm a vigorous shake. Marti had a strong urge to wash her hand, but the sink was attached to the toilet and she would have to wait until the fantastic woman had finished.

"What did you do?"

Marti plopped down on the wall-mounted bunk, sighing heavily. "Nothing."

"*Eso es lo que todos me dicen.* You must have done something." Abuelita gave a small grunt then continued. "I stole some fabric for a new dress," she said, pulling a few squares of toilet paper from a roll. "Too bad, a woman was wearing the fabric at the time, but hey, I saw something I wanted. I took it."

Same here, Marti thought.

When she heard the toilet flush, she figured it was safe to look up.

Abuelita was beautiful. Despite all the makeup, which she obviously didn't need, and her bright and flowing dress, she was stunning. Marti guessed her age to be around fifty and felt a certain kinship with the woman who was similar to herself in height and build.

"Ah, now you understand why I am *little* grand-mother, no?"

"Yes," Marti said, smiling.

"I can eat what a man eats and still, I am little Grandmother. My husband, Ricardo Ennrique Havier Frank Gonzales, used to say, 'Abuelita, *dónde está el beef?*'"

She looked wistful. "He loved commercials."

Marti laughed. The woman was as vibrant as the colors she wore. In no time, they had exchanged stories. At times, she doubted whether the woman's stories were true, but she listened just the same.

"You are wrong, you know."

"What do you mean?"

"The painting. It belongs to *el hombre con dinero* now. It was not yours to take."

"But you said a few moments ago that you saw something you wanted and you took it."

Abuelita ruffled Marti's hair and smiled broadly. "*Sí*, but I never said it was right. Only that I did it."

The multicolored woman rose from where she was sitting next to Marti and paced. Then she looked up toward the ceiling as if something of extreme importance was pasted there. "You see, the world is fated. *Destino*. We all must pay for our mistakes. That is our destiny in life. We do wrong; we pay. We face *destino*.

"You are here because of *destino*. I am here because of *destino*. We cannot escape it."

Marti thought the woman was slowly losing touch with reality. She became concerned until the petite woman lay down on her bunk, curled into a ball, and went to sleep. Before she drifted off, Marti heard her whisper, "*Eso es su destino.*

At two A.M., Marti's cell life changed. An officer escorted a woman down the corridor and into her holding cell. The woman was dirty and reeked of alcohol. Her mouth was as filthy as her clothes and for an hour, she shouted obscenity after obscenity demanding her release. The wretched woman finally quieted down after a firm threat from an officer to place her in a small padded cell.

Astoundingly, Abuelita slept through the entire ordeal. Marti, on the other hand, was tempted repeatedly to say something her mother told her when she was young: "You can catch more flies with honey." But then, as a kid, Marti had always wondered who would want to catch flies anyway. So instead, she remained the quiet observer until, finally, the woman took the center bunk and quickly passed out.

When sleep finally took her over, Marti dreamed of cameras monitoring her every move and the straight hard lines of confinement in doors, windows, stairs, vents, and moldings. Everywhere she turned, cold steel closed in. She jerked from side to side, shuddering in her sleep.

Kenyon sulked quietly in the back seat of a black Mercedes limousine and stared out the window. Anger set his teeth on edge and a low growl escaped his lips every time he thought of the woman in his house. A common thief. Just to imagine her as an artist angered him even more.

The artists he knew were upstanding, respectable, decent people. Some of them were a little quirky and had their idiosyncrasies, but on the whole, they were honest folk dedicated to their craft. Not robbers or hooligans.

"Thank goodness she dropped the commission

money before she left. I'll bet she's in a cell right now wishing that hadn't fallen from her pocket."

"I beg your pardon, sir, but I think she may have left that behind intentionally."

"Just drive, Andreas."

Lush green landscape fell away on his right as they headed downtown. All he wanted was his painting returned.

The congested traffic of Atlanta at midday cocooned them in a mass of cars. He sighed at the memory of Marti Allgood's wide-eyed surprise as he stood before her damp, nude, and pissed. "People have no sense of respect these days, Andreas."

Kenyon thrust out a manicured hand. His close-cut nails caught the light of the sun. He slid his thumb across the tops of his fingers, contemplating order. "Didn't she see the 'No Trespassing' signs?"

"I wouldn't know, sir."

He frowned and placed his hand on his chin. "Didn't she hear you when you told her to wait in the parlor?"

"I can only assume so, sir."

Rascal, he mused. He had always balked at the idea of cutting himself off completely from civilization. He already lived in a secluded area. But to have to fence himself off from society?' People already thought of him as a recluse. What would they say then? And what's more important, how would he feel then?

Like a true isolationist.

But it was obvious that he didn't want a repeat of this recent fiasco. He didn't care how pretty she was.

Pretty? Now where had that come from?

Quiet countryside and winding roads gave way to giant office buildings and hustling people. It had been years since he'd seen this part of the city. The skyscrapers and city blocks made it seem like something new and strange instead of old and familiar. When he was sixteen, several of his private school friends used take joyrides downtown and to some of the then-industrial areas to see how the other half lived.

He remembered with perfect clarity kids like Lance Donaldson and Clarence Powell driving the expensive cars their parents had purchased and hauling a bunch of classmates around so they could laugh and throw insults at those less fortunate.

It was disgusting. Kenyon had only gone with them once. Their cruelty had turned his stomach and forced him to see his friends in an unflattering light. That had been the beginning of the end for him. The end of his belief in the goodness of people, in altruism, in human kindness. Then fifteen years later, after he discovered his family's shameful legacy, he had vowed to become the benevolence he sought in others. As the limo approached the police station, he realized that he was here because of yet another demonstration of selfishness and corruption. He wondered if she could somehow be saved.

Andreas opened the door, and Kenyon stepped out determined to recover something for his trouble. The woman who had the audacity to enter his house and steal his painting, irrespective of the fact that she had painted it, had to be taught some kind of lesson. After all, people who did wrong deserved to be punished.

The April air swirled around him in thick humid gusts. The acrid smells of industry and business stung his nose. As he approached the station, he could almost discern the aroma of greed and voracity, could almost see it in the shadows that followed him to the door. He shivered and went inside.

The lobby of the station consisted mostly of a large office area complete with desks, chairs, copier, coffeemaker, etc. Everything you would expect from an office, with one exception. It was encased in glass. No doubt bulletproof. Kenyon rang the buzzer and stood in front of the area of the glass that held the speaker grid.

"May I help you?" a woman in a dark blue uniform asked.

"I'm Kenyon Williams. Arrangements had been made for me to post bail for Marti Allgood. *Special* arrangements."

"Just a moment," she said, walking back to a stack of papers. After leafing through them, she returned with one in her hand. Her expression was one of deep displeasure.

"Money . . . " she said, pressing a button. A buzzer sounded and the officer motioned Kenyon through a door on the right. Andreas walked with him and Kenyon waved him back. "Wait here," he said.

He joined his police escort and together, the two strode down one corridor and then another. Finally they came to an area secured by a metal door and three officers. Once on the other side, they entered a small cell block.

The cold steel surrounding him belied the heat of the day. Someone needed a bath, someone else needed to shut up, and another person needed treatment for sleep apnea. When they reached Marti's cell, he realized that someone needed an attitude adjustment.

Her eyes were as cold as the steel around them. In spite of the lateness of the hour, she was up, looking out of place and out of patience.

"Come to gloat over your conquest?" Marti lifted her chin.

In her child-sized T-shirt and jeans, she looked like an angry pixie.

Kenyon spoke to the officer. "Can you leave us alone?"

"No," she replied, "I'll stand over here," she answered and walked just a few feet away.

When Kenyon turned his attention back to the woman in the cell, she was standing and had approached the bars.

"You know this is wrong." Her eyes never left his. "I came to talk to you, and you dismissed me like a waif."

"I know."

"You *know*? Well, did you also know that Kathryn Runningbear had no right to take money for my painting? It was not for sale."

"I didn't realize . . . "

"No. Of course you didn't. You were too busy turning your back on a guest in your house." Her hard gaze never faltered. "I'm not a thief, Mr. Williams. I'm just a woman who wants her property returned. Considering the circumstances, surely you can understand that."

Her directness surprised him. Obviously, she wasn't going to plead for his leniency. He wondered if his plan would still work.

"Ms. Allgood, I paid for that painting, which, for the time being, makes it mine. But that's not why I'm here."

Marti stiffened. Smooth voice or no, his words were beginning to annoy her. She could hear the lift of superiority and an aristocratic edge to his tone. It made her grind her teeth.

"What do you want, Mr. Williams?"

"Your talent." He glanced around, not out of nervousness but out of impatience. "I'll be honest with you. I'm fascinated with your work. Captivated is more like it. I think you have something I need. So . . . I will drop the charges against you if take the commission."

Marti couldn't believe her ears. The man before her was obviously crazy or just plain eccentric. Kathryn was right. Wealthy people and their whims.

He stepped closer to her cell. "I don't know if you have fifty thousand dollars just lying around. If you do, that's great. You can get out of here." He fingered a spot at his left temple. "Of course, you'll be coming right back after the trial."

"What a dirty threat."

For a second, he thought he saw a flash of disappointment in her eyes, and it stunned him. But he recovered quickly. He knew he was on to something. And it could be glorious, if only she would cooperate. Imagining a bright new star in the art arena warmed him, almost made him forget the ugliness in the world.

"What do you say?"

"I say you've got me confused with someone who's serious about their craft. I just have a terrible hobby that takes me over sometimes. I'm sorry. I can't give you what you want."

"I'm sorry, too," he said, turning toward the officer, still lurking down the hall. "I know art, Ms. Allgood. You have a gift. And just like the painting I bought, you're trying to keep it to yourself. That's a disservice to others, and to you above all."

He looked back as if to give her one last chance. She had already stepped back from the bars.

"I'll see you in court," he said.

Four

The wall was cool and smooth beneath her nail. However, the place where she had drawn Kenyon's face with the tip of her finger began to warm. If she had had a pencil and a pad, she would have had thirty or so images of his face. Some mere silhouettes, others profiles, and still others the hard planes and angles that made up his entire head. By the time the afternoon came, his features were imprinted on her psyche as if the impression had been heat stamped and steam sealed.

A guard led her and five other women into a common area. Marti and the others quickly walked to the phones to make collect calls. Jacq picked up on the first ring.

"Hello?"

"You didn't call my sisters, did you?"

"No, girl. I know better than that. Them crazy heifers would have been on the ten o'clock news for busting you out of that joint."

She sighed and leaned against cold brick. "I know."

"So, girl . . . how you doin'?"

"Not bad, actually. Anger helps pass the time. Imagining all the ways I want to strangle Kenyon Williams until he begs my forgiveness keeps a sister occupied."

"What did the judge say?"

"It doesn't matter what the judge says. It only matters what Kenyon will pay him to do."

"Hopefully it won't come to that."

Marti took a deep breath. "It already has. He was here this morning."

"Girl, no!"

"Yes . . . he was. He wants me to paint him."

"How can you do that if you're on lockdown?"

"If I do the portrait, he'll drop the charges."

The noise of the other women talking filled the small room, which was Spartan, to say the least. There were no chairs, no clock, and only one small table in the corner. So they had no idea ho long they would be on the phone, even though they each got fifteen minutes.

One woman, obviously hungover, talked with her head down and her shoulders hunched. To her right, an older woman was almost yelling into the phone, arms flailing in the air for emphasis.

"Are you gonna to do it?" Jacq asked.

There was one thing for sure. She didn't have fifty thousand dollars just lying around. Jacq could probably get it from Davis, but then again, their relationship wasn't doing so well these days. Her sisters could probably scrape up the money, but the last thing she wanted to do was involve them. She also knew she could get the money from her brother Zay, but with his first child just weeks away, the last thing she wanted to do was impose on his music royalties.

No. She would handle this the same way she did everything else, on her own terms. Maybe it was impulsive and wrong for her to take the painting off the man's wall, but the thought of her most cherished work in a stranger's house made her crazy

The last time he was in a courtroom, some man was suing Williams Brothers for a skin-discoloring rash he'd developed when wearing one of their suits. Rufus

Porter claimed that chemicals in the fabric caused his breakout and sought to recover the cost of doctor's visits along with compensation for mental and emotional anguish. James Townsend, the Williams's attorney, proved that it wasn't the suit but a disgruntled girlfriend who had created a powder-based irritant and laced his suit with it after their breakup.

Kenyon's glance swept the courtroom for James's familiar and well-compensated face. Just as he expected, his attorney was there, briefcase open, Williams suit buttoned.

The two shook hands.

"She's got a PD, and the judge is a friend of mine. The painting is as good as hanging on your wall again."

James had been known to eat public defenders for lunch. "That's what I want to hear," Kenyon said.

They took seats, each preparing in his own way for what was to come. While James riffled through papers and notes, Kenyon watched people file in like lost sheep. They were in a courtroom that reminded him of a show he'd seen once called *Perry Mason*. The accusing and accused sat in dark wooden chairs like a vast and solemn studio audience. The judge's bench loomed in front of her like a rectangular monolith. He could understand how such a position could be intimidating. But he also understood why his family kept James Townsend on retainer.

After a few more minutes of writing and ruffling through papers, his lawyer seemed ready.

"You paid ten thousand dollars for the painting?"

"Yes."

"Did you bring the receipt?"

Kenyon pulled the yellow slip of paper out of the inside pocket of his denim jacket. He handed it over.

James smiled. "That means we're talking felony offense."

A part of Kenyon's stomach twisted. "A felony?"

"Yeah. The woman could see some serious jail time on this. You wanna go all the way or you just wanna spank her a little?"

Kenyon was appalled. "All I want is the painting."

James sat back, looking all too smug. "Oh, you'll get that."

From a side door, deputies herded out several men and women single file. Last in line was Marti Allgood. She looked tired and angry. The sight of her wrists in handcuffs sent a tremor of unease through Kenyon's body. All this over a painting, he thought. Suddenly everything felt very, very wrong.

As the clerk called case after case, and each grouping of plaintiffs and defendants approached the judge, Kenyon's unease blossomed into stark apprehension. If the woman wanted her painting bad enough to snatch it from his wall then maybe she should have it. He groaned as he sat surrounded by people who had committed far more grievous crimes than taking back their own paintings. Hit and run, drug possession, DWI. Besides, he had his own caseload in his office. Why was he being bothered with a thing as petty as this?

Because, the voice in his head told him, there was a crime committed, and Miss Snatch-and-grab had taken something that was not hers to take.

Yet, his conscience told him, the pint-size woman speaking quietly to her court-appointed lawyer deserved better than this.

Marti was furious. Her court-appointed lawyer, Hogan Gynne, had rushed over at the last minute, in a frumpy jacket and trousers. To top that off, he'd asked her to fill him in on the details of the case. Obviously he hadn't prepared. And the tremolo she'd detected in his hands made him appear just a little too nervous for her comfort. What had she gotten herself into?

She stole a glance at Kenyon Williams seated smugly next to a man who looked like a wolf in expensive clothing. If the man's eyes were any more canine, she wouldn't have been able to look at him.

He's taking this all in stride, she mused, wanting to hold on to her anger. But the longer she gazed at Kenyon, the more the anger slipped away, replaced by something warm and sweet. I can't believe he looks that good, she thought, raking her eyes over his sinuous bulk inside the denim outfit he wore. *He looks like he paid a lot of money for his clothes and, even more interesting, looks like he is worth every penny.*

Dang it, Marti! He's the enemy! she reprimanded herself.

But the only thing that tore her gaze away from the dark and handsome man was the clerk of the court calling their case foreword.

Thin slices of trepidation tore through her resolve. She squared her shoulders, determined not to let her unease show. From the corner of her eye, she watched her lawyer toddle his way toward the judge's bench.

As each side presented its case, Marti decided that if Gynne was as inept as she feared, she would ask to defend herself. A few minutes into his presentation, Hogan Gynne sounded as if he were part of the plaintiff's side. Marti flashed him a look of unbridled contempt.

He flinched. "Your honor, may I take a moment to confer with my client?"

"No. You should have done that before you stepped in my courtroom."

Marti closed her eyes and hung her head. Had Kenyon bribed the judge? she wondered.

"Do you have something to say, Miss Allgood?"

She opened her eyes and saw the judge's harsh scowl directed at her.

"N-no," she stammered.

"That's interesting. Because you've been talking during proceedings all morning. But now, when it's your *turn* to talk, you don't have anything to say."

The wolf-lawyer's eyes sparkled. Marti's heart sank. Kenyon must have paid off the judge. She should have called her sisters.

She summoned her courage. "Your honor . . ."

He turned away from her. "We'll come back to you. Now Mr. Williams, explain to the court what happened at your house last Thursday."

"Well, I was finishing my swim when I noticed Ms. Allgood standing in my pool room."

"You'd invited her in?"

"No. She wandered in, I imagine. Probably saw . . ."

The judge shifted in his chair. "What happened then, Mr. Williams?"

"I asked her if I could help her, and she mentioned that she was trying to make an appointment."

"And did she?"

Kenyon blinked. "Did she what?"

"Make an appointment?"

"Well, no."

"Then what happened?" the judge questioned.

"After that, I asked my assistant to show her out."

"So your assistant escorted her to the door?"

"No. She saw herself out with my painting."

The judge's eyebrows rose. Marti thought if they had been yellow they would have looked like the golden arches. "Mr. Williams, do you have a receipt for the painting?"

Kenyon watched as the petite woman standing next to her PD seemed to shrink before his eyes. It was as if his answers had slowly siphoned away her energy. The sight created a dull ache near his heart.

"Your honor?" she said.

"Oh, now you want to *interrupt,*" Judge Hatch said.

She lifted her chin. "Your honor, when Mr. Williams made his purchase, the painting was on loan at the gallery. It should never have been sold. And then when I went to talk to him about it, he . . ."

Her voice broke. "He didn't give me a chance to explain."

"Do you realize that you've been accused of a felony, Miss Allgood? You may have some recourse with the gallery owner. As a matter of fact, both of you might. But you don't have any here."

He raised his gavel. "My judgment is for . . ."

"Please, Your Honor. This isn't just a painting."

Fear and anxiety twisted her stomach into knots. "It's . . . it's . . . My mother passed away and I . . . she . . ." Marti's sobs wouldn't let her continue. Instead she gave in to the anguish building in her chest. *What a cold and cruel man Kenyon is.* To take away her memories and emotions. To be so unreasonable. To . . .

"You *what?*"

The sound of three of the men around her speaking in unison shook her from her misery.

"I said I want to drop the charges," Kenyon repeated, eyes holding on to Marti with soft concern.

The judge frowned and huffed. "In chambers!" he said and marched off toward the back of the courtroom, his black robe swaying behind him.

Marti had always wondered what a judge's chambers looked like. She had imagined everything from a dark and solemn librarylike room to a small Spartan space with standing room only. What she found fit neither extreme. Judge Hatch's chambers were nothing more than a medium-size office complete with modular furniture, two bookcases, and three French windows.

There was room at the long mahogany table for at least ten people. The five of them sat there, a flurry of questions flying between them.

Judge Hatch interrupted the verbal melee. "Let me get this straight. Now you want to drop the charges?"

Kenyon nodded. "That's right."

"Why?" The judge and Kenyon's attorney asked at the same time. Marti's heart pounded like a ceremonial Japanese drum. It was so loud and strong it scared her, and she thought for sure the people outside in the courtroom could hear it.

Kenyon slid a glance in her direction and Marti sensed a touch of compassion on his face. It didn't last long. When he turned away, his facial features looked hard-set and distant.

"Because she doesn't belong in jail."

No matter how many times he turned away, something always compelled him to look at her again. She looked so vulnerable, he thought, glancing back. Vulnerable on top of a layer of defiance. Very attractive.

Before Marti could put together what was happening, her lawyer had risen to the occasion and managed to speak on her behalf. By the time their brief conversation was over, the case was dismissed and she had agreed to do the commissioned portrait in exchange for receiving back the painting of her mother.

Marti didn't know whether to be happy for being released and getting her painting back or sad that she would have to work with Kenyon Williams. But what she did know is that she wanted very badly to take a bath and sleep off the stress in her own bed. She couldn't wait to call Jacq to come and get her.

Five

Marti walked into her spare bedroom like the prodigal artisan. Most of the time she ignored the fact that Frankenstein's laboratory loomed just catercorner from her bedroom. Like something from the movie *Edward Scissorhands* or *Honey I Shrunk the Kids,* she kept a room overflowing with experiments—acrylic starts and stops, half-finished sculptures, abandoned collages, and various works—out of—progress.

No, she thought, looking around. It was more like *Poltergeist* or *The Exorcist.* A room where evil spirits lived and took over if you let them. She pulled out a tall storage container. It was clear plastic and stood five drawers high. She blew the dust off the top and coughed.

Standing in her art room was like hitting a trip wire. Memories of Harvey, Terrence, David, and Frank materialized as if they'd been summoned by witchcraft.

Harvey was her college sweetheart. They had been inseparable until she caught him flirting with her sister Ashley. That incident resulted in her first mosaic. Then there was Terrence. She realized now that he was a rebound from Harvey, but their breakup had hurt her nonetheless. She'd channeled her pain through collage that time. Six of them. They made great Christmas gifts for her family.

Marti had sworn off men after that, until she met

David. David had been her all. After two broken
hearts, she believed she had finally found the one.
But God had other plans. One night when his car had
broken down, David was walking to a gas station to
call for help and was struck by a van and killed. His
death propelled her to brushes and oils so that
stretches of her imagination, fury, and pain could be
flung out across white canvas. Ten paintings in all.
Eight of which leaned now against the rear wall of her
art room.

Her last lingering excursion into creativity happened when she broke up with Frank. They had been
seeing each other for about seven months and it just
wasn't working out. The thought of never finding
someone drove her back to the canvas for abstract
renditions of whatever crossed her mind. Five more
paintings were born.

Since then, she had tried to recapture whatever terrible muse it was that compelled her to art in times of
deep pain. Each time, she could begin a project well
enough, but never had the follow-through to finish it.
Something was always missing, and she didn't know
what.

The only exception was when her mother died.
That loss brought a dramatic finish to several projects
she'd started, including a ceramic vase, a brass statue
of her own hands, and a painting of her mother. Sighing, she realized that she should have never taken that
painting out of her house.

Marti slid the first drawer open. Her hand traced
the smooth lines of the cool wooden brushes, re-
acquainting herself. She had a trove of all sizes and
shapes. Some like new. Others worn and stained with
colors. Red, brown, and a deep dirty green.

Tools of destruction, she thought, picking up a long
slender brush. *Am I crazy?* Sadly she realized that she

didn't even remember painting most of the artwork stacked and leaning against the wall. But here she was again, as if she were responding to a call to arms.

Could she create at will? She wasn't sure. The lines and angles of his physique rose up in her mind, bright and full of light. Like midnight, alive, moving, and powerful, he was already a work of art. What more could she do?

After searching for materials she could salvage and use for the portrait, she made a list of what she would need to purchase. Since she was on commission by one of the richest men in the state, she decided to spare no expense and go to Pen and Ink art store instead of her usual haunt, The Hobby House.

When the phone rang, Marti was headed out the door. She started not to answer it. But since her sister-in-law was pregnant, it might be news of a new niece or nephew. She dashed back and picked up the receiver on the second ring.

"Hello?"

"Miss Allgood."

The ancient voice left no question in her mind. "How did you get my number?"

"You'd be surprised what a smart old man can do these days."

Somehow over the phone, he didn't seem as formal as he did when she was at the mansion. That eased her annoyance. "Well, why is the smart old man calling me?"

"To tell you that I will pick you up at two. Kenny wants to get started as soon as possible."

Marti giggled. The gruff man she'd encountered was as far from a Kenny-type as anyone could get.

"You're not planning to renege now, are you?"

"No," she said when her laughter subsided. "I don't break promises, Andreas."

"Glad to hear it. I'll see you at two."

"Wait!" she shouted as she heard their connection break. "You don't know where I live."

Marti glanced at the clock. 10 A.M. She only had a few hours to get her supplies, grab some lunch, and be ready when Andreas came. She trotted out of her apartment and into her truck.

At one fifty-five she was still trying to get ready. Not exactly sure of what she was getting into, she had packed and unpacked her art case several times. Top that off with the fact that she was nervous for some unknown reason and Marti was one frazzled sister.

She went to the window for the umpteenth time in ten minutes. When she saw the limo, she smiled. Marti remembered when she was young telling her friends every time they saw a limousine, "Gotta go, y'all. My ride's waiting." Now, she could say it for real. Too bad no one was around to hear it.

In a last-minute effort to end her indecisiveness, she grabbed her sketchbook and several charcoal pencils, then headed out to catch her ride.

The smart old man stood next to the long black vehicle. He was actually dressed in a chauffeur's suit. "Miss Allgood," he said, opening the door for her. Several people in the neighborhood stopped to watch her get in. Her landlord, Mrs. Smith, stared out from a window.

She slid a wad of bubble gum to the left side of her mouth. "You can call me Marti," she replied, getting in.

His raisinette face wrinkled into a tight grin. "All right. I will."

I should be angry, Marti thought as the big car floated through the outskirts of the city. Large trees, tall and lush with life, fell away on her right. She realized that strangely, the better part of her frustration had fallen away as well.

She was relieved that her painting would soon be back where it belonged. If she had to paint a stuck-up black man's portrait to get her work back, then so be it. And besides, in the judge's chambers Kenyon Williams hadn't seemed as stuck-up as he had during their first encounter. Maybe there was more to him than his gruff exterior let on. And maybe it was her destiny to rescue the decent man inside.

As they headed toward the river and the Williams mansion, Marti fiddled with all the gadgets at her disposal. CD, DVD, TV, VCR. There was an entire alphabet of electronics in front of her. The right side of the limo held a refrigerator, bar, and something she didn't recognize. She pushed a few buttons, but the cylindrical machine did nothing.

"That was some stunt you pulled."

To her surprise, Andreas had lowered the glass partition. "Running off with that painting. Kenny's not used to that kind of stuff."

"Well, I'm not used to my work hanging in some stranger's house. So, I guess we're even." Marti blew a large bubble and popped it.

The old man's remark made her curious. "Andreas, he's not some kook, right? I mean, he's not getting me to his house on a false excuse, is he?"

She didn't expect laughter, but she got it. A thunder roll of it, as if she'd just uttered the most amusing thing ever said.

"Why is that funny?" she asked, scooting closer to the opening between them.

"I kinda wish he *would* try something with you, Little Miss Marti. But the only concern you should have is how to keep yourself awake in case you get bored."

"What?" she asked, trying to figure out what Andreas meant.

"These days Kenny doesn't have much by way of a personality. But don't tell him I told you."

She let his remark settle into her mind and flipped open the sketchbook. Before she realized it, she had drawn Kenyon Williams's face and shoulders on several pages. On one, she drew his face from several angles, careful to include his large dark eyes and cascading hair. She was surprised at how much detail she remembered and how good her hand felt drawing the hard lines of him. She stopped and closed the book before she got carried away.

When she looked up, Andreas was turning onto the road leading to the front of the house.

Marti knew she must have been a sight, stepping out of a limousine in Keds tennis shoes, hobo jeans, and cropped T-shirt, but she didn't care. It was her style and no one, not even the rich and infamous, had to like it but her. With sketchbook and pencils in hand she accompanied Andreas inside.

The opulence of the Williams's mansion nearly swallowed her whole. This time she took in not just the artwork but the entire decor. Marble from ceiling to floor. Ornate gold trimming practically everywhere. Glass-bladed chandelier. She felt like Cinderella in the prince's palace.

The short man paused at the foyer. "Wait a moment. I'll let him know you're—"

"I know she's here."

Kenyon descended the wide marble staircase, eyes holding hers. This time he was fully clothed. Brown suede boots, faded blue jeans, and a denim shirt. His hair was pulled into a ponytail by a rawhide band.

"I'll put the car in the garage," Andreas said and exited quietly.

Marti felt her eyes go wide. "The *car?* You *own* that limo?"

Kenyon took a deep breath. "It belongs to my family," he said, walking up beside her.

"That's some family you got, mister."

"Kenyon," he said, correcting her.

She stared into his eyes and then looked away, realizing that despite his attire, she couldn't shake the memory of him stepping out of the pool and the waterfall rushing down his body.

"Is anything wrong?" he asked.

"No," she said.

"Good. Then let's go into the study."

She followed him down a lengthy hallway. This one on the opposite side of the pool room. Marti ran her hand against the smooth coolness of the marble wall. "Very impressive."

"Um," he muttered, opening a large oak door.

Marti blew a bubble. It popped like a small firecracker when she walked through the entryway. Like a library, the room had wall-to-wall bookshelves. Above the bookshelves was a second-floor catwalk. Along the walls of the catwalk were huge and elaborate portraits at least five feet high.

"This is where my family entertained. And this," he said motioning toward all the pairs of eyes that seemed to watch them, "is my family."

He moved in closer. "Starting with my great, great, great, great, great, great grandfather Silas Williams and ending with my younger brother Reynard. That gap you see is where my portrait's supposed to be."

He sounded about as enthusiastic as a flu patient.

"It's a family tradition," he said eyes flat and hard.

Then he frowned and Marti felt his unease as if it were walking on her skin.

"Where's your stuff? Your paints and canvas and brushes?"

"Well, if we're going to do this right, I'll need ask you some questions first, get to know you a little bit, and find out what you want."

At that remark, she saw a golden flicker in his jet black eyes. She decided to ignore it and the way it made her feel. "Besides," she said, casting a stiff glance at the black men of various hues all suited up in Williams Brothers' finest, "your family is decked out. You look like you just walked in from the grocery store."

His expression remained unchanged. "That's the point. When you do me, I plan on being as casual as I possibly can."

Marti shifted the book and pencils from one arm to the other. That deep rolling ocean in his voice made her nervous. Especially when he said things like *when you do me.*

"If you wanted something quick and easy, you should have hired a photographer. As a matter of fact, my sister-in-law takes wonderful pictures. I could call her—"

"No, don't." he said, reaching to hold her arm. "I need a portrait."

She wanted to search his eyes for sincerity, but the intensity she found in them cast her gaze away. "Portraits are very special *types* of paintings. They capture the nature of a person, not just the likeness. They aren't moments in time. They're . . . stories, testaments, and lifetimes painted with light."

She stopped chewing her gum. "The canvas might be one-dimensional, but good portraits never are."

Marti moved her arm where it had warmed to

Kenyon's touch. "For me to do a good job, I have to know you: who you are, what you do, your likes, your dislikes, the way you move. If you aren't willing to commit to that, then I might as well leave."

Kenyon's eyes rolled back in his head. He looked like a man pondering two evils. So far, with his reserved demeanor and cryptic responses, she'd pegged him as a private man. Opening himself to get a portrait painted was probably more than he'd bargained for.

Finally, he cocked his head to the side, and Marti could tell he'd made a decision.

"All right," he said, voice smoky and barely above a whisper. "Let's get started."

If it hadn't been so dark in the room, Marti might have been able to tell that nearly everything in it was shining. The wood was polished, the brass was gleaming, and the crystal was shimmering. But in the shadows of curtain-drawn windows, all the objects cast a dull brown aura.

A bubble of excitement burst within her. Kenyon had just given her permission to probe into his life a little. The sudden urge to smile surprised her. Instead of relenting, she exchanged her old gum for a fresh piece and went to work.

"So, tell me about yourself."

They were seated in the library. Marti on a long, blood red couch, Kenyon on the matching chair across from her. It was a few moments before he spoke.

"I'm six feet tall, I weigh one hundred and ninety pounds, and in three months I'll be thirty-nine years old."

Marti raised an eyebrow. "I really wasn't going for

demographics, but I guess that's a start. Tell me something about you as a person."

Kenyon sighed as if he were incredibly bored. Marti wondered why a man who could probably have anything he wanted would be in such a funk. A whim she didn't understand made her determined to see him smile at least once before she left.

He crossed one denim-clad leg over the other. "I have one brother, Reynard. He's a year younger than I am. My parents are Richmond and Beverleigh. They live in Savannah with my brother. I have a host of aunts, uncles, and cousins scattered across the country, but that's the core of my family."

Marti tapped her pencil against the leather cover of her sketchbook. "What about *you?*"

"I just told you—"

"No. You talked about your family. I want to know about Kenyon."

He gave her a blank stare in response.

Exasperated, Marti stood and walked to a bookcase. She pulled a book from the shelf. It was leather-bound with real gold lettering on the cover. *Great Thinkers of the World,* it said.

"Have you read this?" she asked.

"Most of it."

"What did you think?"

"I think if it hadn't been for African philosophy, there would be no great thinkers of the world."

Marti opened the book, flipped through a few pages, then slid back into place. "Why?"

"Because it's too big a coincidence that Aristotle and the rest of those guys came up with all these great ideas at the exact same time when Europeans began sailing to other countries and bringing back everything they could beg, borrow, or steal."

Marti took her seat across from Kenyon and reviewed her observations of his posture. While he talked, his brow furrowed slightly, his head moved in time with his words, and his hands punctuated his sentences.

She opened her sketchbook and created a thumbnail of Kenyon's hands in motion. She smeared the lead on the page a bit with her index finger to create the feature of dark skin. Then she added a few details: fingernails, creases at the knuckles, veins on the back of his hands.

"Don't stop," she said after a few moments. "Keep talking."

"I'm not used to talking about myself."

"No way! I would never have guessed!" She looked up to get his reaction. Not even a smirk. Her hope for a smile dwindled. "Alrighty then."

She decided she'd ask him the question hovering in the back of her mind since her day in court. "Why do you *really* want your portrait painted? I know what you said before, but since you've waited this long, I was just wondering . . . why now? Is it for your wife or girlfriend?"

When Kenyon's jaw tightened and his eyes narrowed, Marti knew she'd ventured into dangerous territory. The phrase *never mind* was on the end of her tongue. Before she could get it out, he answered.

"I'm doing it to get my parents to stop hounding me."

She glanced at the images of Kenyon's family staring straight ahead from the uppermost part of the library walls. "It's obviously a strong tradition in your family."

"It's not the painting they're hounding me about. It's the business." Now the muscles on his face tightened around his eyes, but his hands still worked to periodically add emphasis.

"What about the business?"

"They want me to run it."

Marti's eyes widened. "You mean you don't."

"No. Reynard does."

"Then what do *you* do?"

He recoiled in the antique chair. His movement was slight, but she registered it.

"I collect art."

To keep him talking, she asked him a series of not-so-personal questions about the weather, current events, and the like. She wanted to watch him and get a sense of his mannerisms. All the while, he'd answered her questions with a cool resignation, as if he was talking about one thing, but thinking about another. Marti realized that even though they were sitting right across from each other, he was someplace else, and she didn't like it.

"Let me see you pose," she said.

His head tilted in disbelief.

"No really," she said, springing from the couch. "It will give me a chance to see what I'm working with and get you out of that funk."

"I'm not in a funk. And I'm not going to pose for you like some *GQ* model. All I want is to get my picture painted and get back to life as usual."

"How old did you say you were?" she asked, walking around him.

"Thirty-nine. Why?"

"Because that's much too young for you to act like a such crotchety old man."

"What if I pay you to just shut up and paint?"

Marti blew a bubble, a big one. She suspended it for a while and then popped it as loud as she could. "Mister, you don't have enough money or class to pull that off."

"Okay," the robust voice said. "So what now?"

"Look, you can't just splash some paint on a canvas and call it a painting." Marti rolled the wad of gum from one side of her mouth to the other. "At least, *I* can't. Painting is a planned activity. I'll do some sketches first to make sure I get a feel for what the final product will look like. Then I'll make larger sketches on canvas and soon after that lay on the final oils."

Kenyon looked as though someone had dipped his tongue in turpentine. "Isn't there some way to speed the process?"

"Yes," she said. "Stand over there and shut up!"

The expression on his face was priceless and one she wished she could get on canvas. She could call the work *Bourgeois Shock. Maybe this wouldn't be so bad after all.*

As Marti made sketch after sketch of Kenyon, her mind returned again and again to her night in jail. She discovered it was quite easy to take her anger out on his image on her pad. Kenyon with horns. Kenyon with bucked teeth. Kenyon cross-eyed. Kenyon with one eye in the middle of his forehead. Two-headed Kenyon.

"You're having too much fun. Let me see."

"No! These sketches are just . . ." Before she could cover her work, he was at her side staring at her latest creation. Kenyon with dunce cap.

"That's not funny."

"Oh, yes it is," she said, giggling.

Andreas took that very moment to enter with a silver tray of coffee and biscuits.

She moved to where the old man stood fussing over the snack. 'What do you think of this?" she asked, sliding the picture under his nose.

Marti could tell from his reaction that the grunt he'd made was actually a laugh choked off. He left the room quickly and both Marti and Kenyon turned at the gale of laughter coming from the hallway.

"Obviously you think this is a joke. I don't play games, Ms. Allgood." He walked to the wall and pressed a button on the intercom. "Andreas?"

A few short seconds later, Marti recognized the older gentleman's age-weathered voice coming through the speakers. "Yes, sir?"

"The painter is leaving. Please see to her disposal." Then he turned stiffly in her direction. "I will enjoy your painting of . . . your mother, is it?"

Marti's heart twisted sharply in her chest. "No!" The essence of her mother's love, trust, and legacy would not hang in some stranger's house. She would not have it. She would steal back the painting a million times, face ten lifetimes in jail, and yes, she realized finally, she would even paint the portrait of an egotistical aristocrat whose heart was as black as his skin.

"Wait! Kenyon!"

"No," he said, and left Marti standing in the cold wake of his anger.

Six

Selena Graves typed the last few words to her feature article and hit SEND. She didn't bother to proofread it. She was in the zone, and she knew the article was good.

Better than good. It was award-winning material. Ty would be pleased. Probably take her out to dinner. Steak, of course. Her editor had an affinity for red meat, rare and served up on large platters. As long as he kept her bonuses coming every year, so would she.

"I want a big assignment, Ty," she'd told him over an eighteen-ounce porterhouse once.

"You get all the big assignments," he replied.

"You know what I mean."

After fifteen years as a news reporter in Des Moines, Iowa, she'd learned that even though she loved her job, there wasn't much earth-shattering news to be covered in the city. She could move to a larger metropolitan area, but then she'd run the risk of having to start all over with grunt stories and work her way up. No, she'd put in enough time and deserved to step out into the world of real reporting with real drama and top-notch investigating.

She knew she was up to it. But she'd grown tired of chipping away at Ty's resistance. He was a home grown man with hometown ideals. When Selena'd discovered that there was a meth lab on the outskirts of town, he'd been surprised and delighted with her treatment of that event in her front-page story. Ty couldn't fathom the types of stories she'd dreamed of covering.

His big pink lips closed down over a forkful of blood-red beef. The smile that peeled back his lips looked like infantile bliss. Selena turned away from the stray juice trickling down his chin like a small child running out of a cave frightened and frantic. And she realized that he would never see the need to cover a hard news story. His mind could not conceive of the necessity. She would have to do this on her own. And then, when she was right in the thick of it, she would bring him in. Tell him of all the wonderful things she'd been doing. She could all but see the look of shock and awe on his face as he realized once and for all what a gem he had in her.

By then she would be so far into the story that he couldn't refuse her anything. The sacrifice would be too great. And she would prove once and for all that she was not just a small town beat reporter. She could stand in the tall grass with any feature writer in the country. She would finally make a name for herself.

The ringing phone pulled her from the dry mist of her thoughts. She sat back in her ergonomically correct chair and let it ring. She knew it was Ty. He was calling to express his amazement at her beating her deadline by a week. On the forth ring, just before the call would be shunted into voicemail, she snatched up the receiver, thinking Ty's amazement at her accomplishments was just beginning.

Jacquelyn Jackson walked across the plush carpeting in Davis Van Housen's living room wishing that he had hardwood floors. At least that way she could hear something in the room besides the emptiness of her heart and her own breathing. With Davis gone to work, maybe her own footsteps could keep her company.

That's right, she thought. *Shiny hardwood floors where I could see my reflection and know that I was really here.* But today she felt like a ghost. But then again, even ghosts had houses to haunt.

She had boxes. Eleven in all. Nice, neat, and waiting to be moved into her new apartment on the other side of the city. She couldn't believe that she'd left her home in Lincoln, Nebraska, to shack up with a man she hardly knew. Well, that wasn't entirely true. She knew he was handsome and had money. She also knew he was attracted to her. So she'd thought, why not? Life is too short. And besides, her best friend Destiny had just moved to Atlanta and gotten married. Love was in the air. Or in Jacq's case, an earth-stopping case of lust.

This was all Destiny's fault anyway, she mused, checking the room for anything she might have forgotten to pack. If Destiny hadn't introduced her to Davis, she wouldn't be in this predicament. But who was she kidding? If not Davis, there might have been some other man to dazzle her with good looks and a bank account. At least this way, her best friend was here to help her pick up the pieces.

Jacq made one more sweep of the house and was coming down the spiral staircase when the doorbell rang. Instead of a pleasant tone, the refrain blaring out of digital speakers was, "Who let the dogs out!" Despite herself and her emotions, Jacq smiled and opened the door.

"Hey, hon!" Marti Allgood's bright smile greeted her. The two embraced.

Immediately Jacq felt better and less like Little Bo Peep who'd lost her sheep.

"Thanks for coming," she said, stepping aside so the petite woman could enter. She always thought Marti looked like a Chrissy doll with short, turbulent hair.

"You call me Chrissy one more time and it's you and me," her friend said knowingly.

"I wasn't even thinkin' about that!" Jacq protested, but she knew the signs were on her face.

No sooner had she closed the door behind Marti than a loud honking blared from the driveway. Just for a moment, Jacq allowed herself to believe that it was Davis, driving up at the last minute to stop her from going. She could all but see him getting down on one knee to apologize. If she strained, she could hear his voice spinning a magic spell in her ears with three little words. She jerked the door open to see a very pregnant Destiny Allgood climbing down from the driver's seat of an SUV. The excitement in Jacq's heart popped and deflated like a mylar balloon. She tried to look happy at seeing her friend. It was hard.

"What are you doing here?" she asked as Destiny waddled through the door.

"I came to help you move," she replied.

Marti looked Destiny up and down. "You must be joking. That's my niece you're carrying. I'm not about to let you haul boxes."

"You're wrong," Jacq quipped. "That's my goddaughter she's carrying, so you know she ain't movin' no boxes here!"

They all laughed and Destiny plopped down on Davis's couch. 'Then I'll just hang around for moral support."

Marti tested the weight of one of Jacq's boxes, then replaced it on the stack. "So how's my brother?"

"Tired," Destiny said, smiling. "He won't admit it, though. It's been a long tour. I'm glad it's almost over."

"When does he get back?" Jacq asked.

Destiny arranged the pillows on the couch to provide more support for her back. "He was supposed to fly back next Tuesday, but he called me last night and said that his manager booked him for two more nights. They love him in Japan."

The fact that her best friend married Allgood, R&B's newest singing sensation, still seemed like a fairytale to Jacq. She and Davis had gone to dinner with them on several occasions and at times she still found herself awestruck. But what was even more amazing was how down-to-earth he was and how much in love with Destiny he was. They made an elegant couple.

"Ooh, this child," Destiny said, stroking her big belly. Jacq was amazed at how good her friend looked. Even though she was sure she'd gained about thirty pounds. She carried it well. Destiny was truly all baby.

In less than forty-five minutes, Jacq and Marti had loaded Marti's truck with boxes. Jacq was grateful most of her things were still in storage. Her only accumulations at Davis's house had been clothes and books.

Marti stretched out her back. Jacq was surprised when she heard it pop.

"What did you have in the last box? Bricks?"

Jacq smiled. "Schoolbooks." That's something else she had to be grateful for. Since moving to Atlanta, she'd indulged her interest in physical therapy. Remarkably, she'd taken to it like a bird to the sky. It was challenging study but no career Jacq had ever pursued, and she'd pursued her share, had made her feel so confident, competent, and content.

The two working women finished their task and turned to their friend on the couch. They were not surprised to find that she had propped her feet up on the coffee table and had fallen asleep.

"Look at this heifer!" Jacq motioned toward Destiny. Marti moved closer. "She looks beautiful."

"Just think," Jacq said, elbowing her in the arm. "That could be you."

"No way!" Marti protested, shaking her head. "I'm not ready for children."

"You got that right," Jacq responded, watching her friend blow yet another bubble with the wad of gum she'd been chomping on. "You're still a kid your damn self."

"Forget you!" Marti said.

At her remark, Destiny's eyes fluttered open. "Are we ready to go?" she asked, sleep clouding around her words.

Jacq looked around at the opulence of Davis Van Housen's home. When she'd first laid eyes on it, she knew she wanted to be with the kind of man that could afford such luxury. It was an immature thought, but it was what had brought her 1,000 miles to Atlanta.

Then she got to know the man behind the money and realized that the status of his bank account didn't matter. He was a fascinating man who made her feel like the woman that she was created to be. But something had gone terribly wrong. The closer she drew toward Davis, the more they'd argued. Finally they decided that it would be best if they separated.

Jacq sighed at the unexpected pain that thought caused.

One last glance and she realized that, no, she wasn't ready to go. But there was nothing she could do about it.

Marti knew it was coming. She was shocked that it hadn't come before now. But she was also grateful that Jacq had waited until her sister-in-law was gone before grilling her about Kenyon. Once her brother Xavier got wind that there was a man in her life, any man, he acted like an overprotective parent.

"Not talking, huh?"

Marti grabbed another piece of KFC. "I didn't want to talk with my mouth full."

"Bull," Jacq said, smacking.

They were seated on the floor of Jacq's studio apartment. Their words and the occasional crunch of extra crispy chicken echoed back to them off bare walls.

"I'm just painting his picture, Miss Nasty Thang. We aren't knocking boots."

"Well maybe you should. That way your hair would be messed up for a reason."

Marti stopped chewing. "Now you know that's just wrong."

"No, what's wrong is you sittin' over there pretending that you ain't sprung."

"I'm not sprung!"

"As fine as he is? You can't tell me you don't at least lust after the brother."

Jacq got up and went rummaging through her unpacked boxes. She carelessly tossed bras, panties, slips, and hose out of their neatly packed arrangements until she found what she was looking for.

"I got this from the university library," she said, tossing a magazine at Marti.

"You stole it!"

"Permanently borrowed."

"Trifling. Just trifling."

Marti stared at the 1997 issue of *Black Enterprise* magazine. She picked it up and looked into the eyes of the man she'd seen daily for the past week. He was standing next to a younger, more intense version of himself. *Must be his brother,* she thought.

The dark blue suit fit Kenyon like he'd been dipped in it. He looked very much like a man in charge, commander in chief. His eyes were set, his chin hard and determined, his shoulders square and confident. It didn't take long for the image of his expensive suit to dissolve and Marti could see him quite clearly in the most beautiful suit of all.

"Dang, girl. Lick the picture, why don't you!"

Marti's head snapped up. She'd been found out. She couldn't deny it.

"Okay. So I think he looks good."

Jacq tore a large chunk of chicken away from the bone and shoved it into her mouth, smiling. "Sprung!" she garbled out. "Like a spring!"

The heat of embarrassment warmed Marti's cheeks. "Oh, yeah? Well what about you being sprung on Davis? Let's talk about that!"

Jacq's look of whimsical teasing drained away to nothing.

"I'd rather talk about Ms. Runningboar."

"That's Running*bear*."

"Whatever."

"You know, you two really should try to get along."

"Yeah. And people in hell—"

"I know, I know . . . want ice water."

Marti sensed she'd touched a raw nerve by mentioning Davis. She would be more careful in the future. And she would also be more careful in her future dealings with Kenyon Williams. She knew she wasn't sprung as Jacq had implied. But he was captivating, and handsome, and smoky. If she wasn't careful, she'd be more than sprung. And she'd be doing more than painting his picture—she'd be guarding her heart.

* * *

Davis opened the door to his home and, as he had done for the past three months, checked the air. The scent of her bright and sassy perfume was still there. His feet moved heavy against the carpet as he entered the living room where he could smell it the most. *Night Velvet*. The aroma was faint. Not heavy and alluring like when she was upstairs changing or in his den studying. No, sadly he realized Jacquelyn was gone and gone for good.

Why did he think that she would change her mind? He had wanted so much for her to be waiting for him when he got home. He wanted . . .

Davis sat down in a chair and set his briefcase near his feet. The question raging in his head for the past week bid him no rest now. *What went wrong?*

He reviewed everything in his mind like a painful and infinite algorithmic loop. Their critical path was set—courtship, exclusivity, engagement, marriage, and eventually a family. He could see the milestones like a Gantt chart in his mind. But every time he tried to put the plan into motion, something would happen. They would clash, argue, miss cues. It was almost like Jacquelyn was trying to sabotage their developing relationship. Like she was only along for a joyride. And that's what hurt the most.

When he had had as much as he could take, he suggested that it might be best if they separated. His innermost feelings told him that what he really wanted was for her to refuse his suggestion. To show him in some way that it really wasn't his money, status, or the things he could provide. It was the future they could have together.

But she hadn't done that. She gave him that look. That Jacq look of incredulity and said "Okay," like it was no big deal. Davis couldn't remember bearing a worse feeling in his life.

He swept a glance at his surroundings. He remembered how purchasing each thing, whether it was a painting, furniture, a rug, a lamp, or some other accessory, had given him a sense of accomplishment and satisfaction. He remembered thinking that his clients would be impressed with his lifestyle. But he never considered that one day the things he'd accumulated would mean nothing, and that if he gave them away or burned them, it would no longer matter.

The room he worked in was the smallest in the four-story mansion. Light from the desk lamp splayed softly against the deep mahogany walls. In the shadow of evening, the only other light radiated from a small computer screen on a long desk.

Kenyon's hands swept across his keyboard with speed and deliberation. His latest family tree project was coming along nicely. The Wills family had quite a history and was one of the easiest to trace yet. It seemed they had a long-standing tradition of fire fighting. For the past seventy years, every generation had had a Wills male associated with fire fighting. Before that, it was politics.

Kenyon glanced from the notes in a file folder to documents he'd copied from microfiche and then to pages he'd downloaded from the Internet. As he filled in the information on the latest generation of Willses, he smiled. Gerald Wills had just entered college. Looked like he was majoring in accounting. He worked as a volunteer firefighter for the Philadelphia Fire Department and had pieced together several grants and small scholarships to fund his education.

He finished the last entry on the Wills family tree and printed the document. The culmination of six months' work. Kenyon was getting better. Faster. Each person he identified made it easier to find the next. His routine would soon become second nature.

He packed the papers on his desk into a file folder according to date. The oldest pages went in first, followed by more recent research and study. Each folder he created was filed and locked away in a storage cabinet. A glance into the large cabinet adjacent to his modular desk told him he'd need another storage area soon.

Before closing his computer down, Kenyon opened an electronic file on his desktop that was brand new. The Allgood family tree stared back at him in 32-bit color. Only partially completed, it was a project he had begun on a whim, just to see what he could find out about the little imp who refused to call herself an artist. During the past week he hadn't been able to figure out why she refused to acknowledge the truth.

As soon as they understood each other, they both had settled into the task at hand. He posed as she asked and in return, she drew sketches in preparation for the final portrait. After only the second day, Kenyon realized that if her painting was half as good as her illustrations, he'd not only fulfill his family duty but he would have discovered the next great twenty-first century talent in the art world.

In the cool of his third-floor office, that thought excited him. A spark of life traveled unchecked throughout his body. Stirring thoughts and energies Kenyon hadn't felt in quite some time. He had to see more of her work. And if there was more, then she was truly unaware of her own gifts. But maybe he could persuade her.

Kenyon took the paper from the printer, folded it and stuffed it into his jeans pocket. He was determined to discover the extent of Marti's artistic abilities. Unfortunately, he couldn't do it right away.

He had to remain focused on what had become his life's work. Nothing, not even a talented and spunky woman could prevent it.

Kenyon dialed the numbers to Andreas's extension. The assistant picked up on the first ring.

"Yes, sir."

"Tell Paul to prepare the plane. We're going to Philly."

Seven

Two weeks had gone by and Marti had done little more than a few sketches, mostly of Kenyon's hands, but somehow the pace felt right. His flat answers and air of impenetrability made it slow going, anyway. Even if she had wanted to work faster, she doubted whether he would be more forthcoming about himself and his life. Despite his expressed desire to "get this over as soon as possible," he didn't seem to be in a hurry to allow her to get to know him.

He was dark and mysterious like a smoky night. His deep black eyes, long nose, and marvelous mouth were always set, always stern. She had yet to see him smile. Whenever she came to the mansion, he was always businesslike and treated their time together like one more item to check off his daily task list. And that fact was starting to work on Marti's nerves.

What kind of person never has fun? she wondered. Marti grabbed three charcoal pencils and her sketchbook and headed out to the waiting limousine, determined to find out.

"Andreas," she said, settling inside the large plush vehicle, "how long have you known, uh, Kenny?" She felt funny and a little exhilarated calling the stoic man Kenny.

"Since before he was born."

"Really?" Marti said, enjoying the squish of Bubblicious between her teeth.

"Oh yeah, my family and the Williams family go back a long way. You know the Williamses have been prominent in this area for over a hundred years."

Marti sat forward. "You don't say?"

In the time it took for them to travel from her apartment to Kenyon's mansion, she had learned all about Zachary Williams who purchased his freedom in 1850 and, along with two other freedmen, started making fine clothes for the other freedmen.

"Word of mouth spread all over the South about the James, Clark, and Williams Company. Pretty soon any black who could afford it, and even some who were still enslaved, purchased their outfits.

"With the money he made from selling clothes, Zachary bought his brother's freedom and brought him into the business. Then something happened. Nobody seems to know exactly what, but Zachary and his brother Turner broke away from James and Clark and started their own business: Williams Brothers.

"For a while, Williams Brothers and the James Clark Company competed neck and neck, or so the story goes. But over time, Williams Brothers became more popular and the James Clark Company just couldn't compete and eventually went out of business.

"With the exception of the Depression, the business—that's what Kenny and his folks call it—has been extremely profitable, especially during the Superfly era. Black folks couldn't get enough of Williams Brothers suits back then."

"How are they doing now?"

"Now they're struggling a little. The folks with the buying power are more interested in what I call the thrift-store look. What's keeping the business afloat now is the steady stream of loyal customers like Steve

Harvey, Jesse Jackson, and Michael Jordan. But Reynard needs to do *something* or pretty soon the business will be out of business."

When they arrived at the front door, Andreas turned to her and smiled as if he knew a wondrous secret. The twinkle in his eyes made him appear twenty years younger. She wanted to ask what could cause such an expression, but she noticed Kenyon standing in the doorway. His arms were folded and his expression was that of a man not accustomed to waiting.

Just for that, I'll take my time, she thought.

"You're late," he said, as Andreas helped her from the vehicle.

The authority in his voice gave her goosebumps. Maybe it was a good thing that he didn't talk so much. That way his baritone voice couldn't fluster her so.

"So?"

Kenyon, who had been leaning against the door frame, arms folded, straightened and cast her a disapproving glance.

"I'm not paying you to be late, Marti."

A river of warmth covered her body. *The way he says my name,* she thought.

He looked ravishing in a tan polo shirt and faded blue jeans. With his moccasins and ponytail, he looked very much like a black Seminole. And why did it seem that each pair of jeans he wore fit him tighter and tighter? And why did that thought make her want to remove her blouse and wear only the white tank top beneath?

She needed to change the direction of her thoughts or else she wouldn't get much work done today. "Andreas and I were talking."

"Is that so?" he asked, staring in the old man's direction. But the elder gentleman was already back in the limousine and driving toward the garage.

"This way," Kenyon said. And without another word, she followed him into the house.

"You said you needed to see me in my element." Kenyon stretched his arms out to his sides. "This is my element. Now, I wouldn't classify myself as a recluse, but I do spend the majority of my time here. So, I thought I would give you a tour. Maybe seeing where I grew up and where I spend my time will tell you more about me, about the kind of person I am."

Marti smiled and warmed inside. "Let's go," she said.

"I guess the best place to start is at the beginning," he said, taking her back to the entrance. They stood before the main staircase. To the left and right were all the piece of artwork that always struck a chord of awe in Marti every time she entered the mansion.

"The first floor is designed for what my mother calls informal entertaining. I call it politicking. There are numerous small rooms on this floor created for stand-up receptions and small social gatherings."

Kenyon showed her a drawing room, a study, a breakfast room and a billiard room. As they moved from room to room, Marti was impressed by the exquisite attention to detail in the doorways, windows, and light fixtures.

"How many rooms do you have?"

"Thirty," he said as easily and nonchalantly as if he were telling his age.

"Thirty! My gosh!"

"There were originally fifteen. Then my great-great grandfather decided that the house was too small for him so he had the exact structure built again and attached to the original."

"You're kidding!"

Kenyon's look of seriousness made something in

her stomach feel just a bit uneasy. "I wish I were," he said.

They walked down a long corridor and Marti could see that true to Kenyon's explanation, the west wing of the mansion was a duplicate of the east wing. The smell of chlorine filled her lungs.

"This used to be the servants' hall, but I turned it into a pool room—which," he said, looking at her slyly, "you've already seen."

Marti's cheeks flushed. "Where do the servants sleep now?"

Kenyon winced. "I don't have servants," he said. "Most of those who assist me in taking care of this place have their own homes. Those that choose to live here stay on the third floor with me."

She nodded.

He led her upstairs. The decor became distinctly more elaborate.

"This is where my family held all their formal gatherings." One by one, he escorted her through an elegant ballroom, a dining hall, and the library where her painting would hang. He also showed her some of the other more thematic rooms. The tulip room was decorated with festive wallpaper and cheerful upholstery brimming with tulips. And there were vases clustered everywhere—waiting for fresh-cut tulips, Marti reasoned. The orange room was just that . . . orange. All the furniture, wallpaper, window treatments, and other furnishings were in various shades of orange. The decorative ceramic bowls looked as though they had been fashioned out of orange sherbet. The room even smelled like orange blossoms.

Next, they visited the tea room. Marti drew in a breath, truly feeling like she'd been transported through time. She could almost see women in high-fashion hats adorned with clusters of flowers, long white gloves, long wool dresses, and lace-up boots taking tea and talking about the things that well-to-do blacks talked about in their time. *Did they ring a bell for more tea? Or did their servants wait on them in the room, fussing over them and attending to their every need? It must have been a grand time.*

"How long has this mansion been in your family?"

The light in Kenyon's eyes went dark. "Generations."

They went up another staircase, this one much grander than the other.

"The bedrooms are on this floor. The east suites are where guests would sleep. Andreas, Roberta the cook, and Bullock the groundskeeper sleep there now. My family slept in the west suites." They walked in that direction. "Now it's just me."

The sleeping areas boasted twelve-foot ceilings, carved oak moldings, and wide fireplaces with ornamental mantels. Some of the plasterwork contained 24-carat gold leafing and many of the rooms were adorned with stained glass windows. Marti's artist eye did not miss the craftsmanship or the opulent splendor and care that had gone into creating and decorating each room. How fortunate Kenyon was to be surrounded by beauty and rooms of lavish fare.

"If I lived here," she said, excitement coursing through her veins, "I'd never want to leave."

If she knew how rarely he did leave, Kenyon was sure she'd label him a recluse. He thought about that for a moment and realized that maybe he was.

"And this is the Empire Suite where I sleep," he said, walking into the only room on the floor with opened doors.

Marti entered and couldn't believe her eyes. The splendor she saw made her want to curtsey or ask permission to enter.

From the moment she'd set foot in the house, and every time since, she'd caught what she called the old-house smell. Aromas of aging wood and varnish; the faint odors of people and their activities; the ghosts of dinners cooked, parties hosted, and families raised. They had all settled into the ceiling, walls, and floor. The house breathed them out, released them from pores of plaster, linen, paint, and mortar. No place was the old house smell more pronounced than in Kenyon's room—Kenyon's opulent room with its draped ceiling, richly appointed wallpaper, oversize four-poster bed, two fireplaces, period antiques, hand-woven tapestries, writing desk, armoire, five enormous windows, floor-to-ceiling closet, and floor-to-ceiling mirror.

He showed her the reading area where he often did research, the morning area where Andreas served him breakfast, and the vanity area complete with a double-backed claw-foot tub and a dark marble shower with five massage jets and three shower heads. Her skin tingled when he told her it was designed for two people. The focal point of his bedroom was the stained glass Victorian French doors, eight feet high, that opened onto a carriage house balcony overlooking the courtyard.

"It's breathtaking," she said, thinking of the view, the tour, and the life Kenyon must lead behind the walls of his mansion. Among the treasures she'd seen, the addition of the painting of her mother was no longer an outrage, but an honor. And so it was with her portrait of Kenyon. As she was slowly becoming acquainted with him, her mind formulated ideas for her painting. The tour had been a good idea.

Even though he had opened up to her by showing her the house and sharing that part of his life, Marti could sense something sad and vulnerable in his demeanor. And whatever it was made her wonder why his soul seemed so troubled. It also made her determined to find out. She sensed that Kenyon could be a warm and caring man if he could only free himself from the yoke that kept his mood so dark. Her instinct told her that some of it had to do with the house.

"Let's go outside," she said.

The end of the tour consisted of the grounds. Apparently Kenyon had saved the best for last.

Kenyon's tour of the mansion had been like browsing through a museum, and strolling through the estate grounds was like walking in wonderland. Tall, wrought iron fenced off half an acre of land. Couched in an elegance of another era sat the superbly landscaped sunken garden. As they wandered through the lush greenery, Marti imagined the grand lifestyles of days gone by. The classical details of the spacious courtly estate enthralled her.

The other buildings of the estate included the conservatory, stables, and gardener's cottage, all of which were currently unoccupied.

"Explaining all of this to you makes me realize how grand it sounds."

"You mean it's not?"

"Not when you grow up with it. Not when it's all you know. And then when you're old enough to realize the luxury you have, sometimes it just becomes stuff. Stuff to look at. Stuff to take care of. Stuff that takes up space. Stuff that stays cold even in the summer."

There was pain in Kenyon's voice, a pain that Marti could feel. She wanted to comfort him. Help him see that a brighter side of life was out there and if he would just remove the gloom from his disposition he would see it.

* * *

As they walked the grounds, Marti felt like an eight-year-old child. She had an overwhelming urge to go exploring. She could imagine there were unique nooks and crannies on the grounds. Places where one could go and get lost or see something spectacular. She blew a bubble and popped it. "Take me somewhere," she said.

"Where?"

She stretched out her arms and twirled around. "Anywhere, as long as it's fun!"

"You mean like an amusement park?"

"No! I mean around here." She took off her shoes. The thick and lush grass looked as though it had been combed instead of mowed. The smell of nature and earth surrounded them. "I'm sure there was somewhere you and your brother used to go and play when you were young."

"There is. But what does that have to do with the painting?"

"Everything," she said marveling at how the grass, the shrubs, and the landscaped bushes just smelled *green*. "Take me there."

For a moment, all he did was frown. She wished he would lighten up sometimes. *Why is he always so serious?* she wondered.

"Well, all right. It's over here."

Kenyon led her through a precisely manicured and elegantly sculpted pathway. The pathway rolled and turned into a thicket that grew closer to the Tallapoosa river.

Now and then, Marti would smell flowers, pick a leaf, or touch a branch. It was like walking through the largest greenhouse on the planet. She wondered who took care of everything. Certainly not Kenyon. He was too spoiled and brooding. And not Andreas. He was too old. Whoever it was must have had a great love for nature. It showed in the care and precision of the landscaping.

The thicket continued until they reached a part that opened into a less dense portion of the property. And there she saw a cluster of trees and bushes the resembled a verdant crown growing out of the ground. She stood back in awe.

"Come on. You said you wanted to see it."

She followed him in.

"How did this happen? I mean, is it natural?"

"I don't know. It's so symmetrical. Someone may have planted it like this as a sanctuary away from the house." Kenyon thought about all of the servants his family had during that time. During a time when African Americans were prohibited from gathering in large numbers, this grove might have been created to provide a place where people could come for fellowship, worship, or just plain getting away from work and all the pressures involved with servitude. Since his youth, he'd imagined meetings of families and friends on many occasions.

Marti saw the reverence on Kenyon's face and was warmed by it. It seemed his heart wasn't untouchable after all. You just had to come through the right door. And something about this spot was the right door.

Marti stepped inside the circle. She touched a tree and examined a shrub.

"These trees look young. Maybe a hundred years or so."

"How do you know that?" Kenyon asked, intrigued.

"My father talked about trees when I was a kid. He was fascinated by them, from what I remember. He died when I was very young."

"I'm sorry."

"Me, too."

Kenyon felt a lump of sadness in his stomach. "So you lost both of your parents?"

"Yes," she said.

Deep regret clouded Marti's eyes and Kenyon was afraid that she might cry. But it only lasted a moment and she was back to her spunky, fun-loving self. "So you used to come here as a kid?"

"My brother and I thought that no one knew about the spot except us."

Marti smiled. "Really?"

"Yeah. I'm not sure how we came to believe that. It was like we were the only ones who could see this thick section of the grounds. We thought this place was magic."

Her eyes brightened with the possibility that his child's mythology could be true. He wondered how someone so small could have a smile so big.

"What kind of magic?" She blew another bubble and waited his response.

"Mostly the magic to get us out of trouble."

Marti plunked herself down in the middle of the grove. "This sounds good," she said, pulling her legs up.

Kenyon remained standing. "Whenever our parents would punish one or sometimes both of us, we always wound up here. We'd talk about how we couldn't wait until we were grown or all the terrible things we wish would happen to our parents for doing us wrong." Kenyon smiled. "We even planned to run away one day."

"How old were you?"

He rubbed his dark fingers across his goatee and looked up into the sun. "Let's see, I must have been eleven or twelve. So that means Reynard must have been nine or ten."

He glanced at Marti, a nostalgic grin plastered on

his face. "We had a half-eaten peppermint stick, six slices of bread, and—you would have liked this—some bubble gum. We were going to hike to Marietta by cutting through the woodsy area straight ahead. After that, we were going to hitchhike to California and audition for H.R. Puff-n-Stuff, because . . ." A blast of deep laughter from Kenyon filled the air. "Because he's who you called when things got rough!"

Marti laughed, too. After a few moments, he sat down beside her on the cool green earth.

"I haven't thought about that in years," he said.

Marti hummed the theme song. "I can't remember all the words, but I remember the tune." Kenyon sang awkwardly along with her humming. Some of the words he remembered. Most he didn't.

"Something, something, something, cause you can't something, something," he crooned.

They both broke into hearty laughter.

"Still planning your escape, son?"

Kenyon and Marti's heads snapped around to see an older African American couple standing several feet behind them.

"Marti Allgood," Kenyon said, unease lacing his voice, "meet my parents."

Eight

Even if Kenyon hadn't said anything, there was no mistaking the couple walking toward them. The tall man's moon-dark features and thick jet-black hair. The woman's deep piercing eyes, and fluid form and movement. Kenyon was a perfect physical blend of his parents. Marti wondered if the similarities ran more than skin deep.

She waited for a cue from Kenyon. Would he rise for them?

He didn't.

She sprang up anyway and shook their hands. "Hi!" she said, smiling warmly. "I'm Marti Allgood."

Kenyon's mother, Beverleigh Williams, bent slightly and offered an immaculate hand. Marti took it cheerfully. *Smooth,* she thought. *Just like her son's.* Richmond Williams was a barrel-chested man who stood well over six feet tall and wore a mustache as thick as the hair on his head. His mother had an air of competence and sophistication. Her coppery hair and cinnamon complexion caught the afternoon sun and held it seemingly against its will. She appeared to be the type of woman who smiled only when it was absolutely necessary. Disappointment rumbled in Kenyon's chest. Beverleigh and Richmond Williams never came to the mansion without a purpose. He suspected their visit this time had something to do with a certain small but spunky young woman who had been seen scurrying about the mansion of late. Yes, he was completely certain that someone on his staff had contacted his parents and told them about Marti. And now they'd come to see this woman who was occupying so much of their recluse of a son's life. His time with Marti had made him forget that in the Williams mansion, the walls had eyes.

"Who told you about Marti?" he asked, frustration lowering his already cavern-deep voice.

His parents exchanged glances, then his father spoke and Marti knew where Kenyon's vocal chords came from. "Roberta. She mentioned the extra meals she'd been preparing and wondered if she should increase the monthly grocery order."

Kenyon's face was unreadable as stone. "I doubt that."

His mother huffed. "Be that as it may, we're here now, so be a good son and invite us for dinner."

"And if I don't?"

A smile split his father's ebony face. "We're staying anyway."

Kenyon and Marti walked toward the mansion slightly behind his parents. "What do you want for dinner?" he asked her.

"Why?"

"Because if you're going to endure this agony, you might as well have a pleasant meal."

Her eyes widened in surprise. "Kenyon, I've got plans for this evening."

He eyed her suspiciously. "Cancel them."

She stopped, the audacity of his order bringing her to anger. "You must really be used to getting what you want," she said through tight lips.

His gaze raked over her hotly as if she were naked. The anger she felt dissolved into rising heat.

"Be that as it may," he said, like a leopard speaking in a low growl. "My parents have come to see you."

"How do you—"

"Because I know. Someone must have told them you've been coming to see me. They got curious."

They resumed their long trek back to the mansion. "Don't you have any friends or girlfriends that visit?" Marti asked.

Kenyon didn't miss a beat. "None that my parents don't know."

A lump of disappointment filled Marti's throat. She'd hoped that he would say he didn't have any girlfriends.

Kenyon struggled to be on his best behavior throughout dinner. He didn't want to give his parents any reason to linger, ask too many questions, or come back anytime soon. They would only remind him of how much his rejection of the business disappointed them. And they would ride him about how they thought he was wasting his life away sulking in the mansion. Then he would retaliate by saying something to hurt them the way they had hurt him. And it would be a disaster.

He would not only engage in the age-old game of insults and injury that he and his parents had been playing for years, but also he would embarrass himself in front of Marti and possibly embarrass her. He couldn't stand to let that happen. He respected her too much, and strangely, he liked her too much as well. He refused to let his often-overbearing parents put a ripple in the peace he'd found of late. A peace he strangely associated with Marti.

So he'd remained relatively quiet while Marti, on the other hand, had chattered on like she and his parents were old friends. He kept his eyes on her as she became the center of attention talking about her superstar brother, all the companies she'd created signs for, and her theories about birth order. His parents had laughed when she told them that she was the baby of the family and the fact that they were giving her their undivided attention felt better than if she'd had a glass of champagne.

She was like a tiny beacon in the room shining on his parents, and in her light, suddenly they didn't look overbearing at all. They looked like decent people enjoying dinner and delightful conversation.

Kenyon was in awe.

When Marti excused herself to go to the bathroom, Kenyon shook off the spell she'd cast and focused on finishing his meal.

"She's doing more than painting your portrait," Beverleigh said.

"Mother!" Kenyon replied, shocked at her insinuation.

"Relax. I'm not being vulgar, dear. I'm simply stating that you are obviously smitten with this little girl and perhaps you should marry her or something."

He was too stunned by his mother's suggestion to offer any objection.

"Your mother's right, son. I haven't seen your eyes this alive since . . . since you discovered that your ancestors were less than perfect."

"Less than perfect means making a mistake. What good old Williams and Williams did was commit atrocities," Kenyon said, his voice cold and lashing.

His father's features hardened like stone. "Get over it. Everyone else has."

"Everyone else has what?" a curious voice asked.

Kenyon's head turned toward the sound and groaned. He thought the evening couldn't get any worse. He was wrong. Someone on his staff was going to be sorry for speaking out of turn. He closed his eyes as his brother Reynard strode into the room and placed a perfunctory kiss on their mother's cheek.

"So, where is she? I heard she's as cute as hell."

Right on cue, Marti returned from the bathroom and retook her seat. Reynard's eyes were trained on her the entire time. "And so she is," he said with quiet emphasis. "And so she is."

"Marti, this is my brother, Reynard," Kenyon said, looking up.

Reynard was his mother's son. He'd taken all of her features, her lighter, almost reddish, complexion, hard-set eyes, and hair like auburn embers. Reynard tapped a button on the wall intercom. "This is Reynard. I'll be having dessert with my family."

Kenyon's eyes washed over with deep concern and regret. "I apologize for all this. They're checking up on me. No, that's not true. They are here to check you out. I guess one of my staff—"

"That's nice," she said, interrupting. "I'm glad to meet you, Reynard," Marti responded. And it was true. She'd wondered what Kenyon's family was like, what their relationships were. Now she would find out firsthand.

She was doing it again. After only a few short minutes, Marti had Reynard eating out of her hand. They had all become moths to her flame. The freeness of her spirit, to laugh, to poke fun, and to look upon everything with wonder had captured all their hearts, including his. Especially his. For the first time in years, Kenyon had a decent meal with his family. Despite everything he did, by the end of the night, they all ended up laughing and joking a little. A change that was both small and monumental.

Maybe he was looking at Marti with eyes that were alive. And maybe there was a reason for it.

"What kind of portrait do you want?"

"Are there different kinds?"

A smile tugged at the corners of her mouth. "Yes and no. There are definitely different styles. The style you get depends on why you want the portrait. The purpose," she said with a snap of her gum.

"I need a portrait to shut my parents up, especially my mother."

Marti's childlike features crinkled with confusion.

"It's tradition. While the women in the family are responsible for decorating the rooms in the mansion, selecting themes, and arranging for the care of the furnishings, the men in my family run the business and have their likenesses immortalized in canvas.

"I don't participate in the affairs of the business, a fact that my parents take every opportunity to nag me about. I leave company business for my brother, Reynard. I've also resisted having my portrait painted. The primary purpose of the portraits was to create a record of the business owners for posterity. Since I'm not involved in the business, I saw no reason why my image had to be added to all the rest.

"I'm the first Williams in a long time to balk at the idea of running the company. My parents promised to stop riding me about partnering with my brother if I at least sat for a painting."

He slid a glance to Marti who was watching him with bright eyes, as if she found his every word fascinating. He couldn't imagine that to be true, but the possibility stroked his ego.

"They had a painter already on retainer, but I decided that if I'm going to subject myself to this, I'm at least going to hire my own artist."

"Here's what we'll do, then. I'll need some more time to get to know you a little."

Why did her eyes sparkle like tiny suns when she said that?

"I'll be back day after tomorrow, and just so you know . . . a portrait, a good one anyway, doesn't just capture you for a moment. That's called a photograph. A portrait captures you for eternity. The essence of you, your life, your spirit, your nature, your . . . soul."

Kenyon blew hot breath through his nostrils. The way he felt most days, he wondered if he still had a soul.

"No, don't come out."

Marti walked from one end of the pool to the other, keeping the naked Kenyon in her sight. She had come to spend some time with him. Andreas had told her he was taking a swim, so she'd come into the pool room. She'd found him there, in the middle of laps, as if he were training for a competition.

"I thought you were coming over tomorrow."

"I was. But despite what I tell you about being natural and going about your business as if I wasn't here, I still feel like a part of you is not completely relaxed or letting down your guard. So, I thought I would—"

"Catch me with my pants down," he finished.

She giggled, but his expression never changed. He treaded water with the same stern set to his features that she'd come to recognize every day. Kenyon Williams was just way too serious.

"I just thought that if I showed up unannounced, maybe you wouldn't have had time to put up your brick wall."

The light in his eyes flickered for a moment. Maybe she'd gotten through, she thought. He glided to the edge near her and his tight expression loosened a bit. "Why don't you join me?"

A sudden blaze ignited at the pit of Marti's stomach and rose to her heart. What a tempting idea. If only she had been prepared.

"I didn't bring a suit."

"Sure you did," he said, flipping down into the water and giving Marti a quick glimpse of his round backside. In a few seconds, he surfaced and shook the water loose from his hair. "You always have the best suit with you."

His voice sounded as deep as the pool he swam in. Marti's skin prickled from what Kenyon was suggesting.

"I've never swum nude before."

A smile teased the corners of Kenyon's mouth. "Once you do, you'll never want to swim any other way."

What he was proposing sounded like fun, and Marti did enjoy a good time. But what would he think of her if she just stripped in front of him? What would she think of herself?

"Kenyon, I hardly know you, and—"

"And you've been telling me for weeks that it's your job as a portrait painter to get to know me, right?"

She nodded.

"What better way than to join me in my element? And believe me, unlike my house, water is my main element."

Marti stared at the sketchpad and pencils she'd brought with her. The more she considered swimming with Kenyon, the more foreign they felt in her hands.

"I'm not a great swimmer," she admitted. The fact was, she was a terrible swimmer. She could keep herself afloat, but just barely. A trait she shared with her sisters. Something about water and the asymmetrical hairstyles that they wore growing up didn't mix. So she'd spent only enough time in a pool to learn how to tread water, and not much else. But the idea of being naked and wet with the handsome millionaire was more than appealing. It almost felt necessary. She wouldn't even try to fake herself out by telling herself she was doing it for research. She stepped out of her shoes knowing she was doing it for pleasure, plain and simple.

"There's a changing room in the back," Kenyon said, motioning with his hand.

"Oh," she said. She grabbed her shoes and trotted off toward the back of the pool room.

Marti's body wasn't perfect. Of course, she'd always wanted to be taller. She wished her breasts were larger and her waist slimmer. But it was her body and she'd never been ashamed of it. She just wished she could do a little tweaking here and there. Even her small misgivings vanished when she emerged from the changing room. The look in Kenyon's eyes told her that she was perfect just the way she was.

Marti slipped in at the shallow end and Kenyon swam to meet her. When she was all in, he took her arms and pulled her against the surface of the water. Marti let herself relax and stared into eyes that seemed to be saying, "Trust me." For a few long moments, they simply glided in silence.

The smell of chlorine reminded Marti of summers she spent as a child, trying to keep up with her older sisters. Always wanting to know what they knew. Always wanting to do what they did. Being the baby of the family, she always missed the mark.

"Relax," Kenyon said. "I'm not going to drown you."

Marti shook her head. "It's not that."

Then he did it. He actually smiled. "I'm an art collector. So remember, when I see a naked body I appreciate it for the aesthetic pleasure it gives me, not the sexual pleasure."

Something about that statement disappointed Marti. She liked the idea of being sexually pleasing to Kenyon. He certainly was to her.

The sound of their bodies breaking through the water was peaceful, like nature's tranquilizer. Tension eased out of Marti's body and she felt herself rising. No longer weighted down by stress. Kenyon continued to smile as they moved across the pool. They slid together and apart. As was as if he was introducing her to his world, helping her to get acquainted with every inch of the water. She wasn't swimming. She was flying.

"If this is what it takes to make you smile, I'll swim with you everyday."

"Every day? Even after the portrait is finished?"

Marti didn't have to think about it. "Yes, even then."

The sensation of the water against her skin was heavenly. Better than any bath she'd ever taken. The water covered her over, warming her, caressing her.

As he neared the deep end of the pool, Marti's tension returned.

"No, don't," he said. "Don't go stiff on me. You'll sink like a bag of pennies."

She moved closer to him, glided against him for safety. Then she stopped.

"I don't think I'm ready."

His smile faded. "We'll stay in the shallow end, then."

He guided her back to the other side of the pool. His movements automatic, as if he lived in the water.

"How long have you been swimming?" she asked, suddenly remembering her task.

"As long as I can remember. I can't ever recall swimming lessons. My folks say when I was two, I followed Andreas out to the pool. When I saw the water I just jumped in. When my father dove in to rescue me, I kept swimming away from him."

Marti laughed. She liked the way droplets of water clung to his face and neck. It wouldn't take much for her to lick them right off. Her nipples hardened at the thought. In the warm temperature of the water, the only explanation would be arousal.

Not being able to stop herself, she glanced down into the water to see if Kenyon was having the same reaction to her.

He was.

She looked up, startled.

He offered a soft smile. "Okay. So I'm human." He floated closer. "I'm also respectful. I won't try anything."

Suddenly the thought of being in the pool with an aroused man gave Marti a weird feeling all over. She moved to cover herself. Her arm slipped from Kenyon's grasp, and she plunged face first into the water.

A blast of water shot up her nose. The loud and muffled silence of being underwater swallowed her. Marti's arms flailed. She heard her heartbeat in her ears and then Kenyon's strong arms propelled her up and out of the water.

"Are you all right? What happened?"

She gasped for a few seconds before answering. "I

just slipped," she said, slightly ashamed of her bobble. "I told you I'm not good at this swimming stuff."

He held her waist for a moment, making sure she was steady again in the water. She liked the feel of his hot hands against her skin.

Water coursed down Marti's face. She blinked away droplets from her eyes.

"Come on," he said.

"Where?"

"Down here," he replied and dropped into the water. His body plummeted like a missile. When he reached the bottom, he stretched out his arm for her.

He's crazy, she thought. *I can't just descend into the water like I do this every day.* But Marti forgetting hesitation, and never being one for convention, took a deep breath and followed the same route Kenyon had taken to the bottom. She summoned her nerve and opened her eyes. He was smiling again. Then he took her and brought them leisurely up to the top.

They both came up gasping for air and grinning.

"Why did you do that?" Marti asked.

"You needed to shake off your edge. I could tell you were nervous, a little scared maybe. I figured if you visited the bottom and survived, you wouldn't be so afraid of it, or being underwater." He hesitated. "Or me."

Marti frowned. "I'm not afraid of you!"

They swam together across the pool. "Everybody's afraid of me. They think I'm some kind of ogre."

"Are you?"

Kenyon flipped under the water and came up by her side. "Sometimes."

Marti tread water next to him. "Why?"

"Life isn't as great as we are led to believe. It's full of deceptions and false faces."

Marti frowned.

"Someday, when you get a little older, you may come to understand what I mean."

Astonishment widened her gaze. "Older?"

His look of resolution returned. "Yes."

She let go of him and turned away. "I'll never grow old."

He touched her back. "Marti?"

She turned around, at the same time slamming her hands into the water to create the biggest splash possible.

"Hey!" Kenyon shouted, turning away, but it was too late. She'd doused him.

He wiped a hand down his wet face. "I don't believe you just did that."

"Really?" she asked and did it again. This time with a laugh.

"Aw!" he hollered. "Don't do that again."

"Or what?" she taunted, splashing, splashing, and splashing some more.

Kenyon swam back and put his arms up in protest. "Or this," he said and disappeared beneath the water.

"Uh-oh," Marti said, feeling the warm water lap against her flesh.

She peered into the pool after him, but he'd waded out, further and further from the shallow end. "Kenyon?"

When she reached the part of the pool where she dared not swim any further, she waited. The humidity rising from the warm water dampened her skin even more.

Waves rippled near her ankles. She could tell he was close. Then in a split second, he propelled up out of the water behind her and carried her down.

She twisted away from the shock of his actions, but soon settled against his warm flesh. It was comforting, being next to him in the water. It felt so incredibly right. He let her go and they smiled at each other. They floated that way for a moment. Hovering just an arm's reach away. His beautiful black muscular body and mane of onyx hair. He looked like he was flying. Like God sent an angel and he was flying to her.

She needed air.

Marti shot up to the surface, sucking air. She blinked away the water cascading from her short hair. She placed a trembling hand against her chest, suddenly acutely aware of her nakedness.

Kenyon followed her quick ascent. "What's wrong?"

"Nothing," she said, blinking. She didn't know how he could be so asexual at a time like this. He didn't act the slightest bit interested or attracted to her. She, on the other hand, was having a heck of a time controlling her emotions and her attraction to him.

True to his word, he hadn't made a pass at her. The only emotional outburst came in his uncharacteristically playful antics.

"You've been accusing me of being a stick-in-the-mud for weeks. When I finally, and painfully I might add, lighten up, you clam up. What's that about?"

"It's about this!" she said and dunked him into the water. From that moment, it was on. The two had a water-slopping, face-dunking free-for-all. They wrestled, splashed, and bopped each other with long sponge toys. After much coaxing, Marti even convinced Kenyon to join her in a game of synchronized bubble blowing. When she asked him about water soccer, he declined, admitting he'd had enough fun for a while.

He managed to convince her to join him in the Jacuzzi as a way to cool down the muscles he assured her would be aching tomorrow. Marti settled into the tub and Kenyon excused himself.

"I'll be right back," he said.

She was so content, she felt guilty. *I didn't do a bit of work for the portrait,* she thought. But hadn't she? Images of Kenyon's face drenched with water were etched into her mind permanently. The way he looked at her when she emerged from the changing room had become a permanent part of her soul. Images of him gliding through the water as if he had gills instead of lungs would be with her always. Yes, she'd done her work for the portrait. She'd done her work very well.

Before she realized she was doing it, she started singing. "Little Warm Death" by Cassandra Wilson. She thought the song described the euphoric feeling of ecstasy and likened it to dying sweetly and being born again. How just the touch of a love can change you forever. Her voice rose as she realized she'd been changed . . . forever.

Kenyon returned with champagne bottle and two glasses. "That's beautiful," he said. "Why do you paint if you have a voice like that?"

Marti looked on as he opened the bottle and filled their glasses. "Actually, I have the worst voice in my family." She took the flute from Kenyon as he lowered himself into the water and sat beside her.

She shook her head. "I remember singing with my sisters and my brother when I was a kid. All the grown-ups would ooh and ah for them. For me, they would just smile and pat my head."

"Well, this grown-up thinks they were wrong."

Marti sipped from her glass. "Thanks."

"You've had the displeasure of meeting my family. Tell me about yours."

Marti snuggled down into the churning water. "I have four older sisters and one older brother. My sister Ashley is closest to me in age. She's . . . interesting.

For someone who has never really worked in her life, she's managed to travel to all of the states and to several countries. She's a New Age flower child, always talking about auras, chakras, and karma. Her hair is usually dyed some outrageous color. That is, when she has hair. Sometimes she shaves it all off."

She took another sip of champagne. "We don't get along with Ashley. We can't really figure her out. She's on some Zen-Krishna kind of trip. She's *way* out there. And no one in the family seems to be able to reach her.

"Next is my brother, Zay. He's the singer in the family. His second CD went double platinum. He's on an international tour right now. His wife's a really good friend of mine. They're expecting their first child any time now.

"Impressive," Kenyon said.

"He really, really is. Next is Morgan. She's the beauty in the family. And she knows it. She did some modeling for a while, but she never made it big. She's still into looking good, though. She makes all her own clothes. They look like something you'd see on a French runway.

"My oldest sister is Yolanda. Yolanda has the most beautiful streaks of gray hair you'd ever want to see. She met her husband Eldon when she was in junior high school. They've been married for twenty years, but they've been together for almost thirty. They have one daughter, Amara. Everyone thought that Morgan was the most beautiful girl, until Amara was born. Amara really looks like an angel."

They sat in silence for a moment, drinking their champagne. Kenyon couldn't imagine a more beautiful angel than the one sitting next to him. "You said you have four older sisters. That's only three."

Marti took a deep breath and a long swig from her

glass. "My other sister is Roxanne. She's second to oldest. We're not on the best of terms."

"Why not, may I ask?"

Marti blew hot between her lips. "Ten years ago, when I wasn't nearly as mature as I am now, I told on her."

"What do you mean *told on her*?"

"I told someone something that I shouldn't have, and she's never forgiven me for it."

"After ten years?"

"It was something major." Marti wished she had a piece of gum to chew on. "I've tried to make things right between she and me. She says everything is okay. But she never calls me just to say 'Hey!' like my other sisters do. When she's in town, she never stops by. If we're in the same room, she's civil, but she never intentionally speaks to me. I know it's my fault, so I don't press the issue. But sometimes . . . sometimes I want my big sister back."

"I'm sorry," Kenyon said.

Concerned darkened his features, taking Marti by surprise. *Well, what do you know? Under that gruff exterior lives a person with actual feelings.*

"Thank you," she said.

They finished the rest of the champagne, Marti liking the playful side of Kenyon and he liking the more serious side of her.

She couldn't believe she'd just spent the better part of the afternoon in the nude with Kenyon. She asked herself where her modesty had gone. Then she realized that Kenyon had helped her get rid of it.

Nine

Selena folded back the *Des Moines Register* and turned to page three. Her article on the pack of stray dogs that had been terrorizing the riverside area took up a whole three column inches. Barely enough room to rate above a filler.

"Oh," she sighed, shoving the paper away. "I will never get a choice project by waiting for Ty to assign me one."

On cue, her pet Siamese, Ida B., jumped into her lap and the two of them lay on the couch—one purring, the other pouting. Selena stroked the cat's soft fur. "Looks like I have to do this on my own. Looks like . . ."

She paused when the article opposite hers caught her eye. She read it quickly, as if she were consuming a fine meal. The headline read: "Saint Black Blesses Again."

The short article gave the details of a Philadelphia college student who had returned to his dorm room to find a briefcase with a million dollars in it. The note attached encouraged him to finish his education and not to tell a soul how he'd gotten the money. Apparently one of his friends had leaked the information to the press. The article also mentioned similar cases of generosity occurring over the past few years. At last report, the student was unavailable for comment, but sources said he'd already paid off his student loans and was in the process of having a house built for his mother.

Selena put the paper down once again, ideas churning in her head. She scratched Ida B. behind the ears. "If I can find out who this Saint Black is, I can write the news article of the century and sell it to the highest bidder. That would put me on the publishing industry map. And just think, Ida B.," she said, snuggling closer to the feline, "if this is some old coot on his death bed trying to do good deeds in order to get into heaven and somehow he's managed to radically improve people's lives, we might be talking Pulitzer."

The cat jumped down, circled Selena's feet, and headed off toward the kitchen. With renewed energy, she followed, eager to grab a quick bite to eat and to get to work for the first time in months.

Marti sat in a maroon Lazyboy in her brother's living room. The leather squeaked a bit when she moved to fold her leg and bare foot under her.

Although her brother seemed to be blowing up the music charts these days, the success hadn't gone to his head. He and his wife Destiny still lived like plain ol' black folks. She thought that was good and she was glad the accolades and trappings of stardom hadn't gone to their heads.

Destiny swaggled out of the kitchen with a tray of fruit and crackers, and juice she'd made from a juice machine. Marti was hungry and thirsty.

"Girl, don't you mess around and have that baby while I'm sittin' here," Jacquelyn Jackson said, taking a cracker off the tray before Destiny could set it down on the table in front of them. "Marti, go boil some water. This big cow is makin' me nervous."

"Forget you, buffalo butt." The pregnant woman

eased herself onto the couch. "My daughter is waiting for her father to come home before she makes her appearance."

Marti's gaze shifted immediately to her sister-in-law's round belly. "I thought you said you didn't know what you're having."

"I told the doctor not to tell me, but I have a feeling. The way this child is moving and always active, it's got to be a girl." Destiny looked down and cooed. "That's right, daddy will be home soon."

"Okay, now *when* will my brother be back?" Marti took a huge gulp of the thick, sweet liquid.

"Yeah, girl, you know you can't be without your man for too long."

"First of all, Xavier will be home in a few days."

"I thought Zay was supposed to come home tonight?" Marti interrupted.

"He was, but his manager scheduled him for some signings at a few record stores. And Japan has a show like *Good Morning America,* so Xavier will sing a couple of songs on the show."

"Dang, what's wrong with that manager?" Jacq quipped.

"What's wrong with my brother? He knows you're due any minute."

"That's why he's coming home in a few days. His manager actually has him scheduled for appearances for the next week, but Xavier refused and he said he is definitely flying back Wednesday night. Which leads me to my second point," Destiny said, pointing a pudgy finger at Jacq, "I understand my husband's schedule, heifer!" She popped a small cracker in her mouth, and continued to talk. "But if you want to talk about somebody's man, let's talk about yours. When are you two getting back together?"

Flanked on both sides by two stubborn women, Jacq

rolled her eyes first to the left and then to the right.
"Y'all ain't gonna worry me about Davis." Jacq worked
her neck and threw up her hand. "He has been officially kicked to the curb."

The two women on either side of her leaned forward and smiled at each other. "She still loves him,"
they said in unison.

"Humph," Jacq replied, and sipped a little from her
drink. "See, here's what you don't know. I am over
that fool, and to prove it, I'm going out tonight with
some friends from school. You two can come if you
like . . . watch me get my party on!" Jacq snapped her
fingers a couple of times in the air.

"No, that's okay."

"I'll pass, but I will ask you this," Destiny said. "You
mentioned the word prove. What are you trying to
prove and who are you trying to prove it to?"

Jacq sucked her teeth. "Girl, you trippin'."

"Am I?"

There was silence in the room and both Marti and
Destiny could tell Jacq was upset. But neither were
prepared for the emotional outburst that came next.

Suddenly Jacq burst into tears and rushed into the
bathroom. Her two friends followed and pounded on
the locked door.

"Jacq!" they shouted.

"Let us in!"

"Girl, it's all right! Open the door!"

Jacq's sobs reverberated through the closed door.

Marti turned to Destiny. "Do you have a key?"

"Yes!" she said, and ambled off toward the
kitchen.

Marti could feel Jacq's pain as if it were her own.
Her chest tightened and tears welled up in her eyes.
She pressed against the door. "Jacq, please . . . I know
it hurts. I know it feels like you're . . . dying inside."

"I got it," Destiny said, approaching.

Marti stepped aside and in a few seconds, Destiny unlocked the door. The two rushed inside.

Jacq was sitting on the floor, her face wet and her eyes already puffy. She wept aloud, rocking back and forth.

Marti and Destiny sat down beside her and wrapped her in their arms.

"Why can't I get over him? Why does it hurt like this to be away from him? He's just a man!"

Marti wanted to say, "He's the man for you." But she didn't dare. That might make things worse. So she sat there with Destiny and rocked her friend until her sobs subsided.

Jacq looked up and wiped her damp face. "I'm sorry. That just came out of nowhere."

Destiny just smiled. "Strong feelings usually do."

"How are you doing?" Marti asked.

"Better," Jacq replied, eyes a bit brighter.

"Good," Destiny said. "'Cause I got down here, but it's going to take both of you to get me up!"

The three of them laughed. It was a good, nervous laugh. Marti knew that Jacq had only scratched the surface of her feelings. She was still in denial. It was as if she and Davis were the only ones on the planet that didn't realize they were in love with each other. Something had to be done about that.

Davis removed the document from the printer and frowned. Three times he'd printed the same page of the technical manual he was writing. It wasn't getting any better.

All morning, his concentration had been shot. Like someone had taken a gray balloon and blown it up inside his head. He knew the cause.

Jacq had gotten to him.

Damned if he could shake her loose. He didn't care that they couldn't get along. All he wanted was her back with him, in his house, occupying his space—the same way she occupied his mind.

He reached over and fingered the bandana he'd been staring at all morning. Robust orange, crazy red, and potent purple, boldly slammed together in the print, just like the woman who wore it. Jacq had accompanied him to a seventies house party once. She'd washed her hair, picked it into an Afro, and tied the scarf around it. Then she strode into the party on his arm like the bad mamma-jamma she was. He still remembered the defiant way the ends of the scarf hung down the side of her face. He drew the scarf up to his nose, breathed deeply, then grabbed the telephone and dialed.

"Hello?"

"Uh . . . hey," he said.

Pause. "Hey."

"So, how are you?"

"I'm all right. You?"

He looked at the duplicate pages on his desk. "Not good."

"No?"

"No."

"I'm sorry to hear that."

"I'm sorry to have to say it. Look, I need to see you."

"Why?"

His grip tightened on the receiver. "Because we need to talk."

"No we don't, Davis. We need to be apart. At least for a while."

"Why?"

Jacq groaned. "In case you hadn't noticed, we don't get along very well."

"We can try to work that out."

"Again? I'm exhausted, Davis. All feelings aside, some things aren't meant to be."

He sighed and pounded his fist against his work desk. "But we never really analyzed the problem."

"Maybe you didn't," she answered, her voice quiet.

They both held on in the long and painful silence.

"Well, you left something over here," he said, wanting to follow up with "and you took my heart with you." Instead he said, "A scarf. I can bring it to you."

"Davis, I don't think—"

"Please," he said.

Pause.

His stomach fluttered a little, and then it just ached. "Okay," she said.

I won't cry.

After Davis's phone call, Jacq had dashed into her bedroom and changed out of her Capri pants and sweatshirt into black formfitting pants and short linen crop top. She checked her makeup, rubbed a light coat of oil sheen on her hair, and gave herself a quick spritz of body spray. She'd never cried about a man in all her life. As a result, she felt vulnerable and naked.

Did she want him back? Of course. But not the way he was. He had treated her like an IF/THEN statement for one of his computer programs. But even more than that, she couldn't violate the best friendship she'd ever had by dating Destiny's ex-boyfriend. A few months ago, she came to her senses and realized what a terrible thing she was doing. Her problems with Davis had escalated from that point.

Her head snapped toward the door when the bell rang. She told herself again, *I will not cry,* and opened the door.

He sighed.

She sighed, too. "Come in."

She knew her three-room studio couldn't measure up to his lavish condo, but she didn't care. It was her apartment, her space. And if she got tired of Davis and wanted him gone, she could order him to leave.

He held out the scarf to her. She took the end, but he didn't let go. Instead, he tugged back and pulled her onto him.

"Davis," she warned, but it was too late. His lips were upon her like his life depended on it. Her resistance uncoiled at the intensity. Just as she felt herself begin to float, he pulled away.

"I'm sorry. I shouldn't have—"

"Would you like to come in?" she said, feeling the urgency between her thighs.

He leaned in. "How long can I stay?"

All night, her heart said. Then she remembered her plans. "Just for a while. I have to leave soon."

"Leave?" he said, fingering the side of her face, sliding the scarf against it, sighing. "Where are you going?"

"Out." In an effort to take her mind off Davis, she let her physical therapy study group talk her into going for drinks. They were hitting a hot new club that just opened and had the buzz of the entire clubbing community.

He stepped inside then. "Out where?"

She closed the door behind him. "I'm going to Drego's with Susan and those guys."

"Dregos! That pick-up palace? You don't want to go there." His blood boiled angrily. Some of his friends had already talked to him about that place. They claimed the women came hot and now. He wasn't about to let Jacq go to a place where the men assumed all the women were on the to-go menu.

She whirled on him. "Davis, I've had enough of you telling me what I want and don't want. You ain't my father, brother, or lover." She poked him in the chest with a manicured finger. "You don't control me. You got that?"

He took her finger in his hand and realized that all he wanted to do was suck it. He folded the scarf into her palm and stared into her brown eyes.

"We'll see," he said, turning to leave.

"We'll see? You betta *see* your way out of my apartment! You will never control a thing here, mister!" He was gone before she could tell him what he would see if he stayed.

Jacq stared at the back of her front door, fists balled into knots. "Oooh!"

She stomped into her bedroom and rooted through her closet for a sexy outfit. She was on a mission. She would have fun tonight.

This joint is jumpin! Jacq thought as she strolled in with her friends. She pumped her arms and snapped her fingers to the techno-funk blaring through massive raised speakers. Whoever the DJ was, he or she was definitely off the hook. Drego's was one pulsing arena of sound.

Drego's was a multi-level discotheque with an industrial decor. The walls and steel girders, poles, and railings were painted black, while red, green, and yellow strobes flickered a staccato of flash and light.

There was one main dance floor in the middle of the warehouse-style room, with four bar areas in each corner. The second dance floor was an expansive balcony that ran the perimeter of the room. There was movement everywhere, and the bass in the uptempo song thumped like a strong heartbeat.

Jacq and the rest of her friends threaded through the packs of sweaty dancing patrons until they found a table for five. They were lucky. The place was packed with hips grinding wall-to-wall.

"This place is the bomb!" Jacq yelled.

"Told you!" Susan responded.

Jacq took it all in. The men in suits, the women in dresses, the hot boys in FUBU, the ghetto girls in almost nothing. Talking, drinking, shouting, laughing, toasting, smiling. Everyone was having a good time. And that's exactly what she planned on doing. As a matter of fact, she was absolutely certain that she was going to make some man awfully happy tonight.

When the waitress came, Jacq surprised her friends by ordering a Tanqueray sour. They knew she wasn't much of a drinker, but she just wanted a little something to loosen her up a bit, help her put Davis in a mental closet with all of the rest of her bad experiences.

"Wow," Susan said, above the music and the hum of talk around them. "He can jam!"

Jacq turned to the dance floor and saw a man looking as sleek as spun silk shaking his moneymaker. Dressed in a shimmering gray suit, he had mad dance moves. Jacq leaned toward Susan.

"Makes you wonder if he can do that horizontally!" Everyone laughed.

Jacq liked what she saw. He was clean-shaven, smooth-complexioned, and young. Probably midtwenties. His hair was a sandy brown and he had the most gorgeous green eyes.

That's him, she thought. *Mister Lucky.* "Excuse me," she said to her friends at the table, and strutted on to the dance floor.

She had chosen to wear her little black dress, which really wasn't much more than a small tubular piece of Lycra. On an ordinary woman, it would probably look like a cute but long tank top. But because of all the curves and contours of her body, the soft material accented her shapely form. To add that extra touch, Jacq covered her exposed skin with a thin coat of baby oil. Top that off with black stiletto pumps, and Jacq knew she was the hottest thing struttin'.

The man saw her coming, slowed his movements, and smiled.

"May I cut in?" she asked, her eyes wandering the length of his body.

"Hell no!" his dance partner replied.

The man took Jacq's hand and moved away from the other woman. "It's all right," he said. "I'll hit you back later."

"Don't bother!" the woman replied. She stomped away, a barrage of expletives trailing behind her.

Jacq had to admit that she wasn't that great a dancer, but she knew how to move her hips to let a man know exactly what she wanted.

"Damn, baby!" the man responded. "What's your name?"

"Marie," she said, giving him her club name. "And you?"

"Lance."

Marie and Lance danced together through one song after another. Their closeness and suggestive movements made it plain that they were attracted to each other and what they planned to do as a result. She never took her eyes off the way he moved. He never took his eyes off her breasts. *Men are so predictable.*

The DJ put on a slow song, and Jacq stepped back, looking up with her best "take me" expression. Lance nodded and reached out. "I like you," he said.

Her heartbeat increased. Was she really going to go home with this man? She'd always been wild but never loose.

She stepped into his waiting embrace, and another

man's arms pulled her back. Startled, she realized it was Davis. He spun her toward him and before she knew it was coming, gave her a kiss. But not just any kiss. The kiss to end all kisses. A kiss like the kind she'd imagined when she was a young girl just discovering the magic in the attraction to boys. A kiss that made her feel like a queen being worshipped by her king. It stole her breath, palpitated her heart, and made her forget she was in the middle of a dance floor.

When Davis had his mind set on something, he went after it. His lips and tongue ravaged her possessively. He took and took, until it was obvious. It was her that he wanted. With all her resistance drained away and replaced by a fire of urgency, she knew he could have her—lock, stock, and everything else.

She couldn't breathe, forgot to breathe, didn't want to breathe if it meant pulling away. His kiss deepened and she knew another moment or two and she might actually . . .

Davis stepped back, eyes hot and bold on hers. "Now, you can finish your dance. Or whatever else you were doing out here."

Before she could order her lust-swept thoughts, he was gone.

"You didn't tell me your man was here!" Lance said, storming off the dance floor.

Susan rushed to her side. "Are you all right?"

Jacq felt hung over. "No," she said. "I—I need to go home."

She staggered to the door and a terrifying realization hit her. She hadn't locked away her feelings for Davis, and now they were stronger than ever.

Ten

Portland, Oregon, was as beautiful as its reputation boasted. Lush greenery, colorful flora, and spectacular waterfalls. Kenyon liked it immediately. He stepped off of his family's Lear Jet and inhaled deeply. The air was even cleaner than his piece of the world on the outskirts of Atlanta.

He started off toward a waiting car, his mission clear: observe the Willens family and decide whom he would give the next million dollars to. He felt the same as he always did when he came out to observe— alive, acutely alive, and charged with an electric current hot enough to melt steel. He couldn't wait to see them.

He'd started this philanthropic ritual years ago after an alcoholic binge that had lasted three months. He had stumbled across a part of his ancestry that made him physically ill. On the day he officially became an adult he also discovered that he was the direct descendant of a family of slaveholders. His family's wealth and status, which they had garnered and hoarded for so many years, was built upon a foundation of slave breeding.

Slaves! His temples throbbed at the thought.

He rubbed them and remembered an afternoon from his childhood. *It had been raining. For three days a steady downpour drenched the Atlanta landscape and kept*

*him and his brother inside. They were ten and e[...]
Andreas and their nanny MaryJoan had grown [...] of
chasing after the boys as they romped through the house with
their child's energy. Instead of running after them up the
stairs to the third floor, they had left them alone. So the two
curious youngsters had gone exploring.*

*Back then the corridors seemed unending, doors massive,
and rooms enormous. They'd gone browsing in the blue
room, the sun room, a third library, and a bathroom. When
his brother Reynard went traipsing off into the state room,
Kenyon called him back.*

"Rene, you know we aren't supposed to venture in there."

*"Says who?" he asked, already pulling down books from
shelves.*

"Says Mum."

"And just where is good old Mum?"

"You know Mum's in town."

*"Then she won't ever know, will she? Now come on and
help me get that big one!"*

*Kenyon wandered in, nervousness tightening his stomach.
He'd only been scolded out of the room once. But once was
enough. His father had told him to stay out until he was
twenty-one.*

He'd never forgotten it.

*For a split second, he was tempted to do as his brother
asked. After all, who could know? But even walking past the
state room made his skin feel like there were worms crawling
on it. There was something bad in this room, and he was in
no hurry to find out what it was.*

"Stop!" he said, snatching a book from his brother's hands.

*Reynard shoved him and lunged for the leather-bound
tome. Kenyon, being the older and taller of the two, had no
trouble keeping the book out of his reach. The cold determination in Reynard's eyes told Kenyon that the same thing
made him want to leave the room was the same thing compelling Reynard to stay.*

Kenyon slammed the book on the small desk beside them, grabbed his brother by the scruff of his collar, and forced him out of the room.

"Someone will come looking for us any minute," he told Reynard. "We better get out of here."

They both heard the footsteps coming up the stairs, and their eyes locked in frustration. As Andreas came toward them, Kenyon knew his brother was ready to challenge him. But he would not allow it. Something terrible lived in that room, and he would keep them both from it for as long as he could.

When his twenty-first birthday finally arrived, his father had taken him through a rite of passage ceremony. It had been in their family for generations. He took him back to the room and left him there. His instructions were to start with the last book on the shelf and work backward until he'd read all the books in the bookcase.

"But Father!" he protested. "There must be a hundred books here!"

"Then you'd better get started."

At that, his father turned and left. When he heard the door latch, he knew Richmond Williams meant business but wondered if he hadn't lost his mind. Nevertheless, he picked up the first book and started in.

His mouth opened in shock when he realized he was staring at the company income statement. The first book was a record of Williams Brothers' financial statements for the past ten years. He knew his family was well-off, but he had no idea to what extent.

From what he could tell, it cost them an average of twenty-five dollars to make a suit. Yet the price the consumers paid was at least one hundred times that. The company was making a killing. That's when the first wave of nausea hit.

He continued to read, pouring through book after book with greater intensity. Before he realized it, five hours had passed and he'd gone back sixty years.

It was as if he'd been swallowed into a time vortex and transported through the ages. In the writings, he came across names like Daniel, Roland, Hale, Sarah, and Josiah. His family. People he would never know, but whose handwriting he now touched with his fingers and whose enterprise and sweat he'd benefited from. Slowly, he came to believe that he wasn't alone in the room. The spirits of his ancestors were with him, resurrected with each turn of the page.

Starting at about 1930, the books got thicker and more worn. The records and documentation kept were still thorough, but more personal. Much of them came in the form of wills, deeds, promissory notes, and handwritten letters. It took him longer to get through the information, but the pattern was clear. The Williams family had a long-standing history of cataloging their business transactions and making sure that their wealth passed intact from generation to generation.

The door to the state room opened, letting in a cool rush of fresh air. Already, Kenyon had grown accustomed to the smells of aged parchment and bound leather. Paper, dust, and mildew were now his companions. His new friends were now the words and figures faded like ghosts on the page. He was touching his past and it thrilled him. Sitting at the desk, now time machine, he could almost see the hands that scrawled across the pages—light and callused, stained at the fingertips where the ink had dried and pooled from dipping quills. He ingested it all. Blueprints for the mansion. Deeds to property. Receipts. The past was being reborn in him.

He looked up as his mother came in with a luncheon tray of one of his favorite meals, chicken oscar with asparagus. There was also a generous portion of fruit. For snacking, he surmised. A pitcher of water and a tall glass completed her offering.

She set the tray on a desk beside him, then patted him on the shoulder and left. They knew, he thought. They knew there would be no way he could tear himself away from the chronicles on the shelves until he had devoured them all. His stomach grumbled at the aroma of the piping hot meal. Kenyon turned away from it and went back to his reading, replacing the book he'd just finished with an older one from the bookcase. By the time he turned back to his food, it was cold.

His second surge of queasiness came when he was well into the 1900s files. It hit him when he unfolded a ledger of names along with a list of goods, amounts paid, and amounts owed. After a few moments of skimming, he realized that it was a sharecropper's list he was viewing.

He scanned the names for someone in his family but there weren't any. And that's when the nausea struck. The Williams' land was being sharecropped. His family had employed sharecroppers.

What he knew about sharecropping arrangements was less than admirable. Those that owned the land took advantage of those that worked the land. They misrepresented accounts so that no matter how large the harvest or how many years the land was worked, the sharecroppers would never be able to pay off their debts.

Most sharecroppers were former slaves who could neither read nor write. Even though blacks were free, most whites would not employ them unless it was into another indentured form of servitude. He knew that sharecropping proved a viable way for whites to retain the services of blacks without having to compensate them fairly or worry about the newly freed blacks suddenly leaving. Many black sharecroppers died still owing a trumped-up debt to the landowners. Kenyon's anger flared knowing that his family had been part of that corrupt system.

When he finished reviewing the sharecropper's ledgers, he knew. The third and final wave of sickness struck him before he'd even found proof. He placed the book ending in the late 1800s back on the shelf and for the first time since he started reading, he selected a book out of order. He skipped any books with records that came after 1865 and went back to a leather-bound book with records dating in the 1840s.

His stomach pitched and rolled as he skimmed through the handwritten accounts—purchases, receipts, and a list. His finger trembled, and tears spilled out of his eyes in rivers as he read the names—Bo, Whitaker, CoraJean, Nathan, Henry, Mae. The list went on. A slave list.

He flung the book across the room. Documents carefully sewn into the binding flew out and fluttered down to the floor. The header on the bills of sale read Williams Plantation. His family . . . oh, God help him . . . had been slaveowners!

Kenyon tumbled backward in the chair in a fit of remorse. Blacks owning blacks. He'd heard of it once in a history class and had been appalled. But now he knew his own family had built their entire fortune from . . . from . . . he couldn't think it. His mind wouldn't let him conceive of it.

His head hurt. He righted himself, wondering what kind of family had spawned him. Were they devils? Evil beings? How could you enslave your own people and why? A hurricane of questions spun in his head.

He stumbled back to the desk like he'd been drugged. Maybe there was a reason—a motive. Maybe there were good masters. That word "masters" sliced through him like a hot sword. Maybe they bought people as a ruse, to provide them some semblance of freedom.

He returned to the books, pulling them down two at a time. He had to know the whole story. But in his frantic search for justification, he could find no evidence that his family had been rescuing people. On the contrary, his ancestors had one of the most successful plantations in the Carolinas. But unlike so many others, where cotton had been their mainstay, slave breeding had catapulted the Williams family into the stratosphere of the black elite. Almost putting them on the same level as rich whites. After discovering this, Kenyon knew one thing.

He had to get out of that room.

"Should I park in front, sir?"

The chauffeur's question snapped him back to the present.

The truth of that incident had changed him forever. His contempt for his family legacy had manifested itself in months of drunken carousing. But when he emerged from his stupors, he delved into the history and discovered that it was not at all unusual for free blacks to own slaves, especially in places like South Carolina and Louisiana. But the fact that his ancestors were in some obscure history books as being the most prominent and owning close to 100 black people sent his reason spinning. No other family came close except the Ellisons, who owned just under 75.

"Appalling," he said, stepping into the waiting limousine.

"Excuse me sir," the driver said.

"Nothing," he responded.

He shut his eyes, thinking that all his family's wealth, power, and status came from a cotton plantation and was now alive and well in their clothing business.

Yes, he mused, that little bit of information had sent him into the bottom of a bottle of vodka. Back then, he'd only come out for more vodka and wild women.

The office of Van Housen and Associates was located just off Peachtree Road near Lenox Square in Atlanta proper. Davis Van Housen sat in front of his computer and was falling asleep.

"Man, it's only 10:15. You can't be that tired already."

Davis heard Bill Goodmen's voice and pulled himself back from the slumber that beckoned him.

"I haven't been getting much sleep lately," he said, running a hand down the front of his face. He yawned, stretched, and then got up to get coffee.

"You look terrible. Maybe you should go home."

That's Bill, Davis thought. Always upfront. Always honest. That's why he'd hired him as an associate after they met on one of his consulting projects.

He poured a full cup of Tanzanian dark roast and sat back down at his desk. He knew if he went home, he'd just pine for Jacquelyn. That was his problem now. Pining for her had kept him awake for three nights straight. "I'm better off here," he said.

Bill took a spot on the edge of Davis's desk. "All right, it must be a woman."

Davis smirked.

"The last time I saw you in a sorry state, it was over a woman."

Davis sipped his coffee.

"Come to think of it. You weren't nearly as bad off then as you are now. Back then you kept right on going. But now, man, you're slackin'."

"I've never slacked a day in my life."

Bill rose and pulled a stack of blue bar paper from a drawer in his desk. "I wasn't going to bring this up, but you know the new HRIS system we set up for Southern Comfort Records?"

Davis perked up. "Yeah."

Bill handed him the reports. "The database crashed."

"I know," Davis said slightly irritated. "I talked them through a cold boot with backup tapes."

"Uh-huh. Lawson software can't take a cold boot, remember? Just PeopleSoft. So, after you left, the techs at Southern Comfort called back. The database crashed again."

Davis's chest tightened with anxiety. "For the love of . . . I'll call Tony right now and—"

"Never mind. I took care of it. The database is fine."

A deep sigh of relief told Davis just how tired he was. And now he was making mistakes on the job. It was inexcusable.

"So, spill it, man. What's eating you alive?"

Davis hefted the thick printout on his desk and stared out the window. Slowly he explained his troubles with Jacquelyn and his restless nights as a result.

"Maybe she's afraid of a relationship," Bill said.

"That woman isn't afraid of anything." The only time Davis had known her to be frightened was several months ago when there had been a severe thunderstorm. She had come into his room at two in the morning, eyes bright with fright.

"Can I sleep with you?"

"Baby, I've been trying to get you to do that since day one!"

But the fear in her eyes told him her intentions were something else entirely. "Come on," he said, lifting the covers. And for the first time since her arrival, she lay in his bed.

She slid close against him, trembling at his side. He pulled the sheet up and wrapped her in his arms.

"What's wrong?"

"I don't like storms," she said.

"They can't hurt you," he said, stroking her beautiful face. At that moment, he wanted to make love to her and make her forget the storm. He needed her so urgently. He was a breath away from kissing her when she told him a story he'd never forgotten.

"Storms can hurt," she said. "I've seen it. When I was in junior high school, I was trying out for the track team. The field was almost a block away from the school. And we were out there practicing. It was very windy. We were running around the field and this storm comes from out of nowhere. It just rolled over us like train. It started hailing and we all ran toward the school. I remember the gym teacher blowing her whistle and girls screaming while the boys mainly just laughed.

"Then it got dark. Pitch black. There was this eerie quiet right before an incredible wind. When I looked up clouds were swirling and spinning over our heads. One of them dipped down. It's the most awesome thing I've seen in my life. At first, my thirteen-year-old eyes saw what looked like a giant ice cream cone moving toward us. We knew we wouldn't make it to the school. The building was too far away. So the teacher had us all lie down in the lowest part of the field and cover our heads.

"I've never been so scared as I was at that moment because I knew I was going to die."

"What happened?" Davis asked.

"A miracle. None of us were hurt. The tornado sheared off the east end of the school, then spun in a different direction. It took out a line of houses a block away and then went back up into the sky like it was being sucked up through an invisible straw."

A clap of thunder exploded outside and Jacquelyn wrapped her shaking body around Davis.

"I used to get hysterical when it rained. Now that I'm older, I just get really scared."

Davis realized, as she squeezed closer, if she got any more scared he wouldn't be able to breathe.

Jacquelyn had come to his bed twice after that. Each time at the impetus of a storm. And each time he was a gentleman.

He had made her a promise after that first time.

She'd looked up at him, fear dancing in her eyes and said, "Promise you'll hold me when it rains."

"I promise," he said.

"You are useless right now, man."

Davis came out of his revery and turned his attention to Bill.

"You either need to get her back or get your life back. But either way, you need to get!"

Davis managed a chuckle. "You may be right, my friend." He drained the remaining coffee in his cup and stood. "I guess I *will* go home." He yawned so widely he feared the corners of his mouth might split. "Wow," he said. "I really do need some rest."

When he arrived at home, he thought maybe he would pretend Jacquelyn was in the next room, or on her way home to him, so the sandman would be merciful and he could get some rest.

"I don't know how I let you talk me into this!"

Jacq checked herself in the mirror, a million thoughts swirling in her head.

"Because," Destiny said, arranging the twists in Jacq's hair, "you need to get out and enjoy yourself."

The woman with the large round belly stepped aside and Jacq stared into the mirror on her dresser. She had to admit, her hair was cute. Des had twisted it into numerous long sections of shining tresses. Jacq smiled. "I like it."

And she liked more than her hair. She liked the pantssuit she wore. It was golden brown, and didn't hug her curves like most of the other things in her wardrobe. But it made her look sophisticated and refined.

"Anyway, I know you wouldn't let me be a fifth wheel at the concert."

Destiny's famous singer husband was performing at The Paragon Theatre tonight. Marti was going with her new man. And Jacq was going to keep Destiny company.

"Now for some real jewelry." Destiny reached into her purse and pulled out a cream-colored cloth. She unwrapped the cloth and inside it was a set of pearl earrings with a matching necklace and bracelet.

"Destiny, I have jewelry."

"You don't really want to wear that costume stuff tonight, do you?"

"Look, Heifer . . . up until last year, you were wearing costume jewelry on the regular. Now you tryin' to play like you ain't wit it!"

Destiny laughed. "I guess I am kinda spoiled. Xavier buys me the real stuff all the time now."

Jacq crossed her arms. "Uh-huh."

"Well, all I'm saying is that I know this would look good on you. Now, do you want to wear it or not?"

"Of course I want to wear it. Just don't be so bourgeois about it. Okay?"

"Okay."

Destiny helped Jacq put on the pearls. "I remember when I was going through all those changes with Rico. You never once pressured me to talk about it. But I always knew you were there for me anytime I wanted to open up."

Jacq relaxed a little.

Destiny continued. "I don't know what's going on between you and Davis, but if you ever need to talk—"

"I know," Jacq said, touching her friend's hand. "I know." The guy Destiny had been seeing before she married her husband was a real jerk. Jacq just made sure she was there to pick up the pieces when Destiny finally had enough. She knew her friend was only trying to do the same for her.

When the two were ready to go, they went out into
the living room. Jacq needed desperately to lighten
up the mood. "So what's ol' money bags like?"

Destiny smiled. "I don't know. I haven't met him
yet."

"Me either. But all I want to know is if he's as good-
looking in person as he is in magazines."

"Well, I guess it's our chance to find out. Here they
are."

Destiny and Jacq looked out the window just in time
to see a black stretch limousine pull in front of the
apartment building.

Jacq felt some of her old feisty self returning. "Marti
said he owns that limo."

Destiny ushered her toward the door. "Girl, come
on."

As they walked out, Jacq bent over to Destiny's ear.
"Little Marti, leavin' wet spots in a limo."

"Girl, hush! You are just too foul!"

The two women huddled together laughing their
way outside.

A man who looked older than all of them com-
bined stepped out of the long car and opened a back
door. He helped Destiny in first. She maneuvered her
portly frame into the vehicle. Jacq stepped in next
and could not believe her eyes. Seated in the back
were two incredibly handsome men. One with hair
streaming down his back in jet-black waves. The other
familiar, and chilling.

She stepped out.

"You tricked me!"

"Come on in here!" Destiny hollered.

"'Oh no, girl. You just take your time.' Isn't that
what you just said to me?" Jacq was furious. "You set
me up!"

Destiny poked her round head out of the car. "No I

didn't. Xavier invited him. Now stop making a scene and get in this car!"

Marti hopped out from the other side. She rushed to Jacq's side. "Look, I'm trying to make a good impression on this man and you're not helping. Now please, get in and I'll owe you big time."

Jacq gave the little woman a sideways glance. "Owe me, huh?"

"Yes!"

"Enough to give me one of your paintings?"

"Anything," she pleaded, taking her arm. "Just please, get in the car."

"Is everything all right?" a deep voice bellowed from inside the car. Then the owner of that voice stepped to Marti's side and extended his hand. "I'm Kenyon. Can I help here?"

Jacq could only imagine the fun Marti must have when a man with a voice like that talked to her in bed.

"No," she said. "I'm sorry. Let's just go."

For a minute, Jacq had felt like she was finally getting the treatment she deserved. Stretch limo, a night on the town. But now it was spoiled. She gritted her teeth and stepped inside the long vehicle. When they were all in, the driver closed the door, got in, and began their drive downtown.

"Kenyon Williams, this is my sister-in-law, Destiny, and my friend, Jacquelyn Jackson."

They shook hands. "Nice to meet you," they said, one after another.

Jacq couldn't believe the seating arrangement. Davis, Marti, and Kenyon on one side; she and Destiny on the other. And Jacq was sitting directly across from Davis, who hadn't said a word or acknowledged her presence in any way. *It's just as well,* she thought. *At least now I don't have to pretend to be civil.*

Marti sat vibrant and bubbly as she chattered on

about a new collage technique she'd discovered. Jacq pretended to listen. Destiny seemed genuinely interested as she leaned forward toward Marti as far as her swollen abdomen would allow.

It all sounded like dribble to Jacq. Only the occasional pop of Marti's gum brought her out of her funk.

Davis, on the other hand, was in serious conversation with Kenyon. She pretended not to be listening, but she took in every word.

"Your company has been in business for long time."

"Yes, it has."

"Turn of the century, isn't that correct?"

"Yes."

"When I was told that you would be joining us, I took the liberty of doing some research."

Kenyon's eyes narrowed. "Really?"

"That's right," Davis said, settling back into the leather seat. "From what I can tell, your company is one of the longest reigning black-owned businesses in the country."

"Yes, I guess that's true."

Jacq heard Kenyon say the words. He didn't sound too proud or happy about it.

"That's quite impressive. I own my own business also, and I would love to talk with you regarding your strategy for longevity."

Kenyon couldn't look any more bored if he were in a room by himself. "I really don't handle that. You'd have to talk to my brother about it."

"Wonderful!" Davis reached into his pocket and removed a thin gold case. He took out a card, flipped it through his fingers, then handed it to Kenyon. "Will you give this to your brother? Now, that would be Reynard, correct?"

"You really *have* done your homework, haven't you?"

Davis nodded. "I'm nothing if not thorough."

Kenyon took the card. "I'll see that he gets it."

Davis nodded and smiled. "Splendid."

She couldn't believe it. He never stopped being the salesman. Never turned off the computer guy. She knew his MO like she knew her own name. Pretty soon, Davis would guide the discussion to technology and, slicker than oil on wet cement, he would pitch his services to Kenyon.

But Davis might have met his match with this rich man. He didn't appear to be the type to entertain any ideas frivolously. Jacq had to admit one thing. The magazine pictures she'd seen of him didn't do him justice. Marti had snagged a deep, dark, and sensuous looking man.

"Oh, well. At least somebody is happy!"

When all eyes turned to her, she realized she'd spoken her thoughts out loud.

"Nothing," she followed up. "Never mind."

The ride to the theater was long and tedious. Jacq hardly spoke a word to anyone while everyone else seemed to be having the time of their lives. Now and then Destiny would glance her way, insinuating that she should loosen up. But she couldn't. It irked her that just a few days ago, Davis had been in her doorway, pleading for another chance, and now he was all smiles, all business, and it seemed, all over her. If she felt miserable because of their breakup, he should, too.

Eleven

The front balcony was the perfect vantage point from which to watch the concert. Like being in a sky-box, they could see everything without the distraction of anyone in front of them. The evening could have been better only if Jacq didn't have to be bothered by Davis Van Housen's presence. Why did he have to come and ruin everything?

Since Davis seemed intent on bending Kenyon's ear, he sat in the back row with him and Marti. That left Jacq and Destiny to sit in the front. She whispered into her friend's ear.

"I will never forgive you for this."

Destiny smiled and winked. "Yes you will."

Jacq crossed her arms and sat through the entire opening act in a huff. Three young women. She guessed they were trying to be the next big girl group. From what Jacq could tell, they weren't too bad. She barely registered three-part harmony, midriff tops, hip-hugger bottoms, and new school funk. But most of her time was spent fuming. Just as she was trying to get over him, Destiny was shoving Davis back into her face. And she knew Marti was in on it.

When the intermission came, Jacq stood quickly. "I'm going to the ladies' room."

"Okay," Destiny said, wondering why Jacq was an-nouncing it so loudly.

"You're coming with me," she said, boiling.

Reluctantly, Destiny hoisted her round body out of the seat and followed her friend into the aisle.

"I'll be right back," Marti said to Kenyon and marched behind the two women.

Jacq was hot and ready for a meeting in the ladies' room. When they were inside, she spun on her so-called friends.

"I am so angry, I could slap both of you!"

Marti bristled. "I'm little, but I ain't scared."

"I'm pregnant, but I'm not scared of you either. Now calm down!"

Jacq swallowed. Her anger was getting her in trouble. She regretted her hasty words. She had to get out and get away from this whole scene.

"I'm leaving. I'll catch a cab back to my apartment."

"Wait!" Destiny said, placing a hand on her arm.

Marti crossed her arms against her chest. "Let her go if she wants to."

Jacq's anger erupted. "You're just being smug because your man is sitting out there waiting for you. And you," she stared at Destiny, "you're so calm and content because your husband is only a dressing room away!"

In the hum of conversation in the ladies' room, the three overheard, "See, I told you that was his wife! I know *everything* about Allgood."

Jacq continued, ignoring the groupie. "If you two were single, you would understand."

"We do understand!" they said together.

Destiny waddled in front of Jacq. "Here's what I understand. I understand that your man is out there, too. Whether you choose to believe it or not! Now you can play these childish games if you want to. Heck, catch a cab. I don't care."

Destiny swallowed and took a deep breath. "No, that's not right. I do care. That's why I invited Davis in the first place. You can't fool me with your Miss Thang routine. I know you love him."

"Besides," Marti chimed in. "He hasn't said a word to you all evening. He's too busy trying to get Kenyon's business. So, I don't know why you are so bent outa shape."

Destiny headed toward the door. "I know why, but I tell you what, I'm going to go sit down and wait for my husband to come out and sing to me."

"Go on, heifer!" Jacq snapped.

"Yeah, whatever!" Destiny snapped right back.

A line formed in the doorway and Jacq sighed as the buzz of conversation, women applying makeup and checking hair, and the continual flush of toilets swirled around her. The theater had to be at least eighty years old, and the ten or so stalls in the restroom had what looked like the original wooden doors on them. Jacq felt as old as those doors and just as used. She glanced at Marti, whose head tilted to the side like a curious puppy.

"Are you coming or not?"

"I don't know." She caught sight of her reflection in the mirror. Despite the stern expression on her face, she still looked pretty good.

"You can't let him get to you this way. If you want to trip out later, fine. Destiny and I will come back over and you can have another cry. But for now, you should just try to enjoy yourself."

Marti snapped her gum rhythmically. "My brother is about to come out, and if I know Zay, he's going to tear the roof off."

The little woman had a point. And Jacq had already had one crying incident. She wasn't going to let Davis's presence usher her into another one.

"What do you say?" Marti asked.

Jacq made herself smile. "All right."

The two women locked arms and headed back toward their seats.

"Now, the next time you think about slapping someone—" Marti began, but she was interrupted. The ear-rattling shrieks of about one thousand women cut her off.

"Hurry up," Marti insisted. "I don't want to miss his entrance."

Moments later they entered the balcony area in darkness with the sounds of a strong bass and drums coming from the stage. As they took their seats, Jacq noticed the lights in the arena. One was shining down from the ceiling illuminating the stage and the other was coming from Destiny's face. Jacq knew and understood how truly happy her friend was to have her husband back with her.

She decided right then and there to stop feeling sorry for herself and to start feeling good about being at the concert. Forget Davis.

And then a small lonely thought trickled into her consciousness: *If only I could.*

By the time the concert was half over, Jacq was convinced that he was just keeping silent to unnerve her. When Davis got up and headed toward the men's room, Jacq took off after him.

"Hey!" she said.

He turned slowly. "Yes?"

He looked as calm as she'd ever seen him. Face relaxed and content. Stance loose and flexible. The suit he wore accentuated his broad shoulders, tapered at his narrow hips, and hit ever so snugly at his muscular thighs. The fact that it was a Williams Brothers suit added to his million-dollar looks.

She almost lost her rage, and that wouldn't be

good. What she wanted more than anything was to be angry with Davis. Being furious with him would justify the awful feeling she felt about being apart from him.

"What are you trying to do?" she asked.

"Isn't it obvious? I'm trying to have a good time."

A handful of people, decked out in their finest, milled in the hallway. Some looked like they were on their way to a costume ball. A few looked like they were scheduled to perform instead of Xavier. And others looked like they'd just stepped out of the gym.

"What's obvious is that you're tryin' to get on my last nerve. But I'm not havin' it!"

"Jacquelyn, I haven't said a word to you all evening."

"That's what I'm sayin'."

He clasped his hands behind his back. "I don't see the problem."

"Yes you do." Jacq combed her fingers through her straight black hair. "The problem is: all last week you was blowin' up my phone. Now you tryin' to front like we never kicked it. What's that about?"

"The last time you spoke to me, you told me to leave you alone. So, now I've finally gotten the message, and I'm going to do as you asked and," he said, resuming his walk to the men's room, "leave you alone."

Jacq wanted to scream something obscene. But instead she balled her fists and counted to ten. When she finished, there was a woman standing next to her but staring at Davis.

"Ooh, girl! Is that *you*?"

Jacq swallowed a hard lump of anger, frustration, and resentment. "No," she said.

By the time Jacq walked in a deep sulk back to her seat, there was a commotion in the balcony area. It didn't take her long to figure out that while her best friend's husband was busy singing "Got to Be There" in amazing falsetto to thousands of screaming women, his wife was about to do some screaming of her own since her water had broken and she was on her way to the hospital to deliver a baby.

It had taken some time and effort, but the result was worth it. Selena Graves sat on the floor of her living room surrounded by every article she could find on the mysterious Saint Black. After spending days pouring over any tidbit she could find on the mysterious benefactor, she saw a pattern emerge. One that confirmed her suspicion that she would be taking a leave of absence soon. She couldn't wait.

Following hunches, intuition, and gut instinct, Selena traced the path of the million-dollar surprises back ten years. She'd started with a pile of unexpected financial packages. She ruled out those where people said that someone had miraculously paid off all their bills, or where people had received anonymous checks in the mail for substantial amounts of money. There had been hundreds of those over the years. She glanced at the hill of bills mounting on a small table in the entryway and wondered why nothing like that ever happened to her.

Like an amateur detective, she focused on the incidents that had the same modus operandi: exactly one million dollars, in cash, in a briefcase, left in the person's place of residence, with a note requesting confidentiality.

She'd counted sixteen such occurrences over the past ten years.

Now that she'd identified a pattern, she wasn't sure how to proceed. She thought about interviewing each one of the recipients to see if they had any clue as to

the identity of their guardian angel. She also wanted
to get some information about the briefcases the
money came in. Perhaps it was the same type every
time, and if so, she might be able to trace the purchases.

Maybe she could somehow get all the millionaires
together. She wasn't sure why, but the hairs on her
skin prickled at that thought. It would take money.
When she'd gotten further into the story and could
prove that she had something substantial, she could
start contacting newspapers, see who was interested
and which paper would front her an advance.
Whichever way it happened, Selena knew that it must
happen. She could sense it.

Two weeks later she walked briskly into her den
after a long day of beat reporting. One of the reporters at the *Register* was out with pneumonia and
another was on maternity leave. That left Selena to
cover most of the news of the city for the past two
weeks. After working long hours, she'd gone to bed almost as soon as she'd set foot inside her house. But
today was different.

Today, two interns and one freelance writer had
started to take up some of the slack, and she was
home early. It would be the first time she'd worked on
her after-hours project in days.

Sitting on the floor, she spread the newspaper clippings, microfiche copies, and Internet files in front
of her. She placed a stack of file folders next to the
papers and set about the task of organizing her research.

Selena checked and rechecked her facts. The evidence was indisputable. Someone had deliberately

sought out individuals, African American individuals, and left them million-dollar gifts in their homes.

The mainstream press had yet to pick up the story. But Saint Black was now so entrenched in the black community that he or she was more like a beautiful myth or an urban legend. She'd been following the trail of the story for three weeks, and she found out that kids in inner-city America all had stories to tell about the black angel that swooped down from the sky, came in through the window, and left behind treasures for the poor.

She'd even talked to some older folks who had begun to leave one window open at night in case the angel decided to pay them a visit. It was wild.

As she reached for a folder and label, the phone rang. Selena glanced up at the caller ID box on her desk. Rose Graves. Selena moaned and reached up for the receiver.

"Hi, mom."

"Hello, dear. How are you?"

"Fine, mom."

"I haven't heard from you in a while, and I just wanted to give you a ring."

"Thanks, mom."

"How's your job, sweetheart?"

Selena peeled a orange label from the sheet and pressed it on to the folder tab. "Fine."

"They're not making you cover anything violent, are they?"

"No, mom."

"Well that's good. I don't want you mingling with riffraff."

"Yes, I know."

"And Sylvia . . . have you heard from Sylvia?"

She couldn't understand why her mother and sister weren't on speaking terms. Something about her mother's will and Sylvia not being mentioned enough times in it. Selena tried to stay out of their arguments whenever she could. "Sylvia is great."

"Well, that's good. I know she's not speaking to me, but I still like to know that she's all right."

Selena scanned the first article for the recipient's name. She found it and wrote Willman, Donnetta. "You want me to talk to her again?"

"No! No! If she doesn't want to talk, then fine by me."

"Okay," she said, peeling off and placing another label. On this one she wrote, Williford, Allen. "How's dad?"

"Oh, you know your father. Off with his country club buddies. They're probably sitting in some stuffy room trying to one-up each other with tales of their investments, cars, or something."

Selena thought it was more likely that her father was getting his jollies in an expensive hotel with a woman her age. "Tell him I said hello when he returns."

"Oh I will, dear. And speaking of returning, you will be over for supper soon, won't you? The last time I saw you, you were pencil thin, sweetheart. You can't expect to attract a man, especially a man worth something, if he can't even feel you in his arms."

Selena was grateful that the only trait she shared with her mother was their brilliant green eyes. Annoyed at her mother's prying, she affixed label number three and wrote the name Williams, Verla. "Mother," she said, shifting the phone from her right ear to her left, "there is nothing wrong with my weight. And if you promise never to mention it again, I'll come visit this week."

"I'm sorry, dear. It's just that I care about your well-being, and ... well ... you're getting of the age where you should have a man in your life and I'm just concerned that—"

"Don't be, mother. I can take care of myself."

"Of course you can, dear, but why should you when a man can do it for you?"

Clouds of anger rumbled in Selena's chest. Maybe she could understand the rift between her mother and sister after all. Given the chance, Rose Graves could try anyone's patience.

Selena started the fourth label and stopped midname. "Oh my God."

"What, dear?"

"I . . . I . . ." She flipped through the remaining documents. Williams, Wills, Williby, Willers. With only a few exceptions, the names were remarkable similar. "I gotta go!"

"Selena, are you all right?"

"Yes, mom. I'm fine. I have to hang up now."

"But—"

"I'll be over for dinner on Sunday. Give Dad my love."

"Is it something I said?"

She hung up without responding and stared at the papers in front of her. Why didn't I see this before? Why didn't anyone see this before? Her heart pounded like a mallet in her chest. She was on to something. She could feel it. She would put in her request for leave tomorrow. The sooner she devoted herself to this story full time, the sooner she'd earn her Pulitzer.

Twelve

He missed her most in the mornings. Just as his eyes opened to a new day and his need for sexual release was at its peak. He would turn over to an empty bed with his manhood tight and throbbing.

Kenyon sat up and rubbed the area where he felt the most urgency. It had been a long time since he'd ached for a woman's company. He had been celibate for years. Now and then he would yearn for silky legs, firm breasts, a woman hot and wet for him. Long showers, laps in the pool, or meditation usually cooled his desire. Occasionally, when his need was strongest, he would take matters into his own hands and pleasure himself. Those times were rare. But as he stroked himself now, he knew the sensation was not enough to satisfy him completely. He needed a woman.

He needed Marti.

His mind conjured her—her bright eyes, the warmness of her smile. He stroked himself faster and thought of her laughter and how it sounded sexy and earthy.

He imagined her breasts the same way he had imagined them over and over. Her shirts were always loose, so his imagination had filled in the curves, the roundness, the soft flesh, the dark pointed nipples, and his mouth covering the succulent peaks. He stroked harder.

The last picture his mind drew before he broke apart into lust-shattered pieces was the triangle of her womanhood and what it would feel like to be inside her riding and riding until she screamed.

As he shuddered through his climax, he made up his mind. His days of celibacy would soon be over.

Kenyon got up and immediately went into the bathroom. At the end of his bath there was a large rectangular shower with three showerheads. He could turn on a blast of water from any one of or all three different directions. Today, he chose all three.

The water hit him with such force, he gasped until he became accustomed to the powerful spray of moisture on his skin.

As he lathered his skin, he noticed that his body still thrummed with thoughts of Marti. It was as if her very essence were pulsing through his veins. His need for her was organic, physiological. The very idea angered him.

This is why he had refused to become involved with a woman. Since that fateful day in the state room, he had never, ever had a serious relationship. He couldn't. The thought of extending his shame to another person was unbearable. So after years of prowling the nights, carousing, and treating women like toys to play with and discard, he'd simply stopped. He'd grown tired of the late nights, all the alcohol, and waking up beside women he didn't know and didn't care to know. He'd grown weary of passing out in bars and spending money like it was water gushing from a sieve. But his initial reaction to his family secret had turned him into Mr. Hyde. And he had played the role to the hilt.

One night, while he was as drunk as he could remember being without blacking out, he was staggering down the street at about two in the morning. He'd just left one bar and was hoping to find another when he heard someone crying. An urge he didn't understand made him follow the sounds down an alley. He discovered the sobs were coming from a young girl who was sitting in a puddle of who-knew-what hugging her knees to her chin.

His first thought was lecherous. What he could do with a woman, by herself, in an alley. If she was averse, he could pay her—any sum she wanted. Then she looked up at him with eyes that reminded him of his own. And all the hurt he'd been trying to bury with booze and sex came up to the surface.

He didn't know why, but he reached into his pocket and pulled out all the money he had on him. Probably amounted to about eight hundred dollars. He managed to steady himself long enough to bend down and hand it to her.

Her eyes grew large then. With a dirty, trembling hand, she took the money and Kenyon took heart.

He walked away from her almost sober. He knew his season of wild behavior had come to an end. As he headed for home, a strange question entered his mind. He wondered if by some wondrous act of God, he had just helped a descendant of one of his family's slaves. He allowed himself to believe that he had and from that moment on, he'd been celibate and alcohol free.

It was a quiet session. For days, weeks even, Marti and Kenyon had talked and discussed life, art, painting, history. But today, all she wanted to do was be in his presence and sketch. After much persuading, he'd finally agreed to let her shadow him without his acknowledging her presence.

As she worked the charcoal against the sketchpad, she realized that she'd come to know him. He didn't have to talk to her, tell her what he was doing, or explain his actions. She knew them all.

This morning at breakfast, when he'd tugged absentmindedly at the sleeves on his shirt and at his collar, she knew it was because he felt more comfortable out of his clothes than in them. Clothes were too confining for a man who was used to the kind of freedom he had as a wealthy bachelor living alone. When he'd entered the library and walked to the bookshelf, she knew he would select several books instead of just one. He was probably doing research on rare art and wouldn't be satisfied until he was surrounded by the very essence of the topic he was researching. And now as he sat in the den, surfing his way through the Internet, she could feel that he would much rather be in the pool plunging into water, toning his muscles in the wetness.

Her fingers moved quickly. They had memorized him now. His nuances were committed to memory. The deep-set ovals that were his eyes. The long line and angle that was his nose. The blemish-free midnight that was his skin. The thinned butterfly that was his mouth. And the round divot that was the cleft in his chin. She closed her eyes and sketched from the imprint of him in her mind. Then she set the charcoal aside and smoothed the likeness with the tips of her fingers.

The charcoal stained her fingers black. Like the essence of his skin lifting away and becoming a part of her. She thought of smearing the color against her face and across her breasts. Not only was she drawing Kenyon Williams, she was drawn to him. And wanted to know him intimately. She imagined her fingers moving across his skin instead of her paper. She would have her eyes closed and mouth open to receive his lips and tongue. This man, who seemed so detached, had somehow attached himself to her heart. Marti's craving deepened until his dark voice startled her.

"I can't stand it anymore," he said.

She looked up into his beautiful face. It was almost too beautiful to look at. And in a way, it was painful because she couldn't imagine herself ever being the type of woman Kenyon would want. He had his pick of any woman. He didn't have to be faithful, committed, or monogamous.

She hoped her serious attraction didn't show on her face. She had never been able to hide any of her emotions. They just came out. Spilled over when she least expected it.

"Marti," his voice rumbled.

She turned back to see the emotions churning at the apex of her thighs glowing hot on his face.

"You look," she began, searching for the words, "hungry."

"You look," he said, standing, "like you want to be eaten."

She held his gaze at the risk of giving up her hand. The door was open. All she had to do was walk through it. She stood, wanting so much to kiss the lips of her fantasy. But she would not cheapen herself. She would not become part of a harem or become one of many in a stable of women. No matter what her lust urged her to do. She would stand her ground and not weaken.

"Kenyon, I'm not interested in being a one-night stand or whatever else you had in mind."

He fingered her chin and lifted it. She melted like

ice cream in the desert. "Not even if *whatever else* involves something more . . . long term?"

He bent down, but she found the strength to turn away. He couldn't possibly want the kind of long-term relationship she needed. The kind of relationship that involved commitment and growth toward something special. His expression was wanton, brazen. It had everything to do with sex and nothing to do with a relationship. She didn't want that from Kenyon. She wanted more or nothing.

She wondered what he meant by "long term." Long-term commitment? Long-term sexual liaisons? Certainly not marriage.

She had done some checking into his background. What she found confirmed her suspicions. There were enough magazine and newspaper articles on his assorted affairs with women to fill one of her art supply bins. Kenyon's past was replete with histories of wild parties and a succession of models, actresses, and singers. He and his brother had quite the playboy reputations.

Although news of Kenyon's activities had tapered off considerably five years ago, his brother Reynard continued to generate headlines in the *Enquirer* and *People* magazine. Last year he was voted number four of *Essence's* most eligible bachelors, and number one of those least likely to marry. She wondered how different Kenyon was, if at all. And although he seemed to have dropped off the paparazzi radar completely, she still had her suspicions.

She trembled despite her resolve. "I'm sure your idea of long term and my idea of long term are totally different."

Kenyon stepped closer. He smelled like silk, gold, and diamonds all rolled into one.

"Let's find out," he whispered near her ear. "I know you're attracted to me."

Marti turned to him then, eyes wide with surprise.

"From the second we met, I could see it in your face." He stroked her bottom lip with the pad of his thumb. "Tell me, what do you see in my face?"

She had always been able to tell when a man was attracted to her, but the look in Kenyon's eyes said much more. It said that he wanted to possess her and that any refusal she gave would be challenged. It said that as a man accustomed to getting his way, he wouldn't stop until she was naked and opening herself to his desires.

"You're wrong, Kenyon," she said, thinking of his scandalous past. "I don't find you attractive at all, and the last thing I intend to do is become number who-knows-what on your list of conquests."

He combed a hand through his long waves of hair. "Are you sure that's what I had in mind?"

"Let me ask you a question. How many serious relationships have you had?"

He stepped back. "It depends on what you mean by serious."

Marti squared her shoulders. "Have you ever had a relationship that wasn't based on sex? In other words, have you ever loved someone?"

It didn't take a rocket scientist to tell Marti that the reason she was asking that question is that she was starting to feel something beyond mere infatuation for the wealthy and handsome man. She was treading into dangerous territory now. Her heart was at stake and she would not allow a physical relationship with Kenyon, which would throw her into fits of painting and sculpture if he broke her heart. Those days were over.

She waited for his response.

"If you put it that way, no. I've never been in love. So, if love is what you're looking for, then you're looking in the wrong place. I don't do love."

Marti looked away, pain already tearing at her heart.

He moved into her line of vision. "What's wrong with what we have? Good conversation. Companionship. A shared love of the arts. Heck, we even make each other laugh sometimes. I was just hoping to add another element."

Kenyon spoke calmly, but his lust was screaming. Marti was the first woman his body craved in a long, long time. He knew it was only a matter of time before she gave in to the desires he knew she felt. He just needed it to be soon. Very soon.

"I like the way we've become friends. There's nothing wrong with what we have." She paused, took a deep breath, and said, "Why don't we just keep it the way it is?"

He wanted to say, "Because the most sensitive area on my body feels like it's going to explode whenever I'm near you!" But instead, he simply nodded, unable to speak. He needed her to go now, so that he could retreat to his bedroom and the bottle of body oil in his nightstand drawer.

She glanced down at the sketchpad in her hand, images of Kenyon naked swam through her mind. "I think I should go."

He pulled her to him. "Are you sure I can't persuade you to stay?"

"Yes," she said. His touch had set her blood on fire. And his embrace had encircled her like a velvet blanket. One more second and she would give in.

She backed away.

Without another word, she left the Williams mansion wondering how she could ever return.

The next day, when she was on her way to an assignment from her boss at Sign Language, her cell phone rang.

"Hello?"

"Good morning, Miss Allgood."

She placed her cell phone in the hands-free cradle on her truck dashboard. "Good morning, Andreas. How are you?"

"Very well for my age and condition."

The old man cleared his throat. "Kenny asked me to contact you to make sure that you two were still on good terms."

Marti sighed deeply. Talking with Kenyon's elderly assistant was like talking to her father. She felt comfortable and safe sharing her concerns with him. "Andreas, I think my professional relationship with Kenyon is being affected by . . . something else."

"He anticipated your reaction. He said for me to tell you that he will behave himself from here on out. And I must add, that's the first time I've ever known him to tell a woman that he would be on his best behavior. As a matter of fact, I didn't know he had a best behavior."

The old man's assessment of Kenyon matched her own. She wondered if he was capable of redemption.

What's the use, she wondered. She would have to see Kenyon eventually to finish the portrait. It wasn't Kenyon's behavior she was worried about. It was her own. Would she behave upon seeing him again?

She had to.

"If Kenyon talked you into smoothing everything over, consider it smoothed."

"Splendid. Kenny will be pleased. If you don't mind me saying so, Miss Marti, you do something to him. I don't think he knows it. But he's different when you're here. And afterward, too. I wish you'd come around more often."

"Thank you, Andreas."

"Would you like Kenny to send a car for your next appointment?"

"No. I'll drive myself."

"Very good."

She hung up the phone, wondering how the older gentleman got her cell number.

"Alone at last," Jacq said. She smiled at Destiny, who looked wiped out and wore her hospital gown, toussled braids, and no makeup.

They had just taken her nine pound, six ounce goddaughter back to the nursery. That seemed to clear out the rest of Destiny's family and friends who were visiting in her hospital room.

"So how are you feelin', girl? Your daughter is as big as a linebacker. You've gotta be sore."

"I'm so happy to have her, Jacq. She's healthy. My husband's off the road. I could cry."

Jacq nodded. She was happy for Destiny. Her life was in perfect order, like something out of a fairy tale. She said a silent prayer that if one day she could be half as happy as Destiny, she would go to church faithfully and never miss a Sunday.

"I just needed to be around you," she said. "Your vibe is so positive. I just want to pinch off a piece and take it with me."

Destiny sat up in the bed. "Is something wrong, Jacq? Your mouth has this broad smile on it, but your eyes are so sad. What is it?"

"Girl," she said, trying to cover up her unhappiness, "there is no way I'm going to rain on your parade. You had a beautiful baby girl yesterday. Let's just talk about her."

"Mahalia is fat and happy. Plus she's got people waiting in line to see to her every need. But not us," Destiny said, holding her friend's hand. "We have to take care of each other."

Jacq closed her eyes.

"It's Davis, isn't it?"

Jacq decided to lay all her cards on the table. For months, something she couldn't shake had kept her from allowing her feeling of Davis to fully surface. She had to tell her friend what it was. "I love Davis and I want to be with him. But in the back of my mind I keep thinking that friends don't do other friends' exes."

Destiny's eyes widened. "Is that what's going on with you and Davis?"

"Part of it. I mean, you can't tell me that me being with Davis doesn't bother you on some level. You two were engaged."

"Jacq. You know I've always been honest with you. The first time I realized that you and Davis were attracted to each other, I was jealous. Heck, I'm only human. But then I watched you two together and I noticed something. When Davis is with you, he's with you—completely. When he and I were together, even as friends, his mind was always someplace else. Usually on his business. But with you, he's different. He gives you his complete, undivided attention. I've never known him to be that way with anyone. That's when I realized that you're the one for him."

Jacq struggled to hold her tears in check. She'd never cried over a man. But this man . . . he was conjuring emotions in her she never knew anyone could have.

"And while we're on this topic, let's get everything

out in the open. If you're wondering if Davis and I ever had sex, we didn't. You know how strict my parents were. Besides, you and I have discussed all my escapades in the past. You know I never once mentioned Davis, because there was nothing to mention."

Destiny gave a reassuring pat to her friend's hand. The tears in Jacq's eyes made her eyes sparkle like diamonds. "He loves you."

Now the tears made shiny tracks down the front of her face.

"The question is, do you love him? Because if you do," Destiny's face warmed, and her own tears filled her yes, "then you can't let him get away. Love is too important. Love is too marvelous. And life is too short. You, above all the people I know, deserve to have the love of your life."

The time had finally come. And she was ready after shadowing Kenyon during an afternoon of art research, and even a visit to the suit factory that left her in awe. She was finally at the point where she could layer her experience in oil on canvas. Andreas already waited for her downstairs in the limo she'd somehow allowed herself to become accustomed to. She packed up her tackle box-turned-art-carryall, tarp, canvas, and easel and headed outside.

"Miss Allgood," Andreas said, opening the door for her. "you look a true artist today." He cleared his throat before she got in. "I assume all of that's dry."

Marti swatted his arm playfully, then looked down at her attire. Sky blue T-shirt and shorts, but over them she wore bib overalls splattered with the evidence of many of her previous works. Even the baseball cap she sported backward was speckled with what looked like tiny Skittles of paint.

* * *

For his first sitting, Marti thought Kenyon was doing remarkably well. The often brooding, mostly solemn man cooperated with every request she had.

When she suggested that he maintain the tradition of wearing a Williams Brothers suit, he'd complied. She didn't know the reason why he disliked the business his family was in, but she had expected a strong rejection from him. He didn't give her one. When she asked him to take his hair out of his usual ponytail, he'd done it, quickly, and the onyx tresses fell like a black waterfall to just below his shoulders. And finally, when she'd recommended that he allow a smile, however slight, to shine through his eyes, she'd nearly choked on her bubble gum when he did as she asked.

"I feel like a youngster asking 'Are we there yet?' But are we there yet? How much longer?"

Marti chuckled. "I'm just getting started. You are the one who started posing too early. I was still setting up when you sat down."

"I guess I just want this to be over with."

Kenyon's comment pulled a thread of disappointment through her. "You know Helga sat for Andrew Wyeth for four and five hours sometimes, almost perfectly still."

"I ain't Helga," Kenyon said, thinking back to their earlier discussion of one of America's great painters. "She had a different motivation."

Marti mixed the warm colors on her palette with her putty knife. "Not the appeasement of parents, huh?"

"They were lovers," he said definitively.

She put her mixing on hold and peeked around the canvas. "You don't know that for sure."

"The man painted this woman in secret, and often

in the nude, for fifteen years. His wife didn't know it. Her husband didn't know it. What do you think was going on?"

"I think Helga was his muse and he was obsessed."

Kenyon kept his head in their agreed-upon position, slightly to the right, chin up. "And you think that in all that time they never took a tumble on that couch she often posed on?"

"I'm just saying that I don't know." Marti returned to her mixing and began to block dark brown paint onto the canvas.

"I know plenty of artists who had flings with their models. I hear it's quite common."

She snorted. "Well, don't get any more ideas, buster. You gave me my painting back. I just want to fulfill my end of the deal."

Kenyon didn't know why, but he suddenly felt playful and, something he wouldn't have readily admitted, flirtatious. "So, are you saying you don't find me attractive?"

"What?" she said, placing an unintended slash of umber where Kenyon's head would eventually go.

"Most artists admit that in order to do a good job they have to become fascinated with something, become obsessed as you put it, or fall in love with their subjects." He turned then, his eyes searing a path down her body. "Do I move you to do your best work?"

"Back in position," she ordered, pulse quickening in her veins. "Like you said, my motivation is different."

A cacophony of emotions sounded within her—elation at finally getting to the most important part of her job, uneasiness that she would have to attempt a work without the familiar motivation of pain to propel her through it, and disappointment that her time with Kenyon was coming to a close. Even though she saw him as sulking, secretive, and closed, his mysteriousness drew her. She wanted to know what it was that made his world so dark. The times she'd been able to draw a smile and sometimes even a laugh from him warmed her soul. His reminiscence on his childhood dreams had already become one of her favorite memories.

Earth colors flowed from her brush and she realized just how much she would miss Kenyon's company. More importantly, she would miss the person she became when she was with him—happy, carefree, inquisitive. He'd introduced her to a world she only knew existed on *Lifestyles of the Rich and Famous.* Every evening with him had been a new adventure, each filled with the kind of wealth she could barely comprehend. Being with him made her work at Sign Language seem dull and uninspiring. For the first time, she felt compelled to explore her art and to become part of the community that Kenyon found so compelling.

If she did, if she took his advice and the advice her friends and family had given her her entire adult life, maybe she could keep spending time with Kenyon. Maybe he wouldn't be out of her life. Maybe . . . he would be a permanent part of it.

What am I doing, he wondered. But in a moment, his reason came clear. He wanted Marti. Despite her ability to unnerve him with her childlike optimism, he'd become accustomed to the sparkle in her eye. And he wondered, with everything that made him a man, what those eyes looked like in the throes of passion.

The fact that he'd already seen her naked stoked his desire. It was so easy, even now, for him to mentally undress her and imagine her soft skin against his. When they were swimming, he was still peeling off the layers of asexuality that being celibate causes. But now, after spending more time with her than he had with any woman, he discovered his lust at full power. He couldn't believe that in a matter of days, he wouldn't see her again. Anxiousness rolled like waves inside him.

"What's the matter?" she asked.

"What do you mean?"

"You're frowning. Is something wrong?"

Speaking honestly, he said, "I didn't realize how hard this was going to be."

She nodded. "Posing is serious business. It's not an easy thing to sit still. Especially for a man like you."

"Are you calling me antsy?"

"No. I'm just saying that you are used to doing important things, and compared to that, sitting like a statue probably pushes you past your patience level."

He heaved a heavy sigh. If only she knew how boring his life really was, she'd realize that sitting here, fantasizing about her, was the most exciting thing he'd done in his house in quite a while.

"I've got a good start on your face. Indulge me a few more minutes while I get to a good stopping point and then we'll take a break."

"Fine," he said, needing to change the lusty direction of his thoughts. "What's that smell?" he asked, focusing in on the twangy, tinlike aroma coming from her direction.

She kept her concentration on the canvas, her shoulder and arm moving deliberately. "It's turpenoid. Kinda like turpentine, only not as toxic."

Kenyon sometimes forgot the fact that in the not-so-distant past, painters often died from exposure to the tools of their trade. Oils, turpentine, and other chemicals and fumes still have the ability to kill if used in poorly ventilated areas or if digested.

With that in mind, they had chosen the second library to paint in. It had more windows than any other room in the mansion. And now, they were all open, but still the pungent smell was just strong enough to give him something to latch on to other than the almost-outy belly button Marti had that he'd like to flick his tongue against.

"You're smiling. Why?"

"Because your skin is so beautiful, it's fun to re-create it on the canvas."

"Is that a compliment? No, don't answer that. Even if it's not, I'm going to take it as one."

"Okay, Mr. Williams. You're getting a little antsy now. Let's take a break."

Kenyon moved and moaned. He'd only been sitting for forty-five minutes, but already his muscles were stiffening into place.

"I should have told you that by the time the sittings are over, you're going to need your Icy Hot."

"Icy Hot? I'm not that much older than you."

Marti cleaned her brushes and used towels to wipe away some of the splatters on her box, easel, and hands.

"You just . . ." she scrunched up her face. "You just act like an old man sometimes."

"You think forties is old?"

"When you're thirty-three, yes."

She stepped around the canvas, and Kenyon laughed.

"Is that funny?"

"No," he responded, "But that brown paint on your nose is. Come here."

She sauntered over. He licked the tip of his finger and rubbed it where the oil was still damp on her skin. Then he took his other finger and wiped the area clean.

"That's nasty," she said, feeling a small warmth flushing her cheeks.

"No," he responded, pulling her into his lap. "This is nasty."

He kissed her lips and the anxiety she'd been feeling since she'd arrived melted and gathered in a pool around her heart, then dissolved into pulsating heat between her thighs. His lips seared hers and their tongues found each other at last and rolled together like mates in a moist bed. His tender possession burst like a rainbow in her soul. She'd never felt anything so exquisite. She pressed back as her body shivered with pleasure.

His hand stroked the back of her neck as his tongue moved deeper into her mouth. Through powerful, deliberate movements, Kenyon siphoned her energy. She sighed against him.

Marti opened her eyes and pulled away, the intensity of their exchange quickening her breath. "I've wanted to do that since the first time I saw you step out of your pool."

A smile brightened the dark intensity in his eyes. "What stopped you?" he asked, his lips just a whisper away from hers.

A devil danced in her eyes. "You put me in jail, remember?"

"Oh, that." he said, stroking the side of her face.

He kissed her nose where the paint had been. "I'm sorry about that. I—"

Her lips covered his and stoked the fire of his desire.

"You taste like cotton candy," he said. The change in their relationship energized him. He knew the rest of the sitting would be hell on him. "And you smell . . ." Despite the turpenoid, her scent was heavy in his nostrils.

"It's called Innocent," she said. She wore it because it reminded her of baby powder with a mature edge.

Innocent, he thought. *Not for much longer.*

She placed two paint-smeared fingers against his lips. "I was wrong. I shouldn't have barged in here and been so foolhardy."

He took her hand and kissed each finger. "Yes, you were foolhardy."

"Hey! You were unreasonable!"

"You're right." He did his best impression of a sad puppy. "Can I make it up to you?"

She hopped off his lap. "Yes! By being an outstanding model."

"I'd like to do more than just model, Marti."

She grinned, giddy with the idea that this man of such wealth and power could be just a bit smitten with her. "First things first. I mean, let's finish the portrait and then take our time."

He stood. "Take our time? We've been hanging out for months. How much longer do we need to wait?" He stopped himself from adding, "Especially since I haven't had sex in years."

"That's just it," she said, returning to her paints. "Maybe it's just a proximity thing. We've spent so much time together, it's only natural that we become attracted to each other. Isn't it?"

She picked up a brush. Her hand trembled with her need to be wrong.

"Well then, I think I'll need one more kiss to tide me over."

Why did his voice sound like a dark mist wrapping around her?

She let herself stare into his eyes, lose herself in their depths. His beautiful obsidian face neared hers. She breathed easy. Knowing what to expect now cooled the rush of adrenaline that made her want to jump on him and wrap her legs around his waist.

Instead, she closed her eyes and opened her soul.

This time, Kenyon's kiss came more urgently, as if he were trying to make her take back her suggestion to take things slowly. They embraced. All thought of the portrait, painting, and posing vanished at the deep press of their lips, the eager exchange of passion.

He was taking everything, her sense, her will, her resolve. And heaven help her, what he didn't take, she gave freely. Sliding down into the depths of his embrace, Marti knew she was tumbling too quickly. But the weeks they'd spent together had bonded her to him in a way she hadn't realized until this very moment.

It didn't take long for her to discover she loved kissing him. He kissed her like it was his first time. Like the sensation thrilled him, overwhelmed him, and frightened him at the same time. They kissed like kids finding a new toy, not wanted to end their play.

After several hot minutes of heavy kissing, Marti pulled away, gasping for breath.

"You're good at that," she said, placing a hand over her fluttering heart.

He rolled a few strands of her hair between his fingers. "I'm good at other things, too. At least I used to be."

"Kenyon, let' s not waste what's left of the light," she responded. She wanted to get back on track. She really wanted to finish his portrait. She had something to prove to herself. She wanted to prove that she truly did have talent. That it wasn't just a matter of painful sadness and deep despair that drove her artistic inspiration. She needed to know that she could summon her muse at will and create a decent piece of work when she was happy as well as sad.

She also needed to slow down this thing between them before she did something that she wasn't quite ready for. The way her feelings had been stirred up, she knew if they made love, her fate would be sealed just as it had been so many other times when she'd been driven to the solace of brushes and clay. No, this time, she wouldn't rush headlong into love or anything else. She would take her time. She deserved to take her time.

Since he was up, Kenyon stole a glance at the painting. A warm shiver moved through him. He saw where she'd washed out the white of the canvas with pigment, and how she'd sketched in his likeness with pencil, but what struck him was *him* on the canvas. It wasn't merely an image or a representation. He could see his life in his eyes, in the facial expression.

The reflection of his dissatisfaction with life jarred him. *Is that what people see when they look at me? Or is it what Marti has discovered while getting to know me?* His heart told him the portrait was accurate, but he wondered if this was the way he truly wanted to project himself. Deep down, he didn't think so.

"You said it wouldn't be a snapshot." He gazed into her eyes, a profound sadness sagging in his chest. "You were right."

His spirits were only lifted by the fact that Marti was more talented than he'd imagined. She was probably more talented than she herself realized. It was a shame she kept it all to herself. He had to persuade her somehow to do more.

Marti took several slow breaths to steady herself. She couldn't paint with a shaky hand. While Kenyon settled himself back on the stool, she pretended to take inventory of her tools. On her right, her tubes of paint lay according to color on a waist-high table. She arranged them into two groups: warm colors like browns and reds, and cool colors like blues and lilacs. On her left, another waist-high table held her brushes, knife, rags, lots of paper towels, a big metal jar of turpenoid, and her palette. She loved her palette. She'd made it from a small square of glass that she sometimes held, but more often kept on the table. The smooth surface allowed her to load her brushes much more easily and work with more color.

"Should we call it a night?"

"What?" she asked, bringing her attention back to the business at hand.

"You look dazed."

"I'm sorry," she said, embarrassment warming her face.

He smiled. "Don't be. I'm just grateful that I can still have that effect on someone."

"Don't flatter yourself," she said, knowing he was right. She returned to her work knowing that the sooner she finished, the better. Since they'd spent so much time together, and she'd done so many preliminary drawings, she hoped she could finish the job in about five sittings of two hours each. That is, if they both behaved themselves. If not, the job might take longer. Much, much longer.

Thirteen

For the next four days, Kenyon and Marti met in the second library, opened the windows, and went to work. By the time the painting was almost finished, the two had managed to cool their attraction and keep their minds on completing the work—but just barely.

Once during a break, Kenyon moaned in protest over his stiff muscles. Marti had been more than a little sympathetic.

"I'd rather be swimming," he offered, his voice deep with model's fatigue.

"You're sitting like you've got a board stuck up your back," she replied. Then she walked over to where he was, shaking his arms out and placing her hands on his shoulders.

"Umm," he moaned. "I don't know what you've got in mind, but I like it already."

"Is that humor?" she asked, bending into his ear. "Kenyon, you're never funny."

He laughed. "And you're never serious."

She stood up straight and massaged his neck. "I'm serious about this portrait."

"That's interesting," he said. "Since the first sitting, I decided that the best thing to do would be to have fun with it."

She continued to massage his neck and shoulders.

He moaned his approval. "I have a masseur that comes every other month and he isn't nearly this good."

"Admit it. You just like having me touch you."

"I admit it," he said, closing his eyes.

She laughed loudly and freely. "Come on, let's get back to work."

"Wait a minute," he said, pulling her to his side. "What about you? Is your arm tired from painting?"

"Are you kidding? I wouldn't have believed it a couple of months ago, but this is a big rush for me. So if my arm is tired, I haven't noticed it yet." She blew a big bubble, popped it, and smiled.

"What about your feet?" he asked, determined to return her favor. "You've been standing on them since you arrived today. I could massage them for you."

Now that was a thought. Her mind churned with the anticipation of Kenyon's dark hands kneading her soles and arches. She almost purred.

"Does that light dancing in your eyes mean yes?"

"Yes," she said.

Kenyon trailed a finger down one side of his goatee. "Switch places with me," he said.

She did as he asked and settled herself on the stool. He knelt down in front of her and removed her shoes and socks. Her toes were manicured and polished with a deep rose hue. Her skin was softer than milk.

"You really take care of your feet," he said, placing her right foot in his lap. He rolled the ball of her foot and instep between his fingers.

She closed her eyes, wishing she could lean back against something. "My mom and aunts have crusty feet. When I was a kid, I was always scared of their feet. And my Aunt Verla used to touch me with her feet all the time."

"Why?"

"Because she knew I was afraid of them, that's why." She poked out her lip. "She was mean."

Marti opened her eyes and leaned forward. "You don't have crusty feet, do you?"

Kenyon's deep blast of laughter echoed throughout the room. "My feet are not as nice as yours, but they are definitely not crusty."

He wiggled her toes and she giggled. "No fair tickling," she said.

"You're taking all the fun out of it."

"You don't have fun, remember."

Kenyon switched to her other foot. "I really seem that way to you, don't I?"

"Yes," she said. "For the most part. But I also sense something else, too. You're like a lost soul that has the potential to find himself. But I think you get in your own way."

He grunted in response. Her comment cut too close to his heart. He did feel lost most of the time. Until now, the only exception came when he did research or gave away money. Recently, he had to add whenever Marti was around. If he was lost, she was a lighthouse. His whole soul was at peace when she was near. That realization both elated and frightened him. Yet he stroked Marti's foot, mimicking the beautiful strokes he'd seen on the canvas. Building their intensity. Deepening their tone.

She moaned. And moaned again. Then pulled her foot gently from his hands.

"Let's finish the sitting. We don't have much longer. After that we can decide if the good time we've been having is something we want to continue."

A day later, the portrait was finished. Marti suggested that Kenyon let it dry for three days before framing and hanging it. But Kenyon seemed oblivious

An important message from the ARABESQUE Editor

Dear Arabesque Reader,

Because you've chosen to read one of our Arabesque romance novels, we'd like to say "thank you"! And, as a special way to thank you, we've selected four more of the books you love so well to send you for FREE!

Please enjoy them with our compliments, and thank you for continuing to enjoy Arabesque...the soul of romance.

Karen Thomas
Senior Editor,
Arabesque Romance Novels

Check out our website at
www.arabesquebooks.com

SPECIAL OFFER!
4 FREE BOOKS

ARABESQUE
A PRODUCT OF
BET BOOKS

3 QUICK STEPS
TO RECEIVE YOUR "THANK YOU" GIFT
FROM THE EDITOR

Send this card back and you'll receive 4 FREE Arabesque
novels! The introductory shipment of 4 Arabesque novels – a
$23.96 value – is yours absolutely FREE!

There's no catch. You're under no obligation to buy anything.
You'll receive your introductory shipment of 4 Arabesque
novels absolutely FREE (plus $1.99 to offset the costs of
shipping & handling). And you don't have to make any
minimum number of purchases—not even one!

We hope that after receiving your books you'll want to
remain an Arabesque subscriber. But the choice is yours to
continue or cancel, anytime at all! So why not take us up on
our invitation to receive 4 Arabesque Romance Novels, with
no risk of any kind. You'll be glad you did!

Call us
TOLL-FREE
at 1-800-770-1963

THE EDITOR'S "THANK YOU" GIFT INCLUDES:

- 4 books absolutely FREE (plus $1.99 for shipping and handling)
- A FREE newsletter, *Arabesque Romance News*, filled with author interviews, book previews, special offers, and more!
- No risks or obligations. You're free to cancel whenever you wish... with no questions asked.

BOOK CERTIFICATE

Yes! Please send me 4 FREE Arabesque novels (plus $1.99 for shipping & handling). I understand I am under no obligation to purchase any books, as explained on the back of this card.

Name _____

Address _____ Apt. _____

City _____ State _____ Zip _____

Telephone ( ) _____

Signature _____

Offer limited to one per household and not valid to current subscribers. All orders subject to approval. Terms, offer, & price subject to change. Offer valid only in the U.S.

AN122A

Thank you!

Accepting the four introductory books for FREE (plus $1.99 to offset the cost of shipping & handling) places you under no obligation to buy anything. You may keep the books and return the shipping statement marked "cancelled". If you do not cancel, about a month later we will send 4 additional Arabesque novels, and you will be billed the preferred subscriber's price of just $4.00 per title. That's $16.00 for all 4 books for a savings of 33% off the cover price (Plus $1.99 for shipping and handling). You may cancel at any time, but if you choose to continue, every month we'll send you 4 more books, which you may either purchase at the preferred discount price. . . or return to us and cancel your subscription.

to her suggestion. He just stood in front of the picture and stared. She wondered if he was breathing.

"The posing is over now. You can move."

His gaze slid over to her and the expression on his face was a mixture of shock and admiration.

"Well?" she said.

"You are amazing," he responded. "This is multidimensional. It's like I'm standing in two places. It really is *me*."

Marti recalled being in a trancelike state when she had painted his portrait. She had mixed the colors and applied them to the canvas with focused deliberation. His aquatic nature, his life of luxury, his lost, soulful, hooded and brooding eyes, his distance from his family, his disdain for the business, his youthful dream to run away, even the part of himself he kept from her—especially that—was on the canvas. Every color, every angle of the brush came from her experience with him. Since day one, she'd been committing him to memory. Now, she could close her eyes and see his face better than her own.

"Marti!" he held her shoulders. "Do you hear what I'm saying to you?"

"I'm sorry," she said, realizing she'd zoned out for a moment.

"You need to do a show. We need to do a show because I'll help you."

"You've only seen two of my pieces."

"I've seen every sketch you've done of me, including some that weren't so flattering."

She smiled at the memory.

"I've even seen the ones you've done of Andreas and the flower garden. I know good work when I see it."

"Kenyon—"

"No, hear me out. Kathryn invites me to openings

and exhibits all the time. Sometimes I go. Most of the time I don't. I was supposed to buy your painting that night, Marti. You are a brilliant talent. You should let people other than your family know."

She frowned and a nervous pulse throbbed in her veins. Showing her work would be like opening a vein. All of the pain and anguish she'd felt for the last ten years would be on display. It was a disquieting thought.

Kenyon squared himself in front of her. "You're doing the world a disservice if you don't share your talent."

The doorbell rang for a fourth time. Marti gritted her teeth and stood up. Paint splattered her from head to toe. Her overalls were a mosaic of warm browns, raven blacks, and rich gold. A six-by-twelve-foot canvas stretched out on her studio room floor. She'd been unusually and uniquely inspired to do a mural. She'd chosen to paint the neighborhood where she'd grown up. Kenyon's attentions earlier that day had her adrenaline flowing and she had to channel the energy somehow. But events were working against her. The phone had been ringing off the hook all afternoon, and now there was someone at the door.

Her phone she had eventually turned off, letting her voice messaging service answer. But the door was another matter.

Ring number five came while she was en route to the door.

"Just a minute!" she said. *Now I know why artists go on retreats where there is no phone, no television, no radio, no people. No distractions,* she thought swinging the door open. And there in front of her was the most powerful distraction of all. She grew hot at the mere sight of him.

"Kenyon? What are you doing here?"

"I had to see you."

Marti could still do somersaults and was suddenly gripped by an overwhelming urge to do one now. Instead she stepped aside. "Come in."

You really ought to be a model, she thought, *'cause, brother, you are working that long-sleeve T-shirt and those loose-fitting jeans. Tyson Beckford, eat your heart out.*

Kenyon strolled into the living room glancing left and right, taking in the surroundings. Then he noticed the paintings and various works of art on her walls. He studied each one. "Very nice," he said, turning to her.

"Thanks," she responded.

"Yours?"

Marti's cheeks warmed at his approval and instincts. "Yes."

He walked closer to the self-portrait hanging above an African violet. "A bit narcissistic, aren't you?"

Marti pushed back strands of stray hair from her face with the back of her hand. "Not at all. When I moved out of my parent's house at eighteen, I went shopping for artwork. I couldn't find what I wanted, and the prices stores were charging for what I did like were outrageous. I just thought that I could create exactly what I wanted and it would be cheaper. That's how art became a regular part of my life."

Something was gnawing at the back of Marti's mind and then it came to her. "How do you know where I live? I don't think I ever mentioned it."

Kenyon picked up a small statue of a naked woman and rolled it around in his hand. "Let's just say I'm good at research."

"Please don't to that," Marti said, watching the movements of his hands.

"Why?" he asked, smoothing his fingers over the statue. Then he looked down at the figure in his palm and back up at her. "Is it you?"

Marti shuddered. Everything he did to the statue, she could feel on her body. Everything about the man before her was hypnotic. And the way they clicked was uncanny. She had attempted to do a sculpture of herself on many occasions. She was never quite satisfied with them and so they were scattered throughout her apartment in various places. As if he had prior knowledge, Kenyon had zeroed in on one of the figurines and was having his way with it—just like she wanted him to do with her.

"Yes," she said, realizing her voice had dropped an octave. "It's me."

"Umm," Kenyon said, smoothing his thumb across the face, breasts, and lower extremities of the sculpture. "I like this one." He looked up, eyes serious and dark. "I want her."

He placed the clay figure back where he had gotten it and moved closer to Marti. His approach was fluid, aquatic, as if he were swimming in his pool. When he wrapped his arms around her, she knew she was drowning.

"We have some unfinished business," he said, voice deeper than she had ever heard it. Darker than the ocean, richer than the midnight sky.

A wave of yearning swept over him as he lowered his head to drink from the lips that were sweeter than any wine he'd ever tasted, and just as intoxicating.

Their mouths touched and surrendered. His tongue parted her lips and probed for its mate. Marti groaned and leaned in. The crush of her breasts against him relaxed his body in some places, tightened it in others.

His kiss deepened, and his need increased as he felt her hands moving across his shoulders, his neck, his chest. When they traveled downward and stroked him where his lust was building, the sensation was so exquisite, he threw his head back and roared with pleasure.

Then without warning, Marti pushed away and stood back.

His shirt and trousers were stamped with the brown and gold paint still wet on Marti's overalls.

"I'm sorry," she said, backing away. "Let me get something to take that out."

She hurried into her studio as if she were running from a stranger. Kenyon followed and caught her as she reached the damp mural on the floor.

He wrapped his arms around her and pulled her close. Her heart pounded against his chest.

"What are you afraid of?" he asked.

She couldn't say it. How could she tell him that she already loved him? So fast? This soon? He would think she was crazy. But more importantly, she knew he didn't love her. Maybe he never would.

She turned around to face him. "You," she said, voice quivery. "I'm afraid of you."

He lowered his head once more. "Then let me show you," he said, talking against her lips, "that you have nothing to be afraid of."

When he kissed her this time, her defenses fell away. The man she loved was kissing her, filling her with his passion, arousing her. And for once in her life, she decided to give in to her desires and stop turning away from her needs. She submitted to her urgency and let her own passion build.

A deep moan escaped Kenyon's lips and flowed

into hers. She swallowed it and pressed closer to elicit another. Her efforts were rewarded as he crushed her against him and moaned, "Yes."

She slipped her hands under his shirt, rolled it up over his head, and tossed it into the living room. She did the same with the rest of his clothes and he did the same with hers. In no time, they stood before each other naked and in need.

His eyes glowed with hot lust as he swept a glance down her body. He took a deep breath and the expression on his face grew tender. "You are more beautiful than anything I've ever seen."

His statement rendered Marti speechless. She simply wrapped her arms around him, kissed him deeply, and ushered him down onto the floor.

Kenyon gasped as his back came into contact with something cool and wet. "What?" he said, looking around.

"Shh . . ." Marti said, rubbing her hands across his body.

He shivered, wondering where she would touch him next. She kissed and glided her hands across his arms. Bit his neck and tweaked his nipples until he cried out in pleasure. She kneaded the flesh of his abdomen and the hard muscles there. She skimmed light strokes across his manhood and reflexively he lifted his hips. But she didn't linger. Instead worked her fingers into his thighs, then down into his calves.

"Marti . . . please . . . touch me," he urged.

She obliged by rolling his rock-hard shaft between her palms. Then when she had a tight seal, she slid her hands slowly up and down.

"Ah!" he said, jerking upward. Marti met him mouth to mouth and then ventured lower, until the seal provided by her hands was replaced by a seal provided by her lips.

Kenyon stroked her hair and watched as her head rose and fell at the seat of his desire.

His hips thrust upward and he roared again, then stiffened.

"Stop," he said.

She ignored him and he moaned.

"Stop!" he insisted, voice deep like a coal shaft.

"Why?" she said, looking up.

"Because I'm not ready to come yet."

"Oh," she said.

"And besides," he said, breathing heavily, "We're destroying your work."

It was true. She had lain Kenyon smack-dab in the middle of her mural—one of the few things she'd ever attempted without pain driving her creativity. But Marti didn't care. They were creating a different kind of art now. And she loved it. Just then a strange idea tugged at her arousal.

She dipped her fingers into one of the many bowls of paint on the floor and smeared the cinnamon brown into the palm of Kenyon's hand.

He gasped at the coolness and stared into Marti's eyes.

She continued, using her hand as a paintbrush and created deep waves of brown undulating down his arms and toward his shoulders. She dipped her left hand into the gold and spun her fingers in circles on his chest creating a spiral of color against his dark skin.

Kenyon purred like a leopard and watched, transfixed, as Marti slowly turned his body into a work of art. Each dip into fresh paint brought a gasp from his lips as the cool acrylic touched his skin and heightened his arousal.

Soon he followed suit, dipping his hand into a mocha brown and dancing the tips of his fingers across her nipples until they jutted out, covered in the warm pigment.

He was amazed how soft the paint was and how easily his hands glided over her skin with it. Like a colorful lotion, they were soon bathed in a rainbow of hue and lust. Marti lowered herself toward him and took his mouth. She probed the warm inside until her tongue found his and slid across, around, and against the pink muscle. Then with the acrylics wet between them, she slid her body in kind—across, around, and against his—creating new colors and deeper urgency with each movement.

She held his hands above his head and the remaining color seeped through the spaces between their fingers. He rolled her over and the paint rolled with them, creating echoes of their bodies on the canvas. He kissed her neck and kneaded her breasts. She moaned her pleasure and her need. Her hands slid across his back, forming golden patterns and tracks. His hair fell against the side of her face as he bit her jaw and slid his tongue in and out of her ear.

She dipped her hands once more. This time in a brick brown henna. Then she massaged his strong glutes and ran her fingers down through the area where the muscles parted.

Kenyon growled. "I've got a condom in my pants pocket," he said, positioning himself between her thighs, rhythmically bumping her most sensitive area.

She opened her legs, so eager to receive him. She felt him at her opening, so close, so close.

He urged further, her moist womanspace calling him strongly. "Ah," he said, pushing further inside. He couldn't wait for a condom. He had to have her now.

She wrapped her legs around his waist and he sank inside.

He shuddered with pleasure. "Yes," he said. It had been so long. And sex without protection . . . he'd almost forgotten what the inside of a woman felt like. And Marti was so small and compact and tight. He moved carefully in and out, languishing in the bliss of her femininity molding naturally around his maleness. The feeling stole his sensibilities. *So good,* he thought, pumping faster. *Oh, so good.*

"Kenyon, stop."

He heard her, but what she was asking was impossible. He was caught in the firm grip of pleasure and had become a slave to it. "You're so wet," he moaned, and pumped faster.

"Kenyon, please. We should use a condom," she pleaded.

"I know," he said, ready to fight his lust. But a delicate moan escaped her lips, and he knew she felt powerless, too.

When her back arched and her hips met his, the battle was over. He gave in to the call of her body. "So sweet," he whispered in her ear. "You feel so sweet."

"Ah oh . . ." she whimpered, caught up. He was taking her over. The pressure of wanting him so badly, of loving him, of needing him came to a brilliant and erotic head. She gave in and let the heat rise.

"I'm sorry," he whispered. "I can't stop. Marti, it just feels too good. I can't—"

The impending eruption was upon him. Kenyon pushed himself wildly in and out of her. He was coming. The feeling started from someplace a million miles away and grew stronger the closer it got to him. He shook with the intensity of it and let out one last barbaric roar as he slammed into her with such force he imagined his seed shooting out her back.

Marti cried out, gripped in the throes of ecstasy. Her entire body pulsed with the contractions that radiated from between her thighs and erupted within her like a mighty volcano.

"There's a flower on your back."

"A what?" she asked.

"A flower," he said. "It's beautiful. I don't want to wash it away."

After their colorful lovemaking, Marti ran some bath water and they sat snugly in her tub washing the acrylics from their bodies.

"Describe it," she said, closing her eyes.

Kenyon sat behind her and took a deep breath. "At the base, there are these long dark leaves. Two of them. And they coil upward like invisible fingers are twisting and stretching them. The stem is thick and sturdy. A stormy mix of browns."

"Why stormy?"

"I don't know. It's just a word that came to me."

She nodded.

"The bud is unfolding. A smooth blend of mahogany and gold, like the sun is shining directly on it." He slid his wet hands down the sides of her arms. The sound of the water dripping matched the beating of her heart. "Like I said, it's beautiful."

"I wonder what it means."

He chuckled. "It means we made some wild love."

Marti would ask Kathryn. She would know what a symbol like that meant. Marti hoped it meant that their relationship was growing and blossoming. That he would come to love her as she loved him.

She sank against his chest. He pushed back.

"Sit up, little woman. Let me get the rest of this paint off you."

She did as he asked, disappointed that he wouldn't allow her to rest against him for a moment.

Pretty soon, what started out as clear and warm rose-scented water turned a cool murky brown. They had finished cleaning each other and were ready to get out.

They made quick work of drying each other off and while Marti dressed in fresh clean clothes, Kenyon seemed in no hurry to cover himself. He strolled around her living room from painting to painting, studying closely.

He took in the artwork and she took in the work of art. He was completely comfortable naked and looked like he should be. His body was almost flawless with a swimmer's physique and skin black as thunder. She could stare at him for hours. Just taking in the path of the muscles on his well-toned frame made her wet again. She could easily go another round. In the bed this time. On top this time. She would ride him until he shouted her name and proclaimed his love.

"Marti?"

"Yes," she said, approaching.

"What do you think?"

"I think I want you some more."

She stood in front of him and looked up. She put on her best *gimme-what-I-want* expression. It didn't work. He bent down, kissed her nose, and smiled.

"I'm flattered, but I have to go." He gathered his clothes where they lay strewn in various places throughout the living room. She watched silently as he yanked them on. She felt cold and alone and he hadn't even left yet.

Her heart hurt. She realized she had no real excuse to see him again. The portrait was finished and their painting was over. He'd gotten what he wanted from her and now he was leaving.

He took her in his arms. "All right. If you feel that strongly, I won't mention it anymore."

"What?" she asked. "I think I missed something."

"I asked you if you would reconsider doing a show. Then you got all somber on me."

He looked closer into her face. "That's not it, is it? What were you thinking?"

She almost told him. But she couldn't bring herself to say *I love you, and I think you're shutting me out.* "Nothing," she said.

The worry lines on his face softened. "If you're worried that I have some kind of disease, I don't. I'll have the results of my last physical messengered to you first thing tomorrow."

She faked a smile. "No, that's not it."

He stiffened, and then let her go. "Well then, if it's nothing, I'll get going. You probably want to get back to your work."

Desperation bubbled up inside her. "You want me to give you a ride home?"

"No, that's all right. Andreas is waiting for me." He reached for the door and opened it.

"Oh," she said, nodding. "Then I'll see you later?"

"Sure," he said and walked out.

Kenyon trotted down the stairs and got in the limousine before Andreas could open the door for him. "Let's get out of here," he said.

"Yes, sir," the older man responded, and pulled away from the curb.

Kenyon's body temperature soared. Now he understood what a hot flash was because he could swear he was having one.

He'd needed sex. He'd wanted sex. After being celibate for so long, Kenyon's lustful thoughts of Marti had been driving him mad. For the first time in years, he'd wanted to be with a woman so badly he became aroused every time he was near her. And the way her eyes darkened whenever they were close, he knew it was just a matter of time before she let him into her bed.

He ran a hand through his hair, which was loose and flowing across his shoulders. He felt as if his whole body had just been dipped in ecstasy. That wasn't just sex, he thought, reluctantly. *That was . . . something entirely different.*

"Turn the air on, will you?"

"Yes, sir."

A rush of cool air swirled around him, and he tugged at his collar. *What just happened?* he wondered. He was starting to feel something for Marti Allgood, and that scared him. He could not allow himself to care for her. That would be a disaster. What if she found out about him, about his family? She would shun him. And then his soul would be crushed.

No. Marti Allgood was not the woman of his dreams. She was someone who had allowed him to quench his lust. And that was as much as she would ever mean to him.

Fourteen

Jacq opened her door in shock. Marti never came over unannounced. "What's up, girlfriend?"

The petite woman pushed past her. "Men suck!"

"Uh-oh," Jacq said, closing the door.

Marti flopped on the couch. Her doll-like features wrinkled into angry lines. "Why are men such, such . . . ooh!"

"Is this going to be a long one?"

Marti nodded, and Jacq went to work. She turned off her television and her telephone. Then she went to the kitchen, whipped up a quick cheese-and-crackers tray, took a bottle of Arbor Mist from the frig, and grabbed two glasses from the cupboard. When she returned, she could see her friend was fighting back tears.

Marti snapped her gum incessantly while Jacq poured the wine.

"Here," Jacq said, offering her a glass.

Marti gulped down the fruit-flavored drink and resumed her gum popping.

"Dang," Jacq said. "It's bad, isn't it?"

Marti nodded.

"You want me to call Des?"

"No. Don't bother her. She's got her hands full with the new baby."

Then a terrifying thought gripped Marti. She and Kenyon could have made a baby today. "Oh, God!"

"Girl, what is it!" Jacq demanded.

Marti sighed fitfully and recounted the whole story to Jacq, detail by detail.

Jacq rubbed her chin, then smiled, deep in thought. "Paint, huh?"

Marti cut her an angry glance.

Jacq winced. "Sorry."

She filled her friend's glass with more wine, then took a sip from her own glass. "Are you sure he said, *it* feels good'?"

Marti frowned. "Yeah. Why?"

"Because you may be right about him using you. If he said 'it feels good,' that means he's objectifying. Focusing on the object that's between your legs." Jacq took another sip of wine.

"Now if he was into you, he would have said, 'you feel good.' Focusing on the person he's having sex with."

"I knew it," Marti said. "He couldn't get out of my apartment fast enough."

Jacq saw the pain and distress in her eyes. "I'm sorry, girl. Some men are just dogs. After they get what they want, they toss you away like an old bone."

Marti closed her eyes. She would have given anything for some clay and a potter's wheel right then. Cool clay squishing through her fingers, soft and pliable. Her mind filled with visions of all the beautiful bowls and vases she could make. And she would decorate them with vibrant colors. But instead of paintbrushes, she saw hands dipping into pigment and rubbing on to damp naked flesh. She couldn't escape it. She had given over her soul today and out of it came a flower budding with possibilities. She would not give in so easily. She would make him love her. Or else, she thought as an emptiness gripped her painfully, she would die trying.

"You are straight up sprung, aren't you?"

"Yes," Marti said. "And so is he. He just doesn't know it yet."

Jacq sensed the change in Marti's demeanor and wondered what her friend was up to. "What do you mean, girl?"

"I mean, I'm going to take Kenyon up on his offer and have an art show."

Jacq was appalled. "So he can use you for your talent, too?"

"He wouldn't do that," Marti said, trying to convince herself. "He wouldn't."

"I think that wine got you trippin'."

"Not even," she said, then downed her second glass. "I'm just starting to see things more clearly."

What she thought she saw was a man afraid of his feelings. She would convince him that there was nothing to be afraid of, just like he had tried to convince her earlier that day.

One bottle of Arbor Mist later, and the two women were laughing and joking like they hadn't a care in the world. Jacq picked up the last cracker and drew circles in the air with it as she talked.

"Girl, we could be the princesses of comedy! That's just too funny." She leaned back on her couch, feeling no pain.

They burst into laughter again and almost missed the knocking on the door.

"Who's that?" Jacq asked, staring at the door.

"Maybe it's Davis," Marti said, then snickered.

"You think?" Jacq asked, still staring.

Marti shrugged. "I don't know! Go see!"

"Oh!" Jacq said, laughing.

She staggered to the door and opened it. It wasn't Davis and she sighed audibly.

"Men suck!" Destiny said, and walked past her friend into the living room.

"Uh-oh," the two tipsy women said together.

"More crackers!" Jacq declared.

"More wine!" Marti shouted, lifting her glass.

The women replenished their stock as Destiny griped about Xavier and how he was treating her.

"Your brother was talking to me like I was some groupie he met on the road!"

"Huh-uh," Marti mumbled. "That's not my brother anymore, he's your husband now. Don't try to put him off on me!"

"Well he needs to be put off on somebody, 'cause I told him I'm not going to take that mess!"

"Where's Mahalia?" Jacq asked, stuffing another cracker into her mouth.

"With her father! I left him standing in front of the mirror! I told him I was going out!"

Jacq frowned. "Hey, hey. Squash all that hollering. We hear you, girlfriend."

Destiny stared at the glass of wine in front of her. She wished she could drink it, but she was nursing. Then it occurred to her that she had been pumping regularly so that Xavier could take part in feeding their daughter. There was plenty of milk for Mahalia to drink. And at that thought, she picked up the glass of wine and gulped it down.

"Pour me another," she said to Jacq.

"Now, Des, you know you don't hold your liquor too well."

"I said I want some more!"

"Dag," Marti said. "Get this crazy heifer some more wine!" At that, they all dissolved into giggles.

Fifteen minutes later, the Lady Soul party was in full swing.

It kicked off with a verbal battle over men.

"I've got Denzel," Jacq proclaimed.

Marti scrunched up her face. "Denzel is old now."

"Yeah, but he's still fine!" Destiny chimed in. The three women uttered sounds of agreement. Marti took a sip of wine. "What about some of the younger guys?"

"Like who?" Jacq and Destiny asked simultaneously.

"Like Taye Diggs!"

Jacq sucked her teeth. "Girl, Taye Diggs needs a mustache."

"You got that right," Destiny seconded. She propped her feet on a steel gray ottoman. "I like the older guys, like Sean Connery."

"Ooh, girl!" Jacq said, smiling.

Marti nodded. "Well, I have to admit, that man looks good."

"Just like wine," Destiny said. "He gets better with time."

The women exchanged amens and big wide grins.

"You all don't like any of the younger guys? I mean what I would do to Brad Pitt is shameful!"

"Okay, Marti. You've got a point. There's just something about him."

Jacq shook her head. "Something simian about him. That man looks like a rhesus monkey."

Marti looked devastated. "Well, then whom do you like?"

Jacq spoke up first. "Honey, my husband is Morris Chestnut."

The room erupted with shouts of agreement.

"His mouth!"

"His eyes!"

"His everything!"

A reverent silence fell over the room, as each

woman contemplated the handsome and immaculately groomed man.

"Okay, Okay," Marti said. "My husband is Boris from Soul Food."

"Girl, all those brothers on Soul Food are fine."

"You got that right," Destiny added. "Guess who my husband is."

Jacq and Marti exchanged curious looks, then said in unison, "Xavier Allgood!"

Destiny waved them off. "You know what I mean—as part of our 'fine brother' talk."

Jacq swept a glance at her friend. "Xavier is fine. You know everyone swears he and Eric Benet look just alike."

Destiny rolled her eyes. "He does not look like Eric Benet!"

Her two friends stared unbelievingly in her direction, and she smiled. "He looks better than Eric Benet."

Jacq shook her head. "This heifer is something else."

Destiny sat forward. "Me? What about Davis and his Sheman Moore–looking self?"

Suddenly, Jacq was quiet and then all three women burst into laughter.

Marti spoke first. "I wasn't going to go there, but he sure does look like that brother."

"So!" Jacq snapped. "Let's talk about Kenyon."

Marti stopped chewing her gum. "What about Kenyon?"

Destiny smiled. "Don't tell me you don't realize that man looks like Tyson Beckford with a lion's mane of long wavy hair."

"At midnight!" Jacq added.

Laughter consumed the three women again, and

for a few moments they forgot all the tension being in love can cause.

Destiny sprawled out in the chair, the wine making her feel sedated. "I guess we just snagged us some good-looking men."

"You got that right, my sister," Jacq said.

Marti raised her wineglass. "To fine men!" she said.

"To fine men!" they echoed and each downed the remaining wine in their glasses.

They closed out the party by dancing and singing to Jacq's CD collection. But they only played the selections where women asserted themselves in a powerful way. Marti started things off by singing Whitney Houston's "It's Not Right, But It's OK."

Remembering how many times Davis had called her in the past month, Jacq followed up with, "Bug-a-Boo," by Destiny's Child. Destiny lent her strong voice to "Grapevine" by Brownstone and "Outa Love" by Anastasia. Soon, Jacq's small apartment was rocking like an amphitheater. The three women continued to drink, dance, and sing. Then they took parts and brought the imaginary house down by singing the re-make of "Lady Marmalade."

It was getting late, and Destiny wanted to sing one more song before they called it quits and let the neighbors have some peace. She browsed through the CDs and a familiar case stopped her hand.

A man with cappuccino-brown skin, dreads, and a five o'clock shadow was on the cover. He sat in a train station, staring at a picture. She opened the plastic case and glanced at the liner notes. She knew without looking they were arranged like a photo album and that pictures she had taken were displayed inside.

She couldn't stop herself. She removed the CD, slid it into Jacq's player, and advanced the play list to track six, a cut called "Peace."

At the first note of the bass and piano, Marti and
Jacq groaned. They recognized the song as one the
radio couldn't get enough of.

"Oh no she didn't," Jacq said.

Marti smiled. "Yes, she did."

Destiny closed her eyes and sang along with her
husband, the man she loved more than anything in
this world except her daughter.

I don't want to fight with you
We've got too much work to do
I can't hurt like this no more
Can't we have just a little . . .
Peace
After I talk to you
Peace
After our love is through
Peace
Now that what's said is said
Peace
Like a promise we made in bed
Peace
Dawning with the morning light
Peace
You know that I know it's only right
Peace
Take me down, make me yours again
Peace
Let the end of our end begin

All three women sang the next verse, then a voice
like chocolate thunder boomed from just outside
Jacq's door and snatched the chorus from them. Jacq
and Marti turned toward Destiny. She took a deep
breath, closed her eyes, then opened them.

"Let him in," she said.

While Jacq went to the door, Marti turned off the
stereo. Destiny stood front and center, arms crossed.

When the door opened and Xavier saw three angry women, he knew he was in trouble.

"Where's my daughter?" his wife asked.

He stepped inside. "Our daughter is with Davis."

"Davis!" the three women shouted.

"Even I know better than to leave a child with Davis. He'll probably try to schedule her feedings using Microsoft Project." Jacq stared at him but spoke to Destiny.

Even his sister was hostile. "He's my brother and I love him. But if he's wrong, you gotta check 'im."

Xavier knew better than to respond. That would dig him in a deeper hole, and he would never get his wife back. And besides, the way they were all swaying like there was a breeze in the room meant they had been drinking. He decided to play it safe and took a small step toward Destiny. She stopped him with her eyes.

He cleared his throat. "I don't have anything to say for myself. I mean, there's no excuse for my behavior."

Destiny tapped her foot on the thin creme-colored carpet.

"Baby, I've been gone for months. I was Allgood 24/7. I guess it takes a while for me to stop being a performer and start being a husband and father."

His wife's eyebrows rose. He could hear her saying, "And?" even though she didn't utter a word.

He stepped closer. "Lovely, I'm home now. I'm Xavier now. And I need my family."

She rolled her eyes. He knew he had hurt her. He was hurting, too. "Lovely, please . . ."

She breathed a long sigh and walked into his arms. Their deep kiss left the two onlooking women gawking.

"Dag," Marti said.

"Destiny? Girl, can you breathe?"

The husband and wife pulled apart slightly. "Now I can," Destiny said. They walked toward the door holding hands. Xavier turned. "Thanks for taking care of my wife."

Marti smiled. "You're welcome, big brother."

Destiny rushed back to hug her best friend and her sister-in-law. "The party was wonderful," she said.

After they said their good-byes and the couple had left, Marti made a prediction. "I'll bet they are back to normal by the end of the week."

"Are you kidding?" Jacq asked. "When their child goes to sleep tonight, those two will be in bed trying to make another one."

Under normal circumstances, Marti would have laughed at Jacq's retort. But tonight, it served as a reminder that her actions today could have caused her to become pregnant with Kenyon Williams's child. She pushed away her glass that was half-full of wine, knowing that she would do whatever it took to have the kind of relationship with him that her brother had with Destiny.

Marti lined all the paintings along the walls of her spare bedroom. There were twenty in all, and they spanned the last twelve years of her life. Until now, they were just impulses. Spur-of-the-moment detours into color, light, and emotion. But now, they were part of a plan to bring Marti closer to the man she loved.

She'd called him that morning to let him know that she had changed her mind about having a show. She let him know she wanted to have one as soon as possible.

Kenyon seemed both excited and unhappy. He was glad that she had changed her mind, but he was disappointed that he had to go away and wouldn't be back for a couple of days. He'd told her to go on with her planning without him. She could brief him when he returned.

She had agreed, but reluctantly. All the while her mind was focused on where he could be going and why he made frequent trips out of town with no explanation. Could it be another woman, she wondered.

She pushed that thought out of her mind quickly. The mere thought made her sick to her stomach.

No, Kenyon was her man, even if he didn't know it yet. They just needed a little more time to be together, and her art show would provide the perfect venue.

For the past two months, a kaleidoscope of color had been Marti's constant companion. With the help of her friend Kathryn, she'd gone through all of her attempts at artwork. Some of them Kathryn had seen, others she had not. Although her friend thought that the majority of her excursions into her emotions were candidates for her opening, Marti had her doubts.

While Marti had wanted to go with a theme, selecting paintings that told a story, Kathryn suggested a more versatile approach that would showcase her diversity of skill in various mediums. In the end, they had compromised and agreed upon a theme represented by different types of art: paintings, sculptures, collages, and combinations of the three.

Her spare room had gone from an organized mess to just a mess, with all the work she'd unearthed for possible inclusion in her show taking up space there. There were paintings stacked and pulled away from walls, sculptures taking up residence in a back corner, and a tarp strewn across the floor, where Marti worked on one new piece for the event. Her entire apartment smelled like wet paint.

It took a while to sink in, but the thing she'd thought about off and on for ten years was finally happening—her very own showing.

Kathryn had been a godsend. She'd arranged everything from the refreshments, to the music and entertainment. Kenyon had provided her a list of collectors. Since Kathryn's gallery was private, the guests came by invitation only. When it came time to display her work for the show, Kenyon and Kathryn gave her no say-so in the matter. Between the two of them they argued and compromised until they found the best arrangement. Marti had simply stood back and watched them work.

On the night of the artist's reception, Marti was a bundle of nerves. Jacq came over to help her get ready.

When Marti emerged from her bedroom wearing her sexy little black dress, her friend smiled broadly. "I don't care how short you are, you're walking tall now, girl. I'm so proud of you."

The two good friends hugged.

"Thanks, Jacq. You know all this still seems like it's happening to someone else."

Marti riffled through her silver sequined bag and pulled out a stick of bubble gum. Jacq snatched it away.

"Not tonight, girlfriend. Tonight you're going to be elegant and gracious. No gum snapping."

"What will I use to steady my nerves?"

At her question, her doorbell rang.

Jacq lifted an eyebrow. "Bet I know what that is."

Marti opened the door. Suddenly she had a flashback of playing the game Mystery Date when she was a teenager. She remembered opening the door on the game board and praying that the guy behind it was handsome, well dressed, and ready to take her out for a night on the town. The men in her sister's hand-me-down game were tall but never as dark as she wanted them to be and not as handsome as she dreamed they could be. But the man in front of her now was all that and more. He swept her into his embrace and planted a kiss on her lips that stole her breath and her wits.

When he released her, she swayed a bit, steadied herself, then smiled.

"I see you like that, too," Jacq said.

Kenyon strolled inside, confidence placing his every step. "Evening, Miss Jackson."

"Evening, Mr. Williams. I was just leaving."

Marti turned. "Jacq, you can ride with us."

"Naw, girl. Y'all go and do your thang. I'll check in with you at the gallery. And you tell that inconsiderate heifer Kathryn I don't appreciate not getting an invitation."

Marti walked her friend to the door. "She said that was an oversight."

"Uh-huh. Well I tell you what, nothin' is gonna keep me from your reception tonight, ya hear?"

"I love you, Jacq."

Jacq switched her round hips toward her sports car. "I know. I know."

Kenyon wore a suit, charcoal black. Even though it wasn't made by Williams Brothers, it still fit him as if he were born to wear it. He was just a few feet away, but she felt him. His manliness. His desire. His eyes raked hotly over her. She shuddered as if he'd penetrated her. Suddenly, she was too warm to stand in one spot.

"Are you ready?" she asked, reaching for her bag.

He looked down to where evidence of his arousal peaked clearly and then back to her. "Yes," he whispered like soft thunder.

She smiled. Since they'd first made love on her floor, Kenyon seemed insatiable. She knew his need for her raged within him. Yet he always took her tenderly, as if she would break if he kissed her too hard, touched her too roughly, or thrust inside her too wantonly. She had a feeling all his gentle time taking was about to come to a quick and explosive end.

He grabbed her. "How much time do we have?"

She dropped her purse. "Not as much as I know you want," she said, driving her fingers through waves of his obsidian hair.

"Then hold on," he said, and plunged his mouth into hers.

We they came up for air, Marti offered protest. "I don't mind messing up my hair and makeup, but is it good to be late for my very first showing?"

"I'll make it good," he said in a lust-filled growl.

He lifted her onto the dining room table and once there, quenched both of their uncontrolled desires quickly and completely in a fiery onslaught of passion. It took them several moments to catch their breaths afterward. Then unexpectedly, Marti giggled.

Kenyon removed the condom they had used and headed toward the shower. "I know you're not laughing at me."

"No. It was just that we made a lot of noise. We always make a lot of noise. My neighbors must think I'm a nymph."

"And they would be right," Kenyon shouted from the bathroom. Marti heard the spray of the shower as he turned it on. "Are you coming here or not?"

"I'll wait," she said. "I know how you are when I'm naked and wet. We will never make it to my reception."

Kenyon walked out of the bathroom, naked and

partially erect. He picked her and she squealed in protest.

"You know I'm used to getting my way," he said and carried her into the bathroom where they washed and kissed until they were clean, giddy, and ready for the artist's reception.

By the time they arrived, they were only twenty minutes late. They stepped inside MoonWind Art Gallery in Downtown Decatur amid the lively buzz of a handful of guests. Kathryn greeted them with a warm smile.

"You two look lovely together," she said.

"Thank you," Marti said, her cheeks warming at the compliment. Kenyon nodded in kind.

As they strolled toward the hors d'oeuvres, Marti fought the gigantic grin that threatened to take over her entire face. She was surrounded by her work, which looked surprisingly good on the pillars, odd-shaped sections, and walls of the gallery. Kathryn had designed the space so that guests felt as though they were traveling through passageways of art. Some of the walk space led to areas of the room that were secluded for private viewings of special pieces. The large room was bright white from floor to ceiling. Against the stark backdrop, the colors in each of her works seemed to come alive on the canvas and dance upon the clay of her sculpture. Interestingly enough, the ceiling lights were a bit subdued. However, each piece had its own accent lighting. The effect was more cozy than dramatic. More casual than exclusive. Just the way Marti had imagined it. The faint aroma of incense drifted throughout the room, but not enough to overshadow the smells of wine, crackers, and cheese. Marti couldn't remember a time when her sense of smell had been so acute.

She was starving.

As she made her way toward the food table, she took note of the people, their expressions, and tone of conversation. They were having a good time, but more than that, they were admiring her work. Smiling. Pointing. Nodding. Approving. Marti's heart pounded. Tears stung her eyes. They liked her work.

By the end of the evening, Marti had met more people than she could remember. Many were friends and acquaintances of Kathryn's. Aside from a smattering of her family and friends, the bulk of the guests were art collectors that Kenyon had invited. There was even an art critic, and that had Marti shaking in her boots for fear of a bad review. But Avanda Eldridge, highly respected in the Atlanta art community, had left the affair spouting glowing praise and promising a flattering write-up in *Atlanta Weekend* magazine.

Even Kenyon's brother Reynard made a surprise appearance. He'd come with a lovely woman who had the oddest-looking green eyes Marti had ever seen. Although the two seemed much more interested in making sexual overtures to each other than appreciating art, Reynard purchased one of Marti's statues and requested next-day delivery to his home in Savannah.

All in all, Marti was happier than she could have imagined. Nearly all of her paintings sold and by the end of the reception at least fifty people had shown up. And from what Kathryn told her, they were all the right people.

She couldn't get used to the number of people praising her abilities. Jacq told her to, "Smile and say thank you." What Kenyon told her scared her. He was under the impression that she would just have to flat out get used to it.

She wondered if she could.

"Well?" Kathryn said, closing the door as the last guest left.

Marti hugged herself and bit her lip. Not only had she shown people her work, but for the first time, she'd allowed them to buy it. More importantly, they wanted to buy it.

"Well . . . I'm a hit!" Marti said and ran into Kenyon's arms.

He held her and swung her around laughing. "I'm proud of you, little woman."

When he set her down, she pretended to be dizzy. And then he kissed her until she was.

"And where's my hug?" Kathryn asked, a smug look on her face.

Marti hugged her friend tightly.

"I knew you could do it," Kathryn said. "I knew they would love you."

If her heart swelled with contentment any larger, it would burst happily from her chest. "I feel like celebrating." Marti unwrapped a stick of bubble gum from her purse and popped it in her mouth. She chewed happily, letting the sweet juice fill her mouth.

"I've taken care of the celebration," Kenyon said.

Marti spun on her heel and faced him. "What kind of celebration?"

"When you're ready to go, you'll find out."

Kathryn smiled and took a last sip of wine from her glass. "You two go on. I've got everything from here."

"I want to help clean up," Marti insisted.

"Are you kidding? You were the guest of honor. The guest of honor is not on clean-up detail. Besides, I've got a service. They will be here tomorrow to straighten up all this."

"Are you sure?" Marti asked.

"Of course," Kathryn responded, eyeing one of the paintings. It hadn't been purchased yet and for good reason. Kathryn was saving that one for herself, and she had made it perfectly clear to anyone who had been interested in purchasing the abstract work. For days, she had imagined the gold colors above the mantel in her home. She'd set aside the money to buy it yesterday and couldn't wait to add that to the rest of the money Marti had earned.

"Well, all right then."

Kenyon strolled to the door with his arm around Marti.

Marti felt like the most perfect blessing had just been bestowed upon her. She stopped in the doorway. "Thanks, Kathryn. Thanks for everything."

Throughout the reception, she'd kept reminding Kenyon that he couldn't buy all of her work. That he would have to let others buy if they were willing. It was the only way she would know if people actually appreciated her work.

He'd still bought three of the pieces she'd displayed. He'd taken the smallest painting of the three with him when they left the gallery and upon entering the limousine, he'd given it to Andreas.

The old man's wrinkles flattened out in surprise and then crinkled into a wide grin. "Thank you, sir!" he said.

Kenyon hadn't given Andreas instructions, but he seemed to know where he was supposed to go. The fact that Marti didn't made her just a little nervous.

"What's the surprise, Kenyon?"

"You'll see," he said, tightening his arm around her. Then his eyes burned over her with the same intense heat as earlier that evening. "Have you ever had sex in a limo?"

She giggled. "No!" Then she frowned with curiosity. "Have you?"

He leaned over her and ushered her down onto the back seat. "I think I'm about to."

Kenyon didn't understand the strong compulsion he had to hold Marti Allgood, to kiss her and be inside her. To be near her. The only thing he'd been able to do for weeks was obey that desire.

She made him crazy.

Her mouth tasted sweet and sugary and pink. He kissed her deeply, thinking that the things that had first repelled him—her eternal optimism, her playful nature, her ever-ready smile—were the same things that now drew him close and kept him wanting her. Tonight, during the reception, he had been amazed how, despite her reservations and the nervousness she claimed, she had been the most charming guest of honor he'd ever known. Kenyon had been to artist's receptions before. Had spent a significant portion of his life around art and artists. Many of those he'd met were so full of themselves, he could barely stand it. Or they had been so strange and eccentric that they lived in their own worlds. Marti made it a point to meet and greet everyone. She never acted intimidated, shy, or aloof. She was simply herself and had managed to get a laugh and smile from everyone she encountered. She was like a Nubian Tinkerbell tossing her pixie dust and casting a happy spell on all those in the room. He'd followed her around like he'd been in the dark for centuries and she was the first light he'd ever seen.

Wherever she went, she brought the sun with her.

And Kenyon could not fathom what it would be like to be without that warmth.

His lips rolled down her neck, her throat, and across her shoulders. She moaned. He loved her moan. He did everything in his power to keep that moan coming from her lips. She yielded beneath him. Where she gave, he took, claiming the woman he'd come to need more than anything else in life.

She moaned again and he slipped a hand under her dress, gently kneading her thighs. His fingers grazed the delicate fabric of her chemise, feeling the heat of her flesh rise beneath the silk. She squirmed.

"Kenyon, stop."

He hadn't heard those words since the first time they made love. He'd made sure that they used a condom ever since.

"I've got protection," he murmured, peeling down the top of her dress to reveal caramel smooth shoulders.

"No, Kenyon . . . I don't feel well. Please stop!" she said, pushing up.

She signaled for Andreas to pull over and rushed out before the car came to a stop. Kenyon followed close behind her.

She clutched her stomach, doubled over, and all the wonderful hors d'oeuvres she'd eaten that evening came up forcefully.

"Marti!" he said, rushing to her side. He pulled the handkerchief from his front jacket pocket and wiped her mouth as she stood. "I didn't think the food was that bad," he said.

He didn't get the reaction he expected. Instead she looked up at him and her eyes had suddenly grown tired.

"I'm sorry." He wrapped an arm around her. "What happened? I mean, should I take you to see a doctor?"

"No," Marti said, turning her head and spitting. "I've already been.

"Well, if you were sick, we could have postponed the reception. The guests would have understood, I'm sure."

"I'm not sick, Kenyon."

Suddenly everything around them grew still. The sounds of night quieted. It was as if they were the only two people in the world. Andreas had pulled over on a bridge overlooking the Tallapoosa. The view of the stars was spectacular, but Kenyon's thoughts were trained on Marti and the keen sense of foreboding budding in his chest.

She looked at him, trying to smile through queasiness. "I'm pregnant."

Certainly he couldn't have heard correctly. "What?" he asked, already stepping back, already drawing away.

"We're going to have a baby."

"Marti—"

"I know. I know." She paced a little in front of him. "I was trying to wait for the right time. I mean, I was going to tell you after the reception anyway. And after tossing up my dinner like that, it just made sense to—"

"What are you saying?" Kenyon asked, his euphoria gone, disengaged. He could hear the disconnect in his mind like two freight cars uncoupling.

He couldn't have a child. Not with the legacy of shame that had plagued his entire life. He would not wish that torture on a dog, let alone his own flesh and blood. He would not allow it to happen again.

"I'm saying," she said, sidling up to him and brushing against his shoulder, "our baby is due in April."

He jerked back. "You can't be serious."

Marti looked over at the mess she'd made on the concrete and then back at him. "Yes. I'm serious."

"Everything all right, sir?" Andreas asked.

Kenyon ignored him. "Marti, we only—"

"I know, but it only takes one time." She leaned against the bridge sizing him up. "I thought you would be happy about this."

"I don't know why."

Hurt erased the expression of glee on her face. "I thought we were a couple. I thought we were in love."

Kenyon frowned. "Love? I don't think either of us has ever used that word."

Marti bristled. "You don't always have to use it when you can feel it. I can feel it, Kenyon. Even if you don't say it."

He lowered his head, a storm of turmoil and anguish raging inside him. "You can't have the baby."

Now it was her turn to pull away. She backed up so fast, she stumbled and nearly fell. "You want me to . . . to—"

"Yes," he said, looking up, his voice hissing.

Marti regained her footing and started walking. "You're asking me to commit murder."

"It's not as dramatic as that."

She faced him squarely. Although she was almost two feet shorter than he, in that instant she seemed much taller.

"This is our child!" she screamed. "I can't kill our child!"

She was trembling. Kenyon moved closer and reached out to comfort her. She snatched her arm away. Then a terrible memory invaded Kenyon's mind. It was his father telling him and his brother about money-minded women who could try to trap them by getting pregnant or claiming to be. The elder Williams had gone on to explain about paternity tests and at the end of his talk, pushed the business card of a doctor who could be relied upon to be discreet should ever the need arise. The thought had disgusted him for years, but now . . .

He looked down into eyes he'd begun to trust with his life. "Tell me this is not about my money."

The slap she gave him sounded worse than it actually was. In the night air, the reverberation echoed. In his body, his question was answered.

Sadness gripped him. "Marti, I—"

"Don't talk to me," she said, grabbing her abdomen and lurching away. "Oh, God," she moaned, then bent over and retched up all that remained in her stomach. The ordeal left her weak and flushed.

"Let me take you home," Kenyon offered.

"No thank you," she said, wiping her mouth. "I'll call one of my sisters."

"Don't be unreasonable."

She glared at him.

"Miss Allgood. If you'd like, you may ride up front with me."

Neither of them had realized that Andreas hadn't gotten back in the car.

Marti's breathing was heavy and she felt like crap. She needed to go home and lie down.

An exasperated sigh escaped her lips. "Thank you, Andreas," she said, and headed back to the limo. And not a moment too soon. She was beginning to feel faint and was unsure how much longer she'd be able to stand.

During the ride to Marti's apartment, Kenyon kept the partition closed. He was too busy ruminating to talk. Pregnant! If everything in his life had been one unfortunate situation after another, why should his relationship with this woman be any different? And the fact that she insisted on having the baby turned his stomach into knots.

Without consulting him, she'd already made up her mind. Without considering the possibilities or consequences, she'd made a decision that would impact them for the rest of their lives. It seemed his little woman had a boatload of gall.

Maybe I should tell her, he thought. *I could take her to the state room and show her everything. I could tell her how miserable my life has been. I could explain to her how sometimes I get physically ill at the thought that my family committed horrendous atrocities against people who looked like them. And that every day I live in fear that somehow the truth will come out and my family will be ostracized like lepers.*

It might persuade her that bringing a child into that kind of legacy is not only unfair, it's wrong.

He pressed a button. The glass partition hummed down to its base. "Marti, we need to talk."

"No we don't."

"It's important."

"So is the life of this child, but you don't understand that."

"After what I have to tell you, you may feel differently."

"Nothing you can say or do will change my mind. Now please stop talking to me," she said, and then burst into tears.

"Marti—"

"Maybe you should do as she asks," Andreas interrupted.

"This is not your business, wrinkly."

"You know, I've called you Sir since you were six years old. Now all I want to call you is foolish."

"Shut up and drive!" Kenyon shouted and closed the partition.

Since that night, Kenyon hadn't had much peace.

He certainly hadn't had any success at talking some sense into Marti. She'd refused to see him or take his calls. He'd sent messengers and emails. Still no response. At one time, he considered buying Sign Language and thought when it was time to pay her, he'd refuse until she agreed to speak with him.

When he showed up at her job, she'd shouted something unintelligible about stalking laws and threatened to call the police.

He knew when it was time to give in.

She did agree to see his attorney. James Townsend had gone to Marti's apartment and spoken with her regarding the care of the child. In exchange for Kenyon providing monthly child support, she signed an agreement not to sue him for any reason.

Mr. Townsend's report was that he was very impressed with Marti Allgood and either she expected a contract and was ready to negotiate or she was just that sharp. Kenyon suspected it was a combination of both. One thing the attorney stressed was that outside of the financial arrangement, she wanted nothing at all to do with Kenyon. At one point, she'd suggested that that request be made part of the contract. And then she seemed to think better of it.

Kenyon's heart sank deeper and deeper the more Townsend talked. He slid his fingers down his goatee, unable to believe that the woman he thought he was falling in love with no longer wanted anything to do with him.

Fifteen

Five Months

Marti rubbed her stomach, not ready to get out of bed. She had hoped she would be able to work throughout her entire pregnancy, but the way she'd been feeling lately, she'd be lucky if she made it another month. For the third time in a week, she would have to call in sick.

Morning sickness had become a regular part of her morning routine and to stave off the side effects, she'd created a routine of her own. Before attempting to stand, she ate two saltines and drank a few sips of water.

It had been hard not seeing Kenyon for two months. She'd put up a brave façade when his lawyer had come to see her, but when she was alone, and even when she was with friends, she missed him terribly. And no matter how much she believed she shouldn't, she could only talk about him. Even Destiny had told her to stop worrying about him because he didn't seem to be worried about her.

Sooner or later she was going to have to tell her sisters what was going on. They knew she was pregnant, but they didn't know that her relationship with Kenyon had ended. Whenever they asked about him, she would say he was off on another one of his numerous trips. But she'd grown tired of the lie, and if the cramps she sometimes had didn't let up soon, she might have to have someone come and help her.

None of the books she'd read so far had prepared her for the changes taking place in her body. The tiredness, the tenderness in her breasts, the frequent need to urinate, and most of all the cravings. She had never in her life cared for onions. But since her pregnancy, she couldn't get enough. Fried. Sautéed. Raw. She had them all kinds of ways. Jacq finally bought her a machine to make bloomin' onions and onion rings. She'd eaten them almost every day since.

She stood slowly, then a sharp pain stabbed at her womb area and dropped her back down to the bed. "Ah!" she screamed clutching her abdomen.

Marti breathed shallowly until all that was left of the pain was a dull throbbing sensation. She needed that pain to go away soon, because she needed to get to the bathroom or her bowels would move even if she couldn't. When she saw the ring of red forming beneath her, she screamed until her next-door neighbor called the police.

By the time the ambulance got Marti to the hospital, the bleeding had stopped. The doctors assured her that there wasn't much blood loss and that from what their instruments could tell, the baby was okay. But she was urged to see her Ob-Gyn doctor for extensive testing as soon as possible.

She had called Jacq to bring her some clean clothes and take her home from the hospital. When Jacq got there, she was a nervous wreck.

"Girl, what happened?"

"I don't know," she said, trembling. "I just got these terrible cramps and then I started bleeding."

"Oh, God, Marti. Is the baby all right?"

"They say the baby is fine, but they want me to see my doctor just to be sure."

Jacq slowed her usual speed of fifty-plus miles per hour to a reasonable speed. "Are you all right?" she asked.

"I don't know what happened. I just don't know what happened."

"Well, don't worry, girl. I'll take you to the doctor tomorrow and we'll find out."

Kenyon could count the number of times he'd heard the doorbell ring on one hand. The only people that stopped at the mansion were deliverers and Marti. The deliverers always came to the back and Andreas always met Marti at the front door before she had a chance to approach

When the bell rang again, he got up, wondering if Andreas had somehow fallen ill without his knowledge.

"Andreas!" he called. Maybe the old man was in the bathroom.

He waited a few moments. Whomever was at the door was certainly impatient, as the bell rang incessantly now. Kenyon supposed he would just have to answer it himself.

He entered the vestibule more than a little upset. When he opened the door and saw four angry women standing there, he decided to put his feelings aside for a moment.

He knew who they were instantly. Same caramel complexions, same intense eyes, same high cheekbones and sexy mouths. The only difference was that they were all taller than Marti, but there was no doubt. They were her sisters. He could pick each of them out from her stories.

"Don't tell me," he began. "You are Yolanda," he said, pointing to the woman obviously the oldest, with the streaks of gray in her hair. "And you, you must be Ashley," he remarked to the one who looked like a black flower child. "I'll bet my next fortune that you are Morgan," he said, pointing to the woman in the French designer suit and fashion model makeup. "And that just leaves—"

"Yeah, I'm Roxanne. And I'm not impressed. Now are you going to let us in nicely or should we just kill you where you stand?"

"Ladies, ladies," he said, realizing why Andreas was suddenly so scarce. "Please come in."

He escorted them into the drawing room. While three of them took careful looks at the architecture and artwork, he noted that Roxanne kept her eyes on him.

"Please be seated if you like." He wondered what kind of lashing he was in for.

They remained standing.

"I can have some refreshments brought out if you like. Just let me—"

"Look, Kenyon. We're not here for any refreshments. We just want to get some facts straight and some information from you," Roxanne said.

Kenyon leaned against a marble wall. It was cold at his back. He signed. "All right."

"We understand that you are the father of Runt's baby," Yolanda said.

He blinked. "Who?"

"Marti. You know who. Don't play dumb!" Ashley shouted.

What had he gotten himself into, he wondered. "Yes, I am."

Morgan put her hands on her hips. "But you haven't seen her in two months. Why is that?"

How could he make them understand that he would bring even more shame to her by being at her side? It was best if he just faded from the picture. "I made arrangements to send money."

Roxanne stepped closer. Even though she wasn't the oldest, he could tell she was the leader. "You better do a whole lot more than that, because she almost lost the baby."

He perked up. "That might not be such a bad thing."

The four women moved faster than he could see. When they snatched him and pinned him down on a Princess Anne settee, he realized that his comment was something he should have kept to himself.

Roxanne was in his face then. "If something happens to my sister or her baby, I will take you out. Do you understand?" She backed up a bit, but the others still held him in place.

"What kind of man are you?" She looked him up and down. "And what does Marti see in you? She's so stressed out about this whole situation that the doctor's got her on bed rest for the rest of her term."

A boulder of sadness dropped in Kenyon's stomach. "I didn't know."

She shook her head. "You didn't know! Men never seem to know. Especially when it comes to carrying a child. You are all alike!"

"Roxy," Yolanda said.

Then the tall slender woman seemed to calm down. But Kenyon could see the tears in her eyes. They were many; however, they refused to fall.

She pointed a manicured finger in his face. "I need to know that you are going to do right by my sister. I want the best medical care your money can buy. I want a second opinion. I want nursing assistance. I want prenatal expertise. I want—"

"Okay, Roxy. I think he gets it," Morgan said.

Roxanne turned away, but the others held him fast.

"She'll have the best," Kenyon said. "I give my word."

They released him and moved to Roxy's side. She was shaking. He couldn't tell if it was from anger or tears. He would guess it was a combination of both.

He watched them leave arm in arm. Their conviction floored him. They had such intense love for each other. It was palpable. He admired them, liked them even. For standing up for love and family. For being willing to face down an enemy. For having courage and conviction regarding something other than money. He hadn't known a family like that.

Marti was a lucky woman.

He was still staring after them when an absurd thought crossed his mind. The kind of daring and bravery the four women showed today deserved a brave and daring response.

"Andreas?" he said quietly, knowing that the man had to be lurking somewhere in the shadows.

"Yes, sir," Andreas responded, stepping out where he could be seen.

"Pack a day bag."

"Sir?"

"I'll be staying with Miss Allgood today."

"Yes, sir!"

Sometimes the quickness with which Andreas moved surprised him. He would be ready to leave in no time.

"Now, promise you won't be mad."

Marti shifted herself in bed and gave her friend a heavy look. "I know you. When you start a sentence like that, it means I better not promise and that I'll probably be pissed."

"Girl, come on." Jacq straightened the pillows behind Marti's back.

"Okay. I promise."

"I called your sisters and told them about Kenyon's triffin' behavior."

Marti sat up. "Jacq, you didn't! Please tell me you didn't. Oh, God. I better call him. Warn him that they might try to talk to him."

Jacq lowered her eyes. "I think it's too late. Yolanda said something about going to talk to him this morning. They are probably there right now."

Marti sank back against the bed. She felt lost and tossed away. Like she had no control over anything any more. She was adrift.

Her stomach pitched. Jacq shoved a small trash can under her chin just in time, and her breakfast tumbled out of her mouth and into the plastic liner.

"Jacq," she said, struggling to catch her breath. "As soon as I have this baby, I'm going to kick your butt."

Jacq wiped Marti's mouth and placed the bucket back on the floor. "Yeah, yeah. After that baby comes out of you, you won't want to raise your leg to do nothin'!"

A few minutes later, Marti was feeling better and wanted to rest. Jacq put a few items of Marti's clothing in to wash and stretched out on the couch with a good book. She wanted to be around in case her friend woke up and needed something.

"Andreas?" Kenyon said. He'd been watching the landscape pass by, gradually changing from countryside to cityscape.

"Yes, sir."

"I want a gynecologist, a pediatrician, and a personal assistant on standby. While you're at it, line up two personal assistants—one to remain in the apartment and the other to run errands."

"Yes, sir. But if you don't mind, sir, I would be happy to run errands."

"Good deal. I'm entering unfamiliar territory. It will be good to have a friendly face around. Even one as crumpled and antique as yours. But where will you stay?"

Andreas didn't dare tell him that he had his eye on a neighbor lady. "Rest assured," he said, "That I will never be more than five minutes away."

"Wonderful!" Kenyon said, closing his eyes. He put his feet up on the seat across from him and allowed himself to zone out for a brief moment.

He remembered the woman from the concert and art show. He didn't think she was wrapped too tight, but she was obviously a good friend of Marti's.

"Hello," he said, trying to be friendly. The tight expression on her face had told him that he'd better be as friendly, charming, and appealing as he could.

"What do you want?"

"You're Miss Jackson, right?"

The look on her face resembled a cocked shotgun.

"I'm here to see Marti." He shifted his duffel bag from on hand to the other. "I thought I would visit with her for a while."

Kenyon tried not to let the woman's laughter offend him. "You've done enough!" she said when her giggles subsided. "Why don't you just get back on your high horse and ride the hell on back to your palace?"

He shook his head. "It's a mansion," he corrected.

"Whatever!" Jacq replied, eyes cutting him like sharp blades.

"What's the matter?" a groggy voice asked behind them.

Jacq rushed to her friend's side. "Marti, girl, you know you're not supposed to be walkin' around."

Marti's eyes locked on to Kenyon's. For a moment, he thought he saw relief and a small bit of tenderness. But only for a moment. Then her eyes went rock hard and ice cold. The expression made him shiver.

He reached for her. "Marti, I want to see you. I want to help."

She backed away, looking frail and weary. The long cotton gown she wore seemed to swallow her whole. "My sisters must be slacking. I'm surprised you can still walk."

Her voice was glacial and chilled him even more, but he was determined.

"I've called the best doctors in the county. Let me help you."

At that she stopped.

Jacq stopped too, giving him a once-over. Then she turned to her friend. "That's the smartest thing he's done since you met him."

Marti turned and went into the house. Jacq followed behind her. He followed behind Jacq.

"I don't want anything to do with him or his money or . . ."

Jacq caught Marti by the shoulders. "You're thinkin' about yourself. You don't have that luxury anymore. You have a child to consider now. A child that you're having trouble carrying."

Marti stared up at her friend, blinking back the sadness.

"Girl, I don't like it any more than you do, but if Mister Moneybags here can help you carry this baby to term, then let him." Jacq glanced in his direction, her expression still lethal. "It's the least he can do."

Suddenly, Marti's skin went starkly pale.

Jacq's eyes widened. "Girl, what's wrong?"

As Marti crumpled toward the floor, Kenyon dropped his bag and bolted. He caught her just before she hit the ground.

He held her in his arms, amazed at her light weight. "In here!" Jacq urged.

He carried her into her small living room. Before he could block out the thought, an image of their naked bodies flashed in his mind. He could see them clearly on the carpet, smeared with pigment and hot with lust. *This is where it happened,* his mind registered. *This is where my child was conceived. My child,* he repeated in his mind. It was the first time he'd thought of it in that way.

Her bed had been moved into the living area. He laid her on top of a pink-and-white comforter.

Jacq ran into the kitchen while he stroked Marti's hair, which had been sectioned off into row after row of plaits. Within seconds, Jacq came back with a pan of ice water and a thick washcloth. She sat beside Marti, dipped the cloth in the water, wrung it out, and placed it on Marti's forehead.

"She's anemic. The doctor said that throughout her pregnancy, she'd be prone to dizziness and fainting. Cold compresses seem to help."

Kenyon had never seen anyone or anything more fragile than the woman lying before him. He would spare no expense when it came to her care. He couldn't bear to see her like this.

He sat down on the other side of her. "May I?" he asked, reaching for the cloth.

Jacq eyed him suspiciously, then conceded.

He dipped the cloth in the water. It was so cold, he

thought his hands might go numb if they stayed in the tub too long. He squeezed out the excess water, replaced the towel on her forehead, and held his breath. After a few seconds, she stirred and her eyes fluttered open. Upon seeing his face, Marti gasped. He couldn't tell if she was afraid, offended, or just plain shocked that he was attending to her.

"Don't worry, girl. I'm still here. I'm not crazy enough to leave you alone with this fool," Jacq said.

As soon as he heard the words, Kenyon knew that's exactly what he wanted. To be left alone with Marti. And he wanted it now.

"Jacq, I really need to talk to Marti."

The ghetto fabulous woman rolled her eyes. "She's got ears."

"Alone," he said.

She arched an eyebrow, and he knew she had no intention of leaving him alone with Marti.

"Please," he said.

Marti struggled to sit up. "It's all right, Jacq."

After giving him one last harsh stare, she rose from the side of the bed. "Okay. But, girl, if you need anything, I'm leaving my cell number and my pager number. Plus, I'll be callin' to check on you."

As soon as Jacq left, Marti laid into him.

"So, did my sisters bully you into coming to see me?"

Kenyon placed the tub of water and washcloth on the end table. "No," he said.

"Bull."

"All right. Maybe their coming to see me had something to do with it."

Marti sucked her teeth. "That's what I thought."

"But it wasn't the entire reason." He waited a beat before speaking again. "Why didn't you tell me you were having problems?"

"You made it perfectly clear where you stand," she responded. She didn't tell him her real reason was that she couldn't face the look of gratitude and relief that he might have knowing that there was a good chance she could miscarry.

"I care about you, Marti."

"But not our baby," she countered.

He looked down where the evidence of their love-making was growing inside her. What could he offer the child but a legacy of shame? He'd promised himself that he would not perpetuate his family history of prosperity from oppression. But that's exactly what he'd gone and done. He was appalled by his own actions.

Marti saw the look of disgust on Kenyon's face and a pain worse than any she'd ever felt shot through her. She gasped for breath and felt hot and churning nausea in her stomach.

At her sharp intake of breath, he looked up. She looked deathly ill. "What the matter?" he asked.

"I'm gonna . . ."

Before she could finish, the lunch that she'd managed to keep down for an hour tumbled out of her mouth and onto her gown and bed sheets. Kenyon leapt away from the path of regurgitated food and bile.

"Ugh!" he said, looking at Marti. Her eyes clouded over with embarrassment. She looked like a sick and helpless little girl. The image pained him.

He grabbed the wash cloth from the nightstand and cleaned her face.

"I can do it," she protested, reaching for the cloth.

He frowned. "You're already too worked up as it is. That's probably why you got sick."

Marti was trembling now. She looked more tired than he had ever seen her. He crinkled his nose. If she didn't get cleaned up in a hurry, he knew he would lose his lunch as well. He reached in his pocket for his cell phone.

"What are you doing?" she asked.

"I'm calling Andreas. I've got a personal assistant on retainer. Andreas will send her right over."

Marti stiffened as she unbuttoned her gown and shoved the soiled bed sheets aside. "I don't want some stranger in my house!"

"But Marti, look at you. You're a mess."

"You said you wanted to help. You can start by getting me some fresh clothes and bedding and washing these dirty ones."

A bold wave of unease swept through Kenyon's body. He'd never had to make a bed or wash clothes. His household coordinators did that for him. "Marti, I don't think . . ."

The sight of her breasts silenced him. They were larger than he remembered. Larger. Rounder. Something about them made him want to forget everything he'd ever known and suckle them until he found new memories. Only a short time ago, he had to coax her into his swimming pool without a bathing suit. But the ease at which she had disrobed told him that she was becoming as comfortable sans clothing as he.

"Are you going to help or not?"

He shook himself out of his reverie and helped her out of her gown. Then he pulled away the comforter and wrapped it into a ball.

"There's a laundry basket in the bedroom. And in my bottom right dresser, I've got some pajamas."

"Okay," he said, not wanting to take his eyes off of her body. It has been so long since he'd seen it. Too long. And now, all he wanted was to immerse himself. To sink inside where she had once been warm and moist and aching for him. His reaction was strong and it frightened him. It was as if everything in his life over the past few weeks had been utterly wrong and the truth of his destiny was lying vulnerable before him. His arousal was instant and bold. He didn't try to conceal it. He simply, and with much effort, disengaged from the hold her sexuality had over him and carried the soiled spread into her bedroom.

Once there, he took several deep breaths to steady himself. He wondered how he would be able to stop himself from tasting her once he returned to the living room. He needed her body like he needed air and he knew his painful hard-on would not go away easily.

Sixteen

Imbecile! his conscious shouted. *That's what got you into trouble in the first place.* That realization caused a steady deflation of Kenyon's erection. He stuffed the soiled linen in the clothes hamper and retrieved fresh pajamas from the dresser drawer. When he returned to the living room, Marti had covered herself with a sheet and was lying still with her eyes closed.

"Marti?" he said softly.

She moaned her response. She looked exhausted. Carefully, he pulled back the sheet and dressed her. She mostly kept her eyes closed and moved freely like a limp doll in his hands. When she was fully clothed, he covered her and sat in the chair next to the bed. The gentle sounds of her light snoring disturbed the quiet. He watched her chest rise and fall for several minutes before the insistent lull of deep sleep claimed him as well.

When he awoke, Marti was still sleeping. He glanced at his watch. He'd been out for two hours. He got up, stretched, and looked around. Details he hadn't noticed when his concern for Marti was so thick he could cut it now leapt out at him. Two end tables—one holding the tub of water that was undoubtedly tepid by now, and the other cluttered with medicine bottles, tissue, a pitcher of water, and a thermometer. In the corner of the room, a humidifier released moisture into the air. On the floor at the side of the bed, a pile of books and magazines were stacked up like Jenga tiles. Beside that stood a small trash can with a thick lining of plastic bags. *I know what that's for now,* he thought.

She'd removed a lot of her artwork to make room for her bed. The first time he saw Marti's apartment, he thought it resembled a quaint gallery, the kind he'd visited often in Greenwich Village in New York. But now, her apartment looked more like a hospital room. He winced. Something about that thought made him momentarily queasy.

The transition from art space to recovery room was so stark, it gave him the creeps. And the dry scent of inertia and dust had replaced the flat chalky smell of paints and acrylics. He got up, disquieted by the severity of Marti's condition. He watched her frail form stirring beneath the covers, grateful that he had the means to give her the best care possible.

He pulled out his cell phone and dialed Andreas. The old man answered on the first ring.

"Yes, sir?"

"When will the doctors be here?"

"They have to clear their schedules. However, all are making arrangements to arrive by the end of the week."

"Call me when the itineraries are set."

"Yes, sir.

"And Andreas?"

"Yes, sir?"

"Get that housekeeper over here."

"Oh no, you don't," Marti said, sitting up.

Kenyon covered the microphone on his phone. "Marti, be reasonable."

"I'm pregnant. I don't have to be reasonable. Besides, the doctor told me I should limit my visitors. So if I have to ration my time between my friends and family, I damn sure don't want some stranger in my apartment."

Kenyon sighed. "Andreas, nix the housekeeper."

"Sir?"

"You heard me."

"Yes, sir."

Kenyon closed the cover of the cell phone and put it away. "I see you're feeling better."

Marti stretched and yawned. "Yes, and I'm hungry."

He smiled, digging once again for his cell phone. "I'll have a master chef over here in no time."

"You've got to be kidding," Marti said. "I've got plenty of food in the refrigerator. Ashley bought me enough food to last an entire season. Just go whip up a sandwich and maybe some soup."

Kenyon recoiled. "Me?"

"Is there something wrong with you?" she asked, turning into the Marti he knew and enjoyed having sex with. "Your hands and feet do work?"

"Of course!"

"Then get in that kitchen and fix me something to eat."

Kenyon muttered to himself as he walked into Marti's kitchen. He could count the number of times he'd been in a kitchen on one hand. And it was never to prepare food. He looked around at the cabinets and appliances. A stone of dread fell to the pit of his stomach. Cooking. It couldn't be that hard. If his assistants could do it, certainly he could.

He slid open a few drawers. Foil. Plastic wrap. Knives. Serving utensils.

"What are you looking for?" Marti shouted from the other room.

"Bread," he said.

"It's in the refrigerator, along with the cheese."

"Yeah," he said, the slow heat of inadequacy creating a light sweat over his entire body.

He poked his head into the refrigerator and retrieved the items she mentioned. In no time, he'd managed to create a decent and slightly awkward-looking sandwich.

It was almost dinnertime. The rumbling in his stomach told him that without his needing to look at a clock.

Kenyon battled with calm and anxiety as he searched unsuccessfully for anything that resembled a grill.

Finally, he gave up. "Ah, Marti?"

"Yes?"

"Where's your grill?"

"Very funny," she said, gruffly. "My skillets are in a cupboard under the counter.

"Okay," he called back, hoping he sounded confident and calm.

He looked in the cupboard and found a flat cooking instrument with a handle. *Must be a skillet,* he thought. It looked like it would do the trick, so he took it out.

He turned to the stove. He knew it was a stove. But how to work it was another matter. He figured that the metal coils probably provided the heat supply. Somewhere in his memory, he remembered seeing actual fire coming up from a stove. So he turned one of the knobs and waited.

Nothing happened.

He placed the makeshift sandwich on the skillet, set the skillet on one of the coils, and waited. Still nothing.

He looked at the knobs more closely. He had turned on the right one. Maybe it wasn't working.

He moved the skillet and touched his fingers to the coil.

"Ow!" he shouted, jumping back from the stove. He flailed his burned hand in the air, causing the skillet to topple out of the other. The metal clattered onto the floor, spilling bread and cheese.

"What are you doing?"

Kenyon spun around to see Marti up and standing at the entrance to the kitchen.

"What am *I* doing? What are *you* doing? Get back in bed. You're not supposed to be up."

"You sounded like you needed help." She glanced at his reddening palm. "Are you all right?"

The rising temperature of his skin prompted him to step over the heap of bread and cheese on the floor and move to the sink, where he turned on the water and doused his hand into the steady stream of cold and wet.

"I'm fine," he responded, shuddering from the pain. "It's just a little burn. I'll get this cleaned up and have a great dinner prepared for you in no time."

Concern wrinkled her brow. But he was insistent. "Please, get back in the bed. Everything is all right here." He had no intention of letting on that he was as lost as one of Little Bo Peep's sheep.

She headed back into the living room. "Okay, but if you'd rather not do it, just let me know. I'll call one of my sisters."

Kenyon swallowed. "No. That won't be necessary." The last thing he needed was to be in an apartment full of women who didn't like him. And the fact that Mart had called them because he'd somehow managed to botch dinner would just be one more strike against him.

It was funny, being in a position where what he wanted wasn't merely a servant call away. He turned

off the water and dried his hands on a nearby towel.
The pain in his palm was gone, at least for the moment. As he cleaned up the mess he'd made, the
strange sensation of food in his hand fascinated him.
It was like food in the raw. Uncooked and unprepared. He'd never had the sensation of something
undone in his fingers before. It was new and although
it unnerved him to no end, it was exciting, like discovering you have one more piece of candy when you
thought they were all gone.

He went back to work. He was determined to figure
out this cooking thing. What could be hard about
bread and cheese?

He put together another sandwich and this time
managed to get it into the skillet without mishap. He
watched over the food like a mother hen. He couldn't
tell if anything was happening, but the heat from the
coil told him that it had to be cooking.

As the food got hotter and hotter, he realized that
he would have to turn over the sandwich. He
searched the drawers quickly for some utensil to turn
over the food. Much of what he saw was simply metal
bent into unusual shapes. Nothing registered as familiar. Finally he grabbed a giant fork and jabbed it
into the bread. He maneuvered the fork into the
sandwich, lifted it, and flipped it over. What he saw
brought a long sigh out of his throat.

His creation looked nothing like the grilled cheese
sandwiches he remembered as a kid. Andreas had
brought him golden-brown delights of ooey, gooey
goodness. What lay flat in the skillet looked like dry
leather. He wondered if he could scrape some of the
crusty part off.

Despite the overdone appearance, it smelled good.
He stood back and inhaled, proud that he was able to
make something that created such an aroma. Glanc-

ing into the living room, he saw Marti propped up in bed by at least four pillows. She was flipping through a magazine and looked three notches beyond bored. A faint popping sound turned his attention back to the skillet. He looked down where gobs of cheese oozed out from underneath the sandwich and pooled around the crust edges.

That's the best part, he thought, jabbing the sandwich once more with the oversized fork. Lifting the bread and cheese from the skillet, he scrambled through the cupboards for a plate. He found one just in time. A thick cord of cheddar had started to droop out from between the slices. He plopped the sandwich onto the plate and sighed. He'd prepared his first dish, and it looked like disaster on a plate.

"How much longer?" Marti shouted from the other room.

"I'm coming," Kenyon said, searching around the kitchen. He knew from his own tastes that presentation was everything. He searched to no avail for something that would enhance the presentation of his concoction. The only thing he could find was some pink and blue cocktail umbrellas. He opened three of them and dashed them onto the plate.

He hoped the splash of color would make the dead-looking brown heap on the plate more lively and appealing. And perhaps, despite its appearance, the grilled cheese sandwich was still edible.

He walked slowly into the living room with his creation, not because he was trying not to disturb her, but because he was uncertain of her reaction. Carefully, he lowered the plate to her lap.

Her jaw went slack and she stared unbelievingly into his eyes.

"Here you go," he said, trying to pretend that he wasn't offering her a hot misshapen monstrosity.

Marti gazed down upon the object piled on the plate in her lap. She turned the plate completely around, examining it. And then quicker than Kenyon could ask what was wrong, she snatched the sandwich and took a gargantuan bite out of it.

At her action, he started breathing regularly and relaxed a little.

Kenyon stared in awe as her teeth crunched and her lips smacked. "You must really be hungry."

"I am," she said, after swallowing another mouthful. "Can you get me a napkin and some juice?"

"Sure," he said, his confidence returning. In no time, he was back in the living room with her requested items. When he got back, he saw that Marti had eaten over half her sandwich.

"You've got something on your chin," he remarked, glancing at the place where a thin string of cheese clung to the cleft of her chin. She picked off the slender ribbon of cheddar, looked at it, then tossed it into her mouth.

Kenyon laughed. After her earlier spell, it was good to see Marti put some energy into something, especially something that would keep her and the baby healthy.

"Are you laughing at me?"

He sat on the stiff-backed chair beside the bed. "I'm sorry."

She popped the last corner of the sandwich into her mouth and chewed rapidly. "It's all right. I like the sound of your voice when it's happy. It reminds me of a happy storm. Robust and blissful."

Her words warmed the pit of his stomach.

"You don't laugh enough," she said, just above a whisper.

He handed over a few napkins and a glass of apple juice. "I think I've laughed more since I met you than almost any other time in my life." And it was true. At times he found Marti's carefree, fun-loving attitude irritating as hell. But other times it was like experiencing joy full force. Despite all his efforts to shun that feeling, he was becoming accustomed to it. Found himself needy for it. What an indulgent luxury, to take life on a whim and discard all its weights and measures and dirty doings. To only see the good. He wondered if that would ever be possible for him. He doubted that it could.

"Did you wash my blanket?" Marti asked when she had downed her glass of juice.

"W-wash?"

"You didn't just leave it in my bedroom to stink, did you?"

Damn it! Another domestic request. "I really think you should have a private nurse or a caregiver who can take care of these things."

Marti sat back further against the pillows. The bed creaked with her movement. "Are you saying that you're too good?"

Kenyon was appalled. "No! But I think . . ."

"Stop," she said raising a hand. "I've had enough of what you think. Here's what I think. I think you're going to go into my bedroom and get that hamper. Then you're going to go into the hallway to the laundry area and wash that soiled bedding."

His eyes widened. It always shocked him when someone had the nerve to tell him what to do.

"And in between washing and drying, you're going to make me another grilled cheese sandwich."

He got up in a robotic trance, amazed and a little excited that she would speak to him that way. Kenyon meandered off to the bedroom.

"With extra onions this time!" she added.

Kenyon laughed again. Remembering her comment about him laughing earlier, he let the sensation of giddiness rush over him fully and found that not only did he laugh harder, but he really enjoyed laughing. Maybe Marti was right about him doing it more often.

By the time Marti's friend Jacq came back, not only had he washed and dried the bedding, but he'd made not one but two more grilled cheese sandwiches—one with onion. Although the food didn't turn out a whole lot better than his first attempt, he liked sharing a meal with her and tasting his own cooking for the first time.

"You need anything, girl?" Jacq asked, leaning against the wall.

"No. Kenyon's taken real good care of me."

The indignant woman stared in his direction, a look if disbelief plastered all over her face. "You're kidding."

He couldn't help feeling a little smug. He'd done things today he'd never considered doing. Things he'd taken for granted.

"No, girl. I'm okay." Marti smiled in Kenyon's direction. "I'm in good hands."

Jacq stepped away from the wall and adjusted a black leather purse against her shoulder. "What time do you want me to come back?"

"Do you have to come back?" The thought of having to share his time with Marti with someone else made the inside of his stomach feel soupy. He hadn't realized until today how much he'd missed her. And now that they were together again . . .

"Forget you!" came Jacq's tart reply. "Somebody's got to stay with her tonight. And it's my turn." She rolled her eyes.

"Okay," Marti said, weakly.

"I'll stay with her," Kenyon said.

The two women stared at him with looks of surprise. They couldn't have been any more surprised than he.

Jacq plopped her hands on her hips. "You?"

Her constant attitude frustrated Kenyon. "Do you see anyone else here?"

"Are you getting smart?" the woman in the doorway asked, neck working furiously.

"Jacq, maybe you could take a break tonight. I'll be all right with Kenyon."

"Are you sure?"

"Yes," Kenyon and Marti said at the same time.

Marti swung her legs to the side of the bed. "I'll be fine. Now, get out of here," she said getting up.

"What do you think you're doing?" Kenyon asked, rushing to her side. He couldn't believe the rebelliousness of the woman. She was determined to break her bed confinement one way or another.

"I'm going to walk Jacq to the door."

"I'll do that," he said. He waited until Marti had settled herself back on to the bed before moving toward the door.

"I'll call you first thing in the morning," Jacq said.

Kenyon walked Jacq to the door. Before she left, she whirled on him. "Just so we understand each other, I don't like you. I think you're arrogant and coldhearted. And I don't like what you did to my friend—knocking her up and then walking out of the picture. So don't expect me to jump for joy now that you've decided to come back." Her voice came out low and ominous.

Her eyes moistened. "I'm going to watch you like a housewife watchin' Oprah. And if Marti cries one more tear because of you . . ."

Kenyon stepped closer to the woman having a Kodak moment in front of him. "Just so you understand me, I don't care for you either. But it's not you as a person, just your ghetto-girl personality. Now don't get it . . . twisted. I don't have a problem with people being who they are, but I get the feeling that you're not as confident and bodacious as you would like everyone to believe."

Jacq blinked as if there was an eyelash in her eyes.

"And for the record, I hope you do watch me. Because then you'll see that I care about Marti and I'm going to see that she has the best of everything she needs."

Jacq opened her mouth to speak, but instead she turned and walked out of the apartment.

Kenyon closed the door and pounded his fist against it. Even when he was trying to do good, he was still cast as a villain. He walked back to where Marti was wondering if his efforts were really worth it.

When he'd shown up at her door, it was the answer to a very long prayer. Since the moment she'd suspected that she was pregnant, all she'd wanted, besides a healthy baby, was for Kenyon to realize how much he loved her. The fact that he'd come to her was a first turn in that direction.

Marti was sure that her sisters' visit to his mansion probably had something to do with him showing up. But now that he was here, now that they were back together, he would finally realize that they were meant to be together.

So far, he'd been attentive and helpful. He'd struggled through making her dinner and had even managed to wash a load of laundry. Although she could only hear his fumblings in the kitchen, she could see her small stacked washer and dryer from where she lay. It was almost comical to watch the way

Kenyon carefully read the directions on both the washing machine lid and the detergent. It took him a good twenty minutes to figure everything out. But he didn't balk or complain. He just went to work like he was eager to do anything for her.

Watching him in the laundry alcove, she realized that he was probably washing clothes for the first time in his life. Then she realized that he'd probably never cooked a day in his life either. It warmed her heart even more to know that he was willing to do these things for her. He could have easily called it a night and let Jacq take over. But he didn't. He made himself comfortable, brought her fresh water, and was attentive to anything she wanted. God help her, it made her love him all the more.

She couldn't explain how she knew what she knew. But a strong notion in her soul made her know that she and Kenyon would eventually be together. Her sisters didn't understand it. Her friends, especially Jacq, didn't understand it.

But they didn't have to.

All she had to do was wait. Time would do the rest.

"I've never known you to be this quiet," he said. They'd spent the last two hours in silence, Marti trying without success to read a book and Kenyon glued to the Internet.

"I know," she admitted. "It's strange, isn't it?"

"Yes. It's like having a faucet running constantly and then just when you get used to the sound, it stops."

"So are you saying you've gotten used to me?"

"Maybe," he said, and turned back to the computer.

Marti smiled. It was start. He'd given a little. She would take his small concession, knowing in her heart that others would come.

So far, neither of them had mentioned their time apart. It was as if it hadn't existed, only some strange twist in their relationship that caused them to temporarily act more like friends than lovers.

"Okay, that's it. I can't take this silence. Please . . . talk to me."

She searched her mind for something to say, but the only thought that would come was the thing that had occupied her mind beside Kenyon—their baby. "Today I'm exactly fifteen weeks pregnant." She reached over and pulled a thick paperback book off of the end table. She flipped quickly to a section near the front of the book. "That means that the fetus is ten centimeters long and can make a fist." She closed the book and looked up into eyes dark with seriousness. "It's changing from the stage where it looks like a shrimp into a real live baby."

Kenyon took a deep breath. Until now he hadn't allowed himself to visualize the child growing in her womb. But now, it was hard not to. He remembered taking Human Growth and Development in school and seeing the photographs of a child evolving from embryo to infant. She'd given him X-ray vision with that statement. He could see into her right now—see right into her soul. She really wanted this baby. Already loved it. Even now when it probably looked like something more suited for water than land.

Kenyon glanced at the clock. It was late. He suggested that they get some sleep, partly to change the subject and partly because of the time.

His stomach churned tight and hard. Like it or not, this baby was coming. His baby. He still had trouble with the idea, but tomorrow was another day. For right now, he had a pregnant woman to take care of. He grabbed the telephone from where it sat on the table next to him and dialed Andreas's number. He needed clothes. Lots of them.

Seventeen

He'd had a hard day. Davis propped his feet on his leather ottoman and stretched out from his couch. His muscles ached. He'd spent the morning and the better part of the afternoon helping friends move into a new house. Steve and Rachelle were probably the wealthiest couple he knew, and even though Steve had a good job working for Coca-Cola, Davis knew the primary reason for their riches had been their chintziness.

Since his friends were too "frugal" to hire movers, they had called everyone they knew to help them move from a five-bedroom house in Garden Hills into a seven-bedroom mansion in Tuxedo Park. Of course Davis and a few others had gotten stuck with the heavy work. The real heavy work. Expensive furniture always weighed more, and the Foxalls only purchased the best.

As he reclined on his couch, he remembered how he couldn't wait to get home to soak in his Jacuzzi to ease his screaming muscles. And that's exactly what he'd done.

Now, the serene sounds of Enya flowed out of his speakers and relaxed him even more, but something was wrong. Something had been biting the edges of his thoughts all day, but he couldn't bring it forth to see what it was.

Oh well, he thought closing his eyes. *It will come to me.*

Davis breathed deeply as the melodic voice soothed him and eased out his tension. In no time at all, he was asleep.

When the tree branch crashed into his bay window, Davis was deep into REM sleep. He dreamed that he was in a boat in the middle of a vast sea. It was hot and he had caught nothing all day. Then floating just beneath the surface, he saw the face of a woman. He looked closer, realizing it was the face of the woman he loved. She was smiling and holding her arms open for him.

She wants me back, he thought and jumped into the water, just as the sounds of shattering glass pulled him out of her embrace and out of his dream.

"What was that?" he asked to an empty room.

He blinked and sat up to bring himself to full consciousness. A roaring gust from outside mixed with the soft piano-playing coming from his CD player like a bizarre symphony. *The wind,* he thought, hearing a clamorous rustling. But the sound he heard was too loud. He turned and let out a sharp curse when he saw the shattered glass on the floor and the dark, craggy tree limb jutting through the space where the window used to be.

He cleaned up the mess as best he could while the wind raged on outside. The evening sky had grown pitch-black with clouds as dark as the universe. Davis turned on the television as the biting feeling returned with a vengeance.

The Weather Channel charted the path of a severe thunderstorm approaching the Atlanta area. Davis's muscles tightened. If the storm hadn't gotten there yet, then what was going on outside? *If this is a preview, we're in trouble.*

He remembered Steve saying earlier that day that he wanted to get his move over with before the storm rolled in. He studied the weather report for several minutes, unable to turn away. A hard rock of anxiety fell in his stomach. *Why am I on edge?* he wondered.

The uneasiness gripped him tightly. He stared unblinkingly as the radar displayed an image of the storm that was nearly on top of Atlanta now. In seconds, large drops of water hit his house. They sounded like iron pellets being shot out of a gigantic bazooka. *Rain!*

The biting in his mind stopped, replaced by lips, Jacquelyn's rich lips garnering a sacred vow from him. "Promise me you'll hold me when it rains."

Davis bounded from the couch, snatched a jacket from his closet, and raced outside into the storm.

It was as if Atlanta had been swallowed by a black cloud. The streetlights and other illumination coming from houses and buildings barely created enough light to see with. Between the clouds and downpour, visibility was worse than poor.

Cars ahead of him pulled over, surrendering to the storm's fury. Davis switched on his high-beam lights and pressed on through the deluge.

Tree limbs and other debris cluttered the street ahead of him. Several times he swerved wildly to avoid crashing into objects falling in front of him. His heart pounded in his ears, rivaling the thunder outside. *Okay, hot shot. Slow down. You can't do her any good if you get into an accident.*

Hail replaced the driving rain. It was small at first, then the closer Davis got to Jacquelyn's apartment, the larger it became. By the time he pulled up into the parking lot, the hail pelting his SUV had grown to the size of golf balls.

Pulling his jacket over his head, Davis leapt from his parked vehicle and dashed into the apartment. At first, he'd questioned his thinking. Maybe she wasn't even home. But on the way over, he knew that the weather forecast had probably kept her in her apartment all day. Her blue Geo Metro in the parking lot confirmed his suspicions.

Davis pounded on the door. He imagined her collapsed into a tight ball and trembling. When she didn't answer, he ran around the side of the building. With hail pummeling his body, he entered Jacquelyn's apartment through a side window.

"Jacquelyn!" he shouted, racing from room to room. As he neared her bedroom, he heard the distinct sounds of sobbing, even above the raging storm. Fear surged through his veins and quickened his pace into her bedroom.

His imagination was precise. Jacquelyn was huddled on the floor, hugging herself, and rocking back and forth. Tears the size of raindrops from the storm tracked down her cheeks.

"Jacquelyn," he said, sinking by her side.

Her frightened eyes looked up at him, and then she threw her arms around his neck. "Oh, Davis!" she said, shaking.

He cradled her. "It's all right now. I'll protect you . . . from this storm." He stroked her hair and kissed her forehead. "From everything."

And he knew it was true. Arguments or no arguments. Jacquelyn Jackson was his woman, now and forever. And he would protect her from anything that dared to harm her.

She didn't know it, but he was in love with her. As soon as the storm ended, he would show her just how much.

While Destiny finished setting the table, Xavier answered the door. A bright exchange of "how are you's" ensued. Then a blast of Xavier's laughter caught her attention and she glanced back. But instead of something humorous, she saw the unsettling advance of Davis and Jacq as they hobbled into the living room.

"Oh my, Lord! What happened to you two?"

Xavier continued his laughter. He shook his head, held his stomach, and staggered gleefully into the kitchen.

"What's going on?" Destiny asked, feeling left out of the joke, although she failed to see the humor in two people who were obviously in pain.

Jacq and Davis looked like two Cheshire cats who'd just swallowed a crazy secret.

"Davis, come in here, man!" Xavier's voice boomed out of the kitchen.

Destiny stared on as Davis limped into the other room. She immediately went to Jacq's side. Before she could ask what was wrong, her concern was halted by a ring of dark marks around her friend's neck. "Are those hickeys?" she shouted.

Jacq eased down into a chair. "You damn skippy."

Destiny decided to lower her voice this time. "So you and Davis finally—"

Jacq grinned remembering with girlish excitement the pile of condom wrappers they'd left ripped open on her nightstand. "All . . . night . . . long."

"Well, why are you hobbling like you've been in a car wreck? Because . . . oh my gosh."

"Girl, it was like we couldn't stop doin' it. Sideways. Upside down. Right side up. I'm so sore. And I'm sore everywhere."

Now Destiny understood why her husband was laughing. She let out a small snicker of her own. "You guys must have really been carrying on."

"Girl, like Klingons." Jacq had to laugh herself. "You know that cheap little bed I bought?"

"Yeah."

"Girl, we broke that thing."

Destiny covered her laughter with her hands. It didn't do any good. She knew Xavier and Davis probably heard her in the kitchen. She just hoped she didn't disturb the baby, who was asleep in a nearby bassinet.

"We heard this loud pop. Heck, I thought it was Davis, with as much noise as he makes. But a second later the bed had split and the mattress was on the ground. But did that stop us? Hell, no. We kept right on going. As a matter of fact, that was the best or—"

When he heard the topic of their conversation, Davis cleared his throat. "All right, enough girl talk!"

Davis and Xavier emerged with grins smeared across their faces. For a few seconds, no one spoke. Then the room erupted with laughter and the four friends walked into the dining room and finished setting the table for their meal.

Later that night, Davis stroked the soft shoulders of the woman stirring in his arms. "Hey, Miss Lady." A slow warm smile crawled across his face. He was contented, blissful. Straight crazy-happy.

"Hey, yourself," she said, purring like a cat being scratched behind the ears.

She was up against him, snuggled in tight. Had been all night. "You know you talk in your sleep?"

"I do not."

His smile broadened to a grin. "Yes, ya do." He chuckled. "You kept saying, 'It's yours, baby. It's all yours.'"

"You lie," she said, snickering under the covers.

"You didn't say it, huh?"

"Naw."

"Well let's see." He licked his middle finger, then placed it softly at the most sensitive spot on Jacq's body. She jolted as if struck by lightning, then sucked in a breath. It sounded like a bird cooing.

"It's yours, baby," she moaned. "It sho is yours . . .

He laughed and covered her lips with his own, determined to kiss her silly. When he'd had all he could stand without taking her again, he pulled back and stared into her eyes.

"You know what I want?"

She stared back. "No. What?"

He placed his hand over her heart. "I want this to be mine." He planted a tiny kiss on her forehead. He'd never wanted anything so desperately in his life. Not his clients. Not his business. Not his condo or cars. Nothing. "Give me your heart, Jacquelyn. Be mine forever."

At his words, her eyes softened in a way he'd never seen. Had he ever noticed how round and liquid they were? No, he didn't think so. But he was determined, now, to commit every inch of her to memory. To etch her into his life permanently.

"You took my heart the first time you called me Jacquelyn. I was yours from that moment on."

Davis felt like someone had just given him the keys to the world. He kissed her then. Seriously. Marking her for all time with his love.

"Why did it take so long for us to get here?" he asked.

Jacq's eyes went misty. "Because I felt like I was violating the first rule of relationships. Never go out with your best friend's ex-boyfriend. Isn't that what they call sloppy seconds?"

Davis grimaced. "Ugh. What a horrible thing to say."

"But it's true."

He held her tighter then. "Here's what's true. We were meant to be together. I believe I met Des because I was supposed to meet you. Destiny and I are good people, decent people. So naturally we gravitated to each other. But it didn't work. It wasn't supposed to work. I'm supposed to be with you. I was meant for you."

Jacq stiffened in his arms. "Then will you stop treating me like a line of code? And will you stop treating our relationship like a project you're trying to manage?"

Davis laughed and smiled. "I only did that because I wanted us to be us—a successful us."

"I know, but it's driving me crazy."

He kissed her forehead. "Okay, Jacquelyn. From now on, I will take off the systems analyst hat when it comes to our relationship."

Happy tears spilled over her cheeks.

Davis kissed them away. "Can we make love now?"

She grinned and spread her legs. "Oh yeah, Big Daddy. A vigorous romp in the hay is just what I need!"

He laid her down and kissed her smooth neck. "No, baby. I want to make love. Nice and easy. Take you in stages. Make you cry."

"Ooh Davis," she whimpered, already wet, already anticipating.

He peeled her clothes off slowly, piece by piece as if he were afraid any sudden move would harm her. She, in turn, removed his, just as delicately. Then he kissed, sucked, and nipped every place on her caramel-brown skin until she could barely move, only shudder and moan under his deft attentions.

"I can't move,'" she whispered, paralyzed by the sensation of Davis's warm moist tongue dipping in her mouth, sweeping over her nipples, and plunging into her core.

"Then don't."

He took a few seconds to protect her with a condom, then with a long hard kiss, he entered her an inch at a time.

She pulled at him. "Davis, please . . ."

But he wouldn't give in. After weeks of memorizing her body, he'd become attuned to her desires and knew he was driving her crazy—giving her the kind of pleasure she'd never had before. He could have easily plunged himself inside her. But instead, he made her wait, turning her into a mass of quivering need beneath him. He continued his slow slide into her feminine depths.

Jacq moaned. He wasn't even all the way inside her and she was crying uncontrollably. She loved him with all her heart and soul. And to know he loved her and that they could share each other like this overwhelmed her. She lay helpless, weakened by Davis's luxurious foreplay.

When he was completely inside her, she cried out. Nothing had ever felt so good. She gazed into his eyes. She'd never seen them so dark and intense.

"I love you, Jacquelyn," he said, moving inside her. "I love you. I love you."

"I love you," she said, nibbling his neck, pulling him close.

"I love you," he responded, sucking a nipple, plunging deeper.

They repeated the three-word mantra over and over until they were both consumed by the ardor they felt and Jacq regained her strength to move.

Then it was Davis's turn to whimper and moan as Jacq caught his gentle rhythm and matched it. In their tender joining, they moved as one, loved as one, and finally, when they could take no more, exploded as one.

Eighteen

Kenyon leaned over the toilet, dazed and confused. He'd barely made it into the bathroom before the remnants of last night's dinner lurched up from his stomach and spewed out of his mouth. He was so disoriented by the experience that for a moment or two all he could do was sit on the floor and gasp for breath. Then, as quickly as it came, his nausea disappeared and he felt nearly back to normal.

After flushing the toilet, he splashed water on his face and rinsed out his mouth. The last time he'd been sick had been four years ago when he had a horrible bout of stomach flu. He remembered being laid up for days, spending most of that time in the bathroom, weak, with his body purging itself from both ends. His mother had sent him a nursemaid who insisted he eat soup and drink water even though neither stayed on his stomach for very long.

He said a silent prayer that he never go through that again.

"Are you all right?" Marti asked.

"I am now." He sat down in the chair where he'd slept all night. "I hope that grilled cheese from last night is okay. Otherwise, we may both be in for an interesting morning."

Marti smiled. "I feel surprisingly good today. Sometimes I wake up with a bad case of morning sickness."

She held up a box of Zesta saltines that she kept by her bedside. "Before I stirred around too much, I ate a few of these. They must have done the trick because there's not an inkling of morning sickness in sight."

Kenyon's stomach gurgled. He stiffened. "Let me have a few of those crackers."

He stood and pivoted slowly to stretch the kinks out. After a not-so-comfortable night sleeping in a chair, he could really use a deep swim in his pool.

"I've been told that chair is a bugger-bear to sleep in."

"That's one way to put it."

"Yolanda has a cot she's been bringing over for weeks. I haven't seen it yet."

"Maybe she's forgotten."

"Nah. Yolanda is just like that. She means well and all, but she's really wrapped up in her family, and so everything else comes second a lot of the times."

Marti talked like that was a bad thing. He would have loved to come first in his parents' lives. But with them, it had always been the business.

"Andreas should be here any minute with fresh clothes and toiletries for me. Do you need any help changing?"

"No. But . . . well . . ."

"What?"

"I usually take a shower in the morning and then get dressed. The doctor recommended that I limit the time that I'm up to five-minute intervals. So, Jacq or one of my sisters usually helps me in the shower."

Kenyon hoped he disguised his hard swallow. Seeing Marti naked was the last thing he needed. He'd just gotten to the point where his body didn't ache for her every minute. Now it was more like every other minute. He knew seeing her in the shower with hot water coursing down her skin would make him hard for sure. And then where would he be? There was probably no way she would let him back into her bedroom—unless he could persuade her.

"Well, since they're not here, I guess that duty falls on me."

Marti eyed him suspiciously. "You don't mind?"

"I stayed because I want to help you." He stood. "So, let me help you."

She nodded and threw back the blanket. When she stood, Kenyon noticed a white plastic sheet covering the middle portion of the bed.

"What's that?" he asked.

A piercing hurt descended into Marti's eyes. "It's a soil guard. For . . . you know."

Kenyon sucked in a breath as if someone had just prodded him with a hot poker. Of course. In case she started bleeding again. Suddenly he realized just how serious and frightening it was for Marti to be on bed rest and for her to have to endure a high-risk pregnancy from almost day one. He went to her side and guided her into the bathroom.

Once inside Marti's small square-shaped bathroom, Marti turned on the shower and with her back to him, removed her loose-fitting PJs. He tried not to moan or make any sound that would give away just how badly he'd longed for her or just how keenly seeing her nude sent Eros ricocheting through his veins. That might lead her to her believe that the entire reason he'd stayed was inappropriate and selfish. She pulled back the shower curtain and stepped in. He almost reached out to touch her cashew-brown backside. But he resisted. He knew his time was coming.

"Tell me what to do," he said, eyes following the water as it cascaded from her neck and chest to her thighs and below.

Marti took a sponge from a shower rack and handed him a wash cloth. "I'm not supposed to lift, stoop, or bend, so I'll take the top and you take the bottom."

She squirted some liquid soap on to his cloth, some onto her sponge, and went to work.

Being this close to her again momentarily froze him into place. All he could do was watch the lather build up on her skin and her hands, making foamy circles on her brown flesh.

"We've only got five minutes. Don't wait for me to finish."

He nodded and stroked her thighs with the soapy cloth. At first, he was truly making an effort to wash her, giving the cloth a squeeze here and there to absorb more water and release more soap. He used long strokes to make sure her legs got clean within the five minutes' time. But the soap reminded him of their lovemaking and what she always smelled like right before he ravished her—how the scent rose right off her skin and wafted into his nostrils, drugging him with her aroma. All of the ways in which he could take her now played in his mind like film footage from an erotic movie channel. Blood rushed to his groin and stiffened him.

His strokes on Marti's skin took on a more leisurely yet deliberate pace. With his other hand, he reached around to her back and rubbed the suds in.

"Kenyon, what are you doing?"

He kept reaching around until he'd massaged her arm and finally a nipple. Marti gasped. "Kenyon!"

Her breast was silky beneath his fingertips. He slid his fingers back and forth through the soap and against her flesh, soft and moist from the water.

"I have a confession to make," he said, now rubbing her other breast. "Helping wasn't the only reason I wanted to come in here."

"No?" Marti responded, her head falling back just a little, face transfixed with pleasure.

"No. I've missed you, Marti. I've missed holding you and kissing you."

Marti moaned.

"I missed making love to you."

Marti moaned louder and trembled.

Kenyon wanted to take her now. Needed to. But there was one thing he had to know. "What did your doctor say about sex? I mean . . . is it all right?"

She stiffened and grabbed his wrists, stopping his movements. "I don't know. He never mentioned it." She sighed deeply and dropped her head. "Just to be on the safe side, we better stop."

Kenyon groaned his disappointment, but he understood. "Let's ask the doctors when they come on Friday."

Marti nodded. At first, she was embarrassed at how quickly she had succumbed to Kenyon's touch. Without protest of any kind, she had turned herself over to his familiar and sorely missed pleasuring. But after a few seconds, her embarrassment faded as she realized that she had nothing to hide. She loved Kenyon. And he knew it. She would not pretend that she didn't. If she were his wife, there would be no reason for her to curtail his advances or prohibit his touch in any way. The excitement calmed in her flesh as she contemplated what the doctors would say. With her luck, intercourse would be another item on a long list of things she couldn't do until after the baby is born. She sighed. If that happened, the intimacy she longed for to bring them closer together would be impossible.

Lines of disappointment frowned Kenyon's dark features. She could tell he was struggling, too. He had come back to her. He even wanted her. And she couldn't have him.

Life had a terrible way of serving up cruel events.

They finished the job of washing her, got her dried off and into fresh clothes. They walked back to her living room with the thrum of unquenched desire beating between them.

When they settled back into the living room, Kenyon fidgeted a bit, unsure of what he should do. "What do you do here all day?"

"Besides pull my hair out and go bonkers? Not much." Marti unconsciously rubbed the place at her abdomen where life was growing. "Usually there's someone here with me which helps me to not be so bored. My family and Jacy care for me in shifts. This week is Jacy's week. But each of my sisters have had a turn." She lowered her lashes. "Except Roxanne."

"She was pretty outspoken with her demands. I'm absolutely certain she cares a great deal about you."

Marti blinked. "Really?"

"Really."

A solitary tear tracked down her cheek. She sniffed and wiped it away.

"What's wrong? I thought that was good news."

"It is," Marti said, voice shaky. "I'm sorry. I've just been so emotional lately. And from what I read, it could get worse."

Kenyon swallowed. That's all he needed—an emotional pregnant woman. With sisters who were ready to pulverize him for the slightest transgression.

His stomach growled. He glanced at the clock. Eight-thirty. Except when he was out of town, and sometimes even then, he had breakfast promptly at six-thirty in the morning. Andreas would check with him the night before to see if he had a taste for anything special. Most often, he ate what the cook prepared. Roberta Pointer had been cooking at the Williams mansion for as long as Kenyon could remember. After so many years, she knew his tastes. He couldn't recall ever having one disappointing breakfast.

He had the dreadful feeling that in order to eat, he was going to have to go back into Marti's kitchen and whip something up. The thought made his stomach churn with cold apprehension.

"What's the matter?" she asked.

"Nothing," he said, getting up.

"Where are you going?"

"To get better acquainted with your kitchen. I'm starving."

Marti smiled and watched as Kenyon bumped and fumbled into her tiny kitchenette. She tried to look the other way while he banged and clattered his way through her pots and pans. She chewed the inside of her jaw to keep from laughing at all his exclamations and expletives as he burned and cut his way through breakfast. After about an hour, he emerged with something that looked like it was supposed to be an omelette. He brought it to her on a tray and she accepted it gladly.

He went back to the kitchen and returned with his own omelette, then sat down with a grunt.

"Are you sure it's safe?" she asked, then sniffed the egg concoction.

"No, but I'm too hungry to worry about safety." He cut away a forkful of flat and almost fluffy egg and shoved it into his mouth.

Marti waited. "Well?"

Kenyon chewed rapidly and swallowed. "It's not Sylvia's, but I don't think it will kill you."

Marti dug in. The man she loved had prepared a

meal for her. She savored it and thought it tasted delicious.

It didn't take them long to finish their breakfast. Marti was the first one done. Kenyon looked surprised.

"I guess you were hungry, too."

"I guess so."

He stood and took their plates into the kitchen. He placed them into the sink alongside several dishes that were already there. He wondered what he should do with them. Did people throw away old dishes when they were finished with them? Surely not.

"What do you want me to do with these dishes?"

"Wash them," she called out.

Of course! Kenyon thought. He looked around for a dishwasher. He thought he'd seen one before on television.

Stove. Refrigerator. Microwave. Cupboards. He rubbed his chin, the hairs of his thin goatee brushing the back of his hand. "Marti?"

"Yes?"

"Where's the dishwasher?"

He didn't like the sound of her laughter.

Through her giggles, he thought he heard the words 'you are the dishwasher' but that couldn't possibly be right.

"What?" he said, poking his head out into the living room.

"I said, you are the dishwasher!"

"What do you mean?" he asked coming forward, the feeling of dread slowly returning.

There's some dish soap on top of the counter. Plug up the sink, run the hot water, and squeeze some in."

He didn't like where this was going. "And then what?"

"And then, when it gets full, you take a dish cloth and wash the dishes."

He shook his head. "I was afraid you were going to say that."

When he went back into the kitchen, Marti laughed some more. Her ringing phone interrupted her laughter.

Hello?"

"Haaay!"

"Hey, Jacq."

"How you feelin'?"

"Bored."

Kenyon, who must have been eavesdropping, cleared his throat from the kitchen.

"Is he still there?"

Marti smiled. "Yeah. He's taking good care of me. He cooks and everything!"

"That man has never cooked in his life!"

"I know. I'm pretending not to notice."

"Girl, don't slip up and let the man poison you."

She chuckled. "I won't."

"Now, do you need anything?"

"Nope." she said. And she didn't. She had her baby and the love of her life. The only other thing she wanted was for her baby to be healthy and carried to term. She realized that if things got rough between her and Kenyon and the safety of her baby was at stake, she would swiftly tell him to remove himself from her life.

"When do you want me to come back?"

Now that was one thing she was unsure of. When Kenyon arrived yesterday, she had hoped he would stay for a while. When he'd offered to stay the night, she'd been elated. She assumed that he would stay with her until the doctors came. She'd wanted to ask to be sure, but she was afraid that even broaching the subject might make him uncomfortable—uncomfortable enough to leave. *God, please don't let him leave.*

"Kenyon . . . um . . . how long are you staying?"

He looked out from the kitchen like he'd been ambushed by a pop quiz he was unprepared for. "Well, at least until the doctors come on Friday, I guess. That is, if my cooking doesn't kill us. You've got to let me order out. And this is the first and last time I'm ever doing dishes!"

Marti laughed and returned to Jacq, who was waiting patiently on the other end of the line.

"Jacq, I'm good until the end of the week."

"Girl, are you sure? I wouldn't trust him. I'll probably pop over there sometime anyway, just to make sure."

"All right."

"Get some rest. And I know you'll be surprised to hear me say this, but, don't even think about doin' the nasty. That might harm the baby."

"I know."

"Um-hm," Jacq replied. "I'm out."

"Bye, Jacq."

Marti placed the phone back into the charger, and Kenyon stepped out of the kitchen, hands covered with suds. "I don't think she likes me," he said, in that well-deep voice of his.

"She doesn't like what you represent," Marti said.

"And what's that?"

"Potential pain."

Kenyon ran a hand through his hair. It fell loosely against his shoulders.

"She doesn't like to see her friends hurt, and you hurt me, Kenyon. She'll never forget that. Even if I do."

Bubbles dripped from his knuckles onto the carpet. "Marti . . ."

She turned away, not willing to deal with the pain of the memory. "I can't talk about it now," she said.

He stared at her—so small and vulnerable on the bed—and realized that he was truly sorry for hurting her. Sorry for whatever effect his actions may have had on the state of her pregnancy. He returned to the dishes waiting for him in the sink, determined to make everything up to her.

"Cheater!"

"Nah-uh!"

"Yes, you are, Marti. You said you didn't have any twos."

"Don't get mad at me because you can't play cards."

"Please! I can play cards. I'm just not used to playing with someone who cheats."

"You're just mad because you're losing."

"No, I'm not." He closed the cards up in his hands. "Let's play something else."

"Oh, come on." She had already beaten him at black jack, Crazy Eights, and two-handed spades. "This is the easiest card game I know."

A dark rumble of his laughter filled the room. His mouth opened wide and his eyes sparkled. After a few moments, Marti laughed with him.

"What are we laughing about?" she asked.

"You, me, this. I mean, it's so . . . so ordinary. Normal even."

Marti smirked. "Something wrong with normal?"

"No. I've just . . . never had it before. It's . . ." He paused and gave her a look that melted her like the grilled cheese sandwiches he'd made last night. "You make me happy, Marti. I'm not used to being happy, that's all."

He got up then, put his cards on the table between them, and walked toward the bathroom.

Kenyon closed the door behind him and leaned against the sink. He stared into the mirror. A shadow of annoyance crossed his face. *What's wrong with me?* A torrent of emotions competed for dominance in his mind. He cared for her. Really, really cared. She did make him happy. Made him smile when he didn't want to. Made him consider the error of his ways. *Damn.* She made him feel comfortable in his own skin. That was something no one in his life had ever been able to do.

She was drawing him closer, as if a thin string were pulling him. And the worst part was that part of him wanted to go.

"Kenyon?"

"Yes," he said, flushing the unused toilet.

"Andreas is here."

He came out to find the old man standing in Marti's living room with three suitcases.

Kenyon's gaze roved sharply over the leather luggage. "I said I wanted an overnight bag with a few days' worth of clothes."

"Yes, sir. And you have that, along with a few other things. You never can tell what you might need."

Kenyon eyed his wrinkled assistant suspiciously. The man avoided eye contact and smiled at Marti. "How are you doing, Miss Allgood?"

"I'm fine," she said, returning to the bed.

"I could have answered the door, Marti."

"I know, but I had to get up. I'm supposed to get bed rest, not bed sores."

Andreas took an envelope from his jacket pocket. "Here is the doctors' itinerary."

"Thanks," Kenyon said.

"Do you need anything else, sir?"

"No. Thank you, Andreas."

The elder gentleman took short steps to the door.

"Andreas," Kenyon said.

"Yes?"

"Call a plumber. We need a dishwasher installed here right away."

"Kenyon, this is an apartment. I don't own this space. I can't just install kitchen appliances on a whim."

He nodded. "Good point." He turned back to Andreas. "Andreas, buy this building, then call a plumber and get a dishwasher installed in here as soon as possible."

"Yes, sir," he said, and disappeared out the door.

"Kenyon!"

"I told you, short stuff, I've washed my last dish ever in life."

Marti warmed inside. He hadn't called her short stuff since the art show. Normally, she chafed when people made fun of her height. But she took Kenyon's remark as a term of endearment. Suddenly she felt dreamy and dotty.

"I'm going to take a nap," she announced, sliding down under the covers.

"All right. I'll hold down the fort," Kenyon said.

Marti drifted off, sensing his dark eyes on her. She'd let herself smile. He loved her. She knew it. And she knew it wouldn't be long before he knew it, too.

While Marti slept, Kenyon turned on the television and watched Food TV. He'd never been one to do anything half-assed, and he figured if he was going to be cooking for the next few days, he damn well better learn how to do it right.

He looked on, enthralled, as Yan, Emeril, and Two

Fat Ladies prepared mouthwatering dishes in no time at all. It looked easy.

He noticed that the chefs often referred to recipes and cookbooks. Impulsively, he searched the kitchen for a recipe file or a cookbook. When he found a small book of recipes on top of the refrigerator, he returned to his spot on the love seat and continued watching with renewed interest.

The shows held his fascination. They used spices and ingredients to create dishes using utensils he'd never heard of. The result was delicacies he'd eaten but had no idea what it took to make. His respect and admiration for Roberta grew ten times in the span of three hours.

By the time Marti stirred in her bed, Kenyon was back in the kitchen. He thought he would try his hand at chicken Josephine, a dish he'd watched one of the cooks make. It seemed the simplest and one he thought Marti might have all the ingredients for. After following the recipe and burning his hand yet again, he put his attempt in the oven to bake at 375 for two hours.

"What are you doing?" Marti asked, remnants of her nap fogging her voice.

"Making dinner." Kenyon emerged from the kitchen and sank into the chair next to Marti, feeling like he needed a nap.

Marti remembered the grilled cheese sandwiches from last night. They weren't bad, but . . . "Kenyon, if you want to order in, it's okay."

"Relax," he said, leaning his head back. "I'm determined to get the hang of this cooking thing. We're having chicken Josephine tonight, and if I do say so myself, I think it's going to taste marvelous."

Marti imagined that her kitchen didn't look so marvelous.

"I'm tired," he said, closing his eyes. "If I don't wake up when the timer goes off, give me a shake, will you?"

Marti didn't know what to make of this new, resourceful Kenyon. "Sure," she said.

She got up and went to the bathroom. When she returned, Kenyon's light snores vibrated the air in the room.

For a long time, she simply watched him sleep. She'd done it a dozen or so times before. Always mesmerized by the conflict she saw on his face even as he rested. She wondered if he ever truly got a good night's sleep. Somehow now, with him tucked into a corner of her chair, he seemed just a bit more relaxed. The wrinkles in his brow just a little less tense. The scowl across his mouth slightly less pronounced. She had been praying for a long time that he would find peace in his life. Maybe, even with the baby, he was beginning to.

Instinctively, she took a sketchpad and pencil from an end table and drew his face. She followed the model whose features were dark and mysterious, yet drew him as her mind's eye saw him—content, blissful even, with life and his place in it.

She softened the hard lines and flesh points of his face. She removed any traces of dissonance, smoothing out the roughness with her little finger. Only the deep shadows of pitch in his skin remained and the black river of his hair. She sighed, the spirit of her love for him flowing through her.

Like the slow dawning of a new day, Marti realized that if she could find out what it was that concerned Kenyon so and made him at times seem uncomfortable in his own skin, she would know why he rejected any notion of them in a serious relationship and why he was so dead set against being a father. Whatever it was, it scared her. It felt sinister. But that didn't stop her from wanting to get it out in the open and deal with it.

Suddenly, she felt cold. She set aside her illustration and drew the covers up around her. She thought of the tiny life inside her.

"Your father's a good man," she said. "Maybe he doesn't realize it, but I do. And you know what? He loves us."

Marti reached over for the remote control and turned to The Learning Channel. She hoped there was a television program on about pregnancy or child rearing. Lately, she couldn't get enough information on those subjects.

After watching two hours of *The Operation* and being totally grossed out, yet so enthralled she couldn't turn away, the timer on her oven went off. Before she could call his name, Kenyon jerked awake and yawned.

"The alarm went off."

"I heard it," he said, rising. "Time to pay the piper."

She was more than ready to eat. For the last hour, the aroma of garlic, onions, and simmering chicken had teased her into a deep fit of hunger. Her stomach gurgled and growled in anticipation of dinner.

"Ow!" Kenyon yelped from the kitchen. "Your oven doesn't like me," he said.

Marti giggled. "Are you all right? I've got some aloe vera in the medicine cabinet in the bathroom."

"Not necessary. I'll survive."

Then the familiar rumbling of plates and silverware caught her attention. She didn't think he would ever get the hang of it. But he was trying, changing for her. And she was grateful.

It took a while. She almost got up to see what was going on. But Kenyon finally emerged, piping plates in hand. He set hers on a tray in front of her and placed his on a TV tray. It looked marvelous. Baked chicken smothered over brown rice and broccoli.

She smiled.

"Not bad, huh?"

"I won't know until I taste it."

He smiled back. "Well, what are you waiting for?"

She took a small bit of rice and chicken on her fork. Remembering the grilled cheese sandwich, she eased the morsels into her mouth.

Tentatively she chewed until the robust flavor filled her mouth.

"It's good?" he asked, astonishment raising his eyebrows.

"Try it for yourself."

He lifted a forkful into his mouth. Marti could tell by the expression on his face melting with pleasure and surprise that he liked it.

"Well I'll be darned. It *is* good. That B. Smith is a culinary genius."

"Let's just see if it stays down," Marti said.

Kenyon's face flattened with concern. Marti laughed and he joined in. In that instant, something broke between them—something that had been cold and stymied. It wasn't a large break. Maybe only a sliver. But even the air between them flowed differently.

Marti had learned a long time ago to thank God for small miracles. She said a silent prayer of appreciation and set about finishing her dinner.

Nineteen

By the time the first specialists arrived, Marti and Kenyon had fallen into a routine. Five days of being together all day, every day, had them carrying on like they'd been married for years and Kenyon was simply nursing his ailing wife back to health.

He had made honest attempts at cooking meals and cleaning her apartment. His skills in the kitchen improved with every meal. Although it was clear he would probably never master meal preparation, Marti could clearly see a comfort level growing within him.

Other household chores, on the other hand, were not progressing in the same way. He couldn't for the life of him wash a load of clothes without bleaching, bleeding, or just plain ruining an article of clothing. When he complained that the mates to half of their socks had just up and disappeared, Marti laughed until her stomach hurt.

"What's wrong?" he'd asked when she winced.

"I think I laughed too hard. My stomach is sore."

His eyes grew tender. "I can rub it for you, if you want."

An electrical charge like a nine-volt battery surged through her. "That would be nice, Kenyon."

He'd gotten up, gone into her bathroom, brought back a bottle of natural oil, and set about his task.

* * *

The specialists used facilities in Atlanta Medical Center for Marti's doctor's appointment. They gave her a pelvic exam, a blood test, and an ultrasound. By the time the doctors were ready with the results, Marti felt as though every sensitive area of her body had been stuck, invaded, or mashed. She sat next to Kenyon in the waiting room, wide-eyed and fearful.

"Try to relax," he said. "Dexter Page and Kevin Gomez are two of the best doctors in America. They'll tell us exactly what's going on and what to do about it."

When they entered the room, a jolt of fear shot through her. Seeing her alarm, Kenyon instinctively reached out and took her hand. It was cold, as if blood had stopped circulating there hours before. He took both her hands, set to rub the life back in them.

Marti shuddered. "Am I going to lose the baby? Please . . . . tell me. I have to know. I mean, I fought so hard for . . ." She shook her head. "It can't end this way. It just can't."

Doctor Page held up his hand. He was a large man with a boyish smile and thick mustache. "Please calm down, Miss Allgood. Your baby is fine."

She stared unblinkingly. "Really?"

"Yes," Doctor Page said.

Kenyon stopped rubbing her hands but held them firmly. "Then what happened?"

Kevin Gomez stood closer to Marti, his salt-and-pepper hair and olive skin striking in the sterile white room. "You have what's called placenta previa—a condition where the placenta slips out of place and slides down to the cervix.

"There are three types of placenta previa: marginal previa, where the placenta is near the cervix; partial previa, where the placenta partly covers the cervical opening; and total previa, where the placenta completely covers the cervical opening.

"You have marginal previa, which is the mildest form. But what that means is there is a chance for hemorrhage during labor and delivery."

Marti clutched her stomach, her heart fluttering. "Oh my God."

Kenyon swept a glance at her and squeezed her hand tighter. "How do we prevent that?"

"Sometimes these things work themselves out. In about ten percent of cases, the placenta will migrate upward. If that happens, she should be able to have a normal delivery."

"Your OB prescribed bed rest?" Doctor Page said.

"Yes," she said. Her heart pounding now.

"Did she tell you that there is no scientific evidence proving that bed rest prevents prenatal complications?"

"No."

"The good news is, there's no scientific evidence proving that it doesn't. So you are right to give your baby every chance to survive."

Doctor Gomez sat down. He saw the worry lines increasing in Marti Allgood's face. "Here's what we do know. Bed rest reduces cervical pressure which is what caused the pain you experienced. It also increases blood flow to the placenta, and helps your organs function more efficiently. So for you, bed rest is a good idea. At least for the next couple of months, you need to spend your time lying on your left side.

"What we would like to do is hook you up to what we call a HUAM. The HUAM monitors contractions in your uterus that are too faint for you to feel. It creates a report of those contractions and sends it to a nurse via telephone wires. It's just like connecting to the Internet. We'll monitor you for a couple of weeks. If there's no activity, we'll take you off the monitor.

"It's pretty quiet in there now, so we don't anticipate any contractions. It's just a precautionary measure.

"We'll schedule you for regular physical therapy and massage therapy. Being immobile for long periods can weaken your muscles.

"If you have any more changes like bleeding, high blood pressure, or abdominal cramping, we'll have to admit you into the hospital and put you on bed rest there.

"But rest assured, right now, you have a healthy baby. You do what we say, like stay on your side, limit your activity, and no sex, and you'll have a good chance of keeping it that way."

Marti nodded understandingly. "Thank you," she said. Then she remembered the other thing she'd been worried about. "What about Kenyon?"

He waved a hand. "I'm all right. It's probably just tension."

"No, he's not all right. He gets nauseous and throws up sometimes. This morning he was complaining about his back aching."

Kenyon's jaw set angrily. "Please," he said, trying to dismiss her comments.

"He's also been dizzy." She swept a glance his way. "You thought I was asleep yesterday when you got up and had to hold on to the table to steady yourself."

The doctors looked at each other and shared a knowing glance.

"Any tenderness in the pectoral area?" Doctor Page asked.

Kenyon's eyes widened. "Yes," he responded.

"Sounds like Couvade," Doctor Gomez said.

"What's that?"

"That's when the man experiences pregnancy symptoms right along with his wife or significant other."

Kenyon stroked his goatee pensively.

Marti giggled. "You mean I don't have to go through this alone?"

Doctor Page gave her a reassuring pat on the back. "Most of the time, it occurs during the first trimester, then vanishes. But since you're already a bit past that, Kenyon's case might last longer."

"How much longer?" Concern deepened Kenyon's voice.

"I've heard of some cases where it has lasted throughout the entire pregnancy."

"In rare cases, it's gone on through delivery and into post-partum depression."

Kenyon's stomach constricted. "Is there a test for this thing?"

"We can test for increased levels of prolactin in your body, but let me just ask you a few questions. What time of day do you feel nauseous most often?"

Kenyon closed his eyes. "In the morning when I wake up."

"And have you had any cravings recently?"

"He's eaten so many grilled cheese sandwiches lately, I thought he was going to turn into one," Marti said.

"What about weight gain?" the doctor asked.

"Enough!" Kenyon growled. "Can you prescribe something?" Kenyon thought of how miserable he'd been just this past week. "I'll take anything."

"There are no drugs you can take."

"Just eat a balanced diet, get plenty of rest, exercise, and drink plenty of fluids."

Kenyon turned to Marti. "I should have known you were trouble the day you stole my painting." He patted her hands, which were now warm from his body heat, and returned his attention to the doctors. "Thanks, you two. I mean really. I appreciate you coming down."

"Yeah well, you should. My special patients usually fly in to me, not the other way around."

Kenyon stood and smiled. "All right. What do you want?"

"In addition to what you are already so graciously paying us, we were wondering if you would be interested in donating to each of our favorite charities?"

"No problem," he said, twinging just a little inside. He'd withdrawn so much money already, his mother would surely dog his heels for this one. For the first time in a long while, he couldn't care less about his mother's grating behavior. He paid the doctors the fees they asked for.

He thought he was accompanying Marti to a routine checkup and uterine monitor removal. He was certain everything would go off without a hitch. He'd made sure that she spent most of her time on her left side, even though she pouted about it quite often. He helped her with gentle exercise, rotating her arms and legs to maintain circulation and prevent muscle aches, just the way the therapists had shown him. And he was sure his cooking was getting better with each meal he prepared. More importantly, she hadn't complained of a single cramp or contraction, nor had any of significance been recorded on the monitor. He expected that the doctor would remove the monitor and give Marti a clean bill of health.

He realized he was in for a unique experience when Marti insisted he go into the examination room with her. With the specialists, he'd simply waited outside and used the time to read newsmagazines and plan his next genealogical research jaunt. When they finished their exams and were ready with their recommendations, he'd joined her. But to be in the room while another man put his hand on her, in her . . . Doctor or no, he didn't like it. When that part of the examination came, he turned his head.

Strangely enough, everything went smoothly. Her pregnancy was progressing well, she hadn't dilated prematurely, and her blood and urine test results were good.

When the doctor removed the uterine monitor, Kenyon breathed a visible sigh of relief. Then his concern peaked again as the doctor and nurse hooked her up to yet another machine.

"What's that?" he asked.

"It's kind of like Doppler radar," the doctor said. "It's about time we listen to the baby's heart."

"Really?" Marti said, eyes wide with wonder.

The heartbeat, Kenyon thought. He didn't know it could be heard this early in the pregnancy.

The room quieted, but for some reason, Kenyon's heart struck inside his chest harder and harder until he could swear it was the loudest sound in the room. He watched as the doctor moved a small object across Marti's abdomen, which was beginning to show the cutest pudge against her clothes. His mouth went dry and tasted like Alka-Seltzer.

When he first heard the sound, he wasn't sure if he was hearing correctly. It sounded like a strong but distant swish, swish. The doctor turned a dial on the machine and the sound grew louder. It was fast and urgent and real. Dear God. It was the beating of a real, live human being. A little person. Kenyon's entire body grew cold with the shock of it. Like someone had pulled a plug at his feet and all his energy drained down his body and out his toes. He could have been knocked over with a feather.

His glance traveled to Marti, whose silent tears touched his heart. He, on the other hand, felt an overwhelming urge to giggle with joy at the sound of the tiny being he'd helped to create. Instead, he allowed himself a small smile.

"Do you hear it?" Marti said. "I can hear it!"

"I hear it, Marti. I hear the heartbeat." He stood and held her hand. "I hear the baby."

Six Months

She had her sisters around her, and despite the circumstances, she was glad. They doted on her, rubbing her back, propping up pillows, bringing her juice, and reading to her. After all the years of looking on in awe as her older siblings lived the kinds of lives Marti only dreamed of, they had come to her in her time of need and lavished their love generously on her.

Kenyon's short visit of a few hours had extended to a few weeks. He'd taken over where her family and friends had left off. She didn't know if it was her pregnancy, but he seemed changed somehow. More attentive and attuned to her needs. Except for his occasional bouts with morning sickness and backaches, he'd been the perfect companion. Almost like they were a couple. Almost like they were married.

When her sisters insisted that he take a break and let them have their turn at taking care of her, she was reluctant. She was just starting to sense feelings from Kenyon—the kind she'd been dreaming of. The kind that said he not only cared, but was just as much in love with her as she was with him. But a part of her didn't want to push it. Maybe he needed a break from being with her 24/7. And that part of her won the argument. So she had asked Kenyon to take the week off so her sisters could play nursemaid to their baby sister.

Morgan straightened a pillow behind her Marti's back. "I can't believe you let him back in your life."

"He was never really out. He was just . . ."

"Trifflin'?" Yolanda finished.

Sounds of agreement filled Marti's living room, along with the strong aromas of her sisters' various perfumes vying for dominance.

"Now, now, my sisters. All this negative energy isn't good for the baby. Besides, I know he's the man for her," Ashley said.

Morgan laughed. "Did you read that in a clump of tea leaves somewhere?"

"No, silly," Ashley said. "It was his aura. When he's around Runt, it glows a bright blue."

"What does that mean?" Marti asked.

"It means that he's your soul mate."

"Honestly, Ashley, when are you going to join the rest of us on planet Earth?"

"I am on planet Earth. You're just too indoctrinated to see me."

Yolanda held up a hand. "All right! I think Ashley's on to something. I'm starting to feel the negative energy in this room, and that can't be good."

Marti felt the need to change the subject before her sisters started a battle royal at her bedside. "Kenyon said that Roxanne spoke up for me."

Ashley patted her hand. "Her energy was strong for you, Runt."

"She was no joke," Morgan laughed. "I thought she was going to rip moneybags into tiny pieces."

Since her pregnancy, Marti's emotions had ridden through her like a roller coaster. Tears stung her eyes. She clasped her mouth to keep from breaking down.

"Oh, sweetheart!" Yolanda said, stroking her head. "You know how she is."

"I kn-know. I just w-wish things could be like they used to be."

Ashley's bright eyes twinkled with hope. "They will be. They will be."

"Roxy did all the talking. The only thing we did was add the occasional 'Yeah! Yeah!' to her demands. She loves you, girl. Never doubt that," Morgan added.

"She loves me, but she hasn't forgiven me."

Yolanda's gaze softened. "She will, Runt. She's just stubborn. And you know she can hold a grudge."

Marti burst into tears. "That's what worries me," she said, sobbing.

"But one thing about our dear sister: Her heart is guided by eternal truth, so she always comes around," Ashley assured her.

Marti's emotional outburst prompted her to reach for her sketchpad and doodle. Her sisters just smiled and shook their heads. "So where's Roxy now?" she asked.

"She had to get back to work."

"Yeah, she was due in Denver. She couldn't stay."

The youngest Allgood nodded. She knew that Roxanne's schedule could be hectic. But still, she probably could have rearranged it if she'd wanted to. Her conscience cautioned her against bad thoughts. Her big sister had stood up for her, so maybe there was a chance that one day they would reconcile.

"Cheer up, Runt. You've got lots of things to be happy about. You had a wonderful art show."

"Yeah. People all over the country are calling you the latest rage in the art world."

"The Goddess has truly blessed you."

"And you have friends and family that love you and

are going to take care of you until that beautiful baby is born."

"And one of the richest black men in American is standing by you."

"Only after we threatened to make him a eunuch."

The women laughed at their humor.

"So, what's it like having him around? I imagine he's not much help around here."

Marti smiled. "Kenyon is so funny. He's teaching himself how to do housework. I mean, he's never had to do it before, ever. So the first time he tries anything, it's dreadful. Like when he washed the clothes, they all came out with tinged with maroon. Somehow a washcloth bled on to everything."

"That doesn't sound like he's much help."

"Oh, he's all right. Getting better every day." Marti chuckled. "Although to hear him tell it, he's got everything mastered."

"Typical male."

"Yeah, just don't let him make you dinner. It doesn't taste too bad, but everything you put in your mouth is unrecognizable."

Marti held up her sketchpad. She had done more than doodle. She had drawn a striking likeness of Kenyon's eyes. They stared at her, with the same fervor they held while making love.

Ashley took Marti's hand. "Have you had any more trouble?"

Marti knew what her sister was asking. Any more spotting, any more cramps, any morning sickness. She'd shared the specialists' prognosis with them and they were always concerned about her condition.

"Actually, I've been more healthy than Kenyon. I didn't tell you what the doctors said about him."

"What about him?"

"He's got Couvade."

"You're kidding!"

"What's that?"

Marti snickered. "Couvade is when men get the same symptoms of pregnancy as their significant others. Some even gain weight."

"Amazing. So what's he been doing?"

"Well, his morning sickness is worse than mine. He goes to the bathroom a lot, and sometimes he walks funny."

Ashley beamed. "See. You two are connected. You're spiritually linked."

"You think everyone is spiritually linked," Morgan said.

"We are, but some people's connections are stronger than others."

For once, Marti hoped that her sister's strange beliefs were true.

For the next few hours, Marti filled in some of her sketches with colored pencils. She'd done quick illustrations of each of her sisters and hoped they would accept them as thank-yous for helping to take care of her. While she worked, they tidied up her apartment, washed clothes and dishes, and cooked enough food to last for two weeks. They packed most of it in food containers and stacked them in the freezer.

Morgan wiped her hands on a paper towel. "Now you have enough eatable food to last for a while. All you have to do is pop your meals in the microwave and voila! Breakfast, lunch, and dinner."

Yolanda washed and rebraided Marti's hair. Morgan helped Marti bathe. Ashley lit incense, made soymilk tea, and sang Liberian healing hymns over Marti's body. By the time sleep claimed her, she felt safely cocooned in her family's love.

* * *

When Kenyon returned the following week, he brought more than a few sets of clothes with him.

"What's all this?" she asked.

"A wardrobe."

"You look like you're on extended vacation. What's up?"

His jaw clamped shut and his eyes went stormy. Then he relaxed. "I'm here. For the duration."

"What?"

He scooped her in his arms and laid her back in her bed. "I'm going to stay with you, Marti. Until the baby is born. I'm going to take care of you."

This time her emotions were too strong for her to control. Happiness swept her up in its powerful torrent and burst open inside her. Tears gushed from her eyes, and she grabbed onto Kenyon so tightly she nearly toppled him.

"Hold on now," he said pulling away. "Let's not toot the horn yet. I'm just—"

"In love with me. Admit it."

Kenyon's eyes softened with concern. "Marti. I never said I didn't care about you. But what I feel right now is a strong need to make sure you and the baby are all right. That you are taken care of. After that . . . after the baby comes . . ." his voice trailed off. "After that, I'll make sure that you and the baby never want for anything."

"Even if you are part of that anything? What if all we want is you?"

He lowered his eyes. "The baby mustn't know anything about me." He turned from her and walked into the kitchen. "I've been practicing. I make a great Fettuccini Alfredo. Want some?"

Hurt and disappointment lay at the pit of Marti's stomach like a brick. "I'm not hungry," she said.

Kenyon emerged from the kitchen an hour later

with a large plate piled high with pasta. "Are you sure you don't want any?"

"I'm sure," she said.

"So, did your sisters take good care of you while I was gone?"

"Of course."

"And nothing happened while I was gone?" He took a forkful of twirled pasta into his mouth.

"Nothing like what?" she asked and waited for his response.

"I mean, you're all right, right? You didn't have an incident with the baby or anything?"

"No."

He sighed heavily. "Good."

Marti crossed her arms. "Why? Were you worried?"

"I was concerned, yes."

"Well, don't concern yourself anymore. My sisters love me. So, they'll always take good care of me."

"Marti . . ."

"Enough, Kenyon." She slid down on the bed and covered herself with a sheet. "I'm going to take a nap."

Marti folded herself into the sheets on her bed and shuddered. He wasn't drawing any closer to her or the baby. He was still the same remote and distant soul she'd met months back. Barking orders and disregarding her feelings. She'd be better off taking care of herself. At least then her stress level would be much lower.

She closed her eyes and tried to let the tension go. Just then she felt a gentle rumbling in her belly. She gasped, waited, and lay perfectly still. She didn't have to wait long. Another soft flutter came again. She grabbed her abdomen and sat up.

"Oh God!"

"What?" Kenyon said, frowning.

"It's the baby . . ."

He put the plate down on an end table and moved quickly to her side. "What's wrong with the baby?"

"It's moving," she said, smiling. Bright tears danced at the corners of her eyes.

Kenyon's eyes, on the other hand, grew as round as a full moon. "You can feel it?"

"Yes," she said. The word came out like a whisper. "Give me your hand."

"I don't think . . ."

"There it is again. Quick," she said, grabbing his wrist and placing his palm where she felt the movement.

They waited.

If Kenyon had been a gambling man, he would have bet anyone a million dollars that his heart stopped beating at the utterance of those words from Marti. His breath halted in his throat, stuck by the idea of life stirring inside the beautiful woman on the bed. Life . . . that he helped create.

As he pressed his hand against her lower abdomen, he willed it to stop trembling, or the only movement he would discern would be his own.

He stared into Marti's eyes. She stared into his as they waited.

The feeling started small. Only a shadow of motion. Then a sensation, like the quickening of a butterfly's wings, fluttered beneath his hand and awed him beyond words.

"It's the baby," she whispered again. "It's the baby."

A quick giggle escaped her lips. Then her happiness bubbled into bright laughter and glee. Kenyon joined her. His deep laughter tumbled in the air alongside her own.

He smiled broadly, brimming with the amazement of the miracle occurring within Marti. "It's the baby," he said.

Twenty

Marti's apartment was turning into Grand Central Station. With her friends and family migrating in and out, she hardly had a minute's rest. And those who didn't stop by, sent her something. She'd recently received a basket of fiber muffins from her sister Ashley. On the accompanying card, Ashley had written a prayer for healing and said that she'd kneaded that prayer into the dough before she baked it. Marti munched happily. Her older sisters and sometimes her brother Zay wanted Ashley to "come down to Earth." But Marti loved her, just the way she was.

Despite all those that supported her and cared for her, Marti still had bad days. Sometimes she even had bad weeks. Earlier that day, she'd had an argument with Kenyon. A serious one. She was dwelling on the baby, the way she almost always did, and anxiety took over.

"Do you think the baby is going to be all right?"

His head snapped up from reading the paper. "How many times are you going to ask me that?"

Fear and anger twisted into a dangerous knot inside her. "Until I feel reassured of your answer."

"What more can I do? I make sure that the only movement you have to make is your lungs for breathing."

"You don't have to get smart, Kenyon Williams!"

"Well somebody around here better!"

Marti sat up in the bed. "Are you calling me stupid?"

"I'm saying that I've turned into a full-time homemaker-slash-entertainment-director. The only thing I don't do for you is pee. But do I get some kind of acknowledgment? No. But every hour I have to tell you that the baby is going to be fine."

"Listen—"

"No. You talk whenever you want to talk. And when you don't feel like talking, then I damn well better shut up. This time, it's your turn to listen."

Kenyon took a long steadying breath and Marti looked like she needed to let go of the breath she was holding.

"The truth is, I don't know if the baby is going to be all right. No one does except God. Now I'm trying to help you the best way I can, by making sure your bed rest goes as smoothly as possible and getting the best doctors in the United States to consult on your case. But that's all I can do. The rest is out of my hands. And I can't take you asking me over and over again if I think the baby is all right."

"Are you finished?"

"For now."

"Well let me tell you something, you self-righteous opportunist. Don't think that I'm going to be all happy and crap just because you're here helping out. All the stuff you've done for me you should do for me. I'm not going to drool over things like fancy doctors or you taking out the garbage. I deserve those things because I'm carrying your child."

Kenyon rolled his eyes. "I see you've been talking to your sisters again."

"Don't you dare say anything against my sisters. They were here for me when you turned your back."

She propped herself up against two pillows. "As a matter of fact, if it hadn't been for them you wouldn't be here now."

"That's not true."

"It's not? Don't make me get up from here."

"As big as you are, I'd like to see you try it!"

Marti gasped and covered her mouth with her hand. Her dark eyes reflected the sting of his words.

"You don't know what it's like to be pregnant, Kenyon."

"I don't? That's funny. The last time I checked, my nipples were more sensitive than yours. I've gained fifteen pounds, and I've eaten so many grilled cheese sandwiches, I can't see straight."

"Nothing you can experience, even this Couvade, can compete with my reality."

"Which is?"

"I don't feel comfortable in my own body anymore. Every day there's something different, something I can't control."

"Isn't that what it means to be pregnant?"

"Not everybody is as emotionless as you are."

"And not everyone wears their emotions on their sleeve, like you do."

To Kenyon, the room had suddenly turned into a giant mouth and it was swallowing him. He grew warm and his head pounded. He tried to concentrate on what Marti was saying.

"I want to walk around so badly, it's making me crazy. I want to do what other expectant mothers do and shop for my child. I want to buy toys, and clothes, and diapers. But I can't because . . ." Her voice broke. "I want to browse in a kid's store and have a total stranger come up to me, rub my belly, and ask me when I'm due."

He heard her talking, like ghosts floating in the

room with him. A room he had to get out of before he disappeared within its depths. He stood, a rush of dizziness bright and powerful swirling in his head. Then the brightness went away.

"Kenyon!" Marti screamed.

She rushed to his side as he lay sprawled on the floor. He looked up at her from his prone position. "What are you doing up?" he moaned.

"The question is, what are you doing down?"

She helped him to his feet. "Are you okay?"

"Of course," he said, shrugging off the remaining dizziness. "I just got a little light-headed."

Her eyebrows crinkled into a frown. "Please," she said. "You fainted."

"I did not!" Kenyon responded, unease rioting within him. He smoothed his hair, which was threatening to come loose from his customary ponytail. "Look, I'm fine. So sit back down, all right? I'm hungry. I'm going to fix something to eat. You want anything?"

Marti returned to the place that had become more like a prison to her than a place to rest. "No. For once," she said, still feeling the residue of her anger, "I don't want anything from you."

For the next few weeks, Kenyon was more attentive to her than she could have ever hoped for. He rubbed her back. He massaged her feet. Ran her bath water. Even though he was still a little klutzy with the household chores, he did them without so much as a moan of complaint. And in return, Marti fought hard to keep her emotions in check. She didn't gush over him like a woman head over heels in love. She didn't make unreasonable demands. She didn't act like a spoiled brat. And when her moods swung from one extreme to the other, she kept herself on an even keel.

By the time she was twenty-five weeks along, she felt better. Her morning sickness ended. Her energy ramped. Her dizziness and restlessness faded away. And she hadn't had any more spotting, cramping, or any other unusual prenatal discomfort. Aside from the fact that she spent so much time in bed, she was in heaven.

Marti stared down at her round belly. It sat in her lap like a soccer ball. She rubbed it with one hand and held her sketchpad with the other. Her most recent creation was a series of drawings of Kenyon. The first was of his dark features looking out and pensive. Each successive picture changed until the final picture was Kenyon as a leopard looking out over savannah grassland. Besides his portrait, it was the best piece of work she'd done in a long time, including the new pieces she'd created for her art show.

The series represented her thoughts of him lately. She knew he was changing—changing into the man she'd always wanted. Changing into the man she had known he could be. But she didn't think he realized it. Not yet. But like Ashley's prediction, she could feel it coming. She would be patient and wait.

Kenyon opened the door for Marti and helped her inside the apartment. They had just come back from her twenty-eight-week check-up. Everything was going wonderfully well. The baby was right on schedule. Although they would have to stop referring to it as *the baby* and start calling it *he*. When Kenyon watched as the ultrasound revealed the male sex of the baby, his reaction surprised him. But there was no mistaking it was pride, just as big, bold, and macho as you please. A boy. His boy. He'd made a boy. The thought brought a smile to his lips even now.

"That little trip tired me out, Kenyon. I'm going to take a nap."

"While you're out, I'll whip up my famous liver and onions. The iron will do you both some good."

"Onions! Wake me when it's ready!"

Kenyon just stood at the kitchen doorway and watched Marti turn on her side and drift off to sleep.

These days, he couldn't get enough of watching for her, caring for her, being with her. The same things that annoyed him about her when they first met now brought him the only joy in his life. Her energy, despite her condition. Her childlike wonder. Her spunk. Even her determination to have their child.

He had no idea God made women like her.

Where his world had consisted mainly of the cold gray shadows of his mansion and his guilt, now it was vibrant with every color of the rainbow and full of promise.

He entered the kitchen knowing that although he couldn't change the past or the bloodlines from which his child flowed, he could take care of the future and make sure that for his child looking forward was much more appealing than looking backward.

Kenyon took liver out of the refrigerator, onions from the vegetable bin, and rice from the cupboard. His back ached. His bladder felt full again. His nipples hurt. And he would have paid a thousand dollars, swum the most turbulent ocean, and beaten a man down for the turtle fudge cheesecake he was craving. But he was happy.

* * *

Seven Months

Kenyon placed the small clear Tupperware bowl on top of the stack. It completed a nearly two-foot high stack of plastic containers left behind by family and friends who had dropped off meals and desserts within the past two months. Marti had labeled them all with the names of their respective owners. He had no idea how she kept track of such things.

After their argument, they'd come to an agreement. The pregnancy was taking a toll on both of them and Marti's bed rest was putting each of them on edge. In the past week, Kenyon and Marti had made an effort to release their frustration—Marti by sketching and drawing, and Kenyon by reading.

When Andreas had showed up at her door with a stack of books and magazines on pregnancy, Marti thought for sure they were for her. Then Kenyon explained that they were for him and Marti had been so delighted, she'd been unable to speak.

Since he'd been staying with her, Marti had periodically filled their conversations with the things she discovered while reading all the information she'd acquired on pregnancy and child rearing. Now and then, Kenyon would pick up a magazine or two, but other than that, he hadn't seemed very interested.

But now, he poured over the information and, surprisingly, seemed to enjoy reading it. Marti thanked God for small miracles.

Over the next few hours, she watched him periodically over the top of her sketchpad. His face played out a full spectrum of emotions—from casual curiosity and dubious confusion to blatant surprise and eye-widening shock. He seemed to be absorbing it all, glancing sometimes in her direction and staring as if couldn't believe that what was detailed in the book

was actually happening inside her body. Marti
thought about trying to hide the grin spreading wide
on her face, but decided against it. It was her happiness and she wanted to let it shine.

Her hands moved deliberately against the paper.
She'd grabbed her colored pencils from her art bin at
the side of her bed and let her emotions rule. She'd
started to think that maybe things would be all right
after all.

Over the past few months, requests for her artwork came in steadily. Kathryn had come over
several times to visit. When she left, she would always take some of the work Marti had done prior to
her exhibition. Kathryn even took a few of the drawings Marti had made while on bed rest. Even Kenyon
had been contacted by acquaintances in his art circle wanting more work from Marti. It didn't take
long for her stockpile of artistic expression to be
depleted. She'd kept a few pieces for herself and
one especially for Jacq, but aside from that, everything else was gone.

It was strange at first. Being without her work was
like being without her friends, like being without her
children. But now that she was having a child of her
own, the real life inside her was filling the void she'd
attempted to fill with her work. She knew that she still
loved to have her hands in wet clay, or clumped by
paper maché, or stained with acrylics. But her muse
had changed. Even this very moment, she was creating out of her joy, not her pain. Her love for Kenyon
and their child had transformed her.

She was overjoyed and started to sing.

Kenyon looked on, not saying a word as she sang
the first song that came to her mind, "Jesus Loves
Me." She sang it for her child, unborn and develop-

ing in her womb, but knowing still the Lord loved him and would protect him.

When she finished, she held her drawing out to get a better look. Her thoughts drifted to the doctors that came at Kenyon's request. They had used the latest ultrasound technology that enabled them to get a four-dimensional picture of the baby inside her. It was like watching a movie of him in almost perfect color. This was no black-and-white distorted image of their son. She and Kenyon knew exactly what he looked like. Out of that image came the one in her hand. Without fully realizing it, she'd sketched a perfect likeness of her baby. Aside from the real thing, she thought it was the most beautiful thing she'd created.

Her hand trembled until another, larger hand covered it. Kenyon knelt at her side, his dark features serious in the afternoon light.

"I'm sorry," he said. "I was angry because I was frustrated, because I was tired."

"Kenyon, we already discussed this."

"Yes. But I want you to know that I really am sorry. And that I'm in awe of you. I'm in awe of what you're doing for this baby. To sacrifice your mobility for the life of your, our, child . . . it's the bravest thing I've ever known anyone to do."

His gaze bore deep into her eyes. "Thank you," he said.

Marti awoke to a strange commotion in the room. She yawned and stretched a little, realizing she'd fallen asleep with the drawing of her child in her arms.

"Shh," a voice said. "You'll wake her up."

"Too late," she said, sitting up. She wiped her eyes

and her vision came into focus. Scurrying in the room in front of her was Jacq and Kathryn. Morgan bustled around near the corner of the room. Kenyon was nowhere to be found.

"What's going on?" she asked, propping herself up.

"Girl, I can't call you Little Bit no more. You are as bug as a house! How can you move?"

Kathryn and Morgan glared at Jacq for her remark.

Marti just laughed. That was all she could do. She was tired of feeling sorry for herself and not acknowledging her body for the wonderful miracle that was occurring inside it. If it meant saving her son's life, she'd get as big as two houses.

Kathryn rolled her eyes at Jacq. "Kenyon had a brilliant idea and called us to see if we would make it a reality."

Marti looked around, noticing for the first time upon waking that the furniture had been moved. It was all pushed away from the bed.

"Okay, what's going on?" she said feeling a little uneasy.

Morgan came and sat down beside Marti on the bed. "Your Mr. Rich-and-Famous thought that since you can't go shopping, he'd bring the shopping to you."

"What?" Marti said. Her pulse quickened with tension. "I can't think about that kinda stuff. What if something happens to the baby? I don't want to have—"

"But you're so close now," Jacq said, scooting over an end table. "You're bound to carry to term now."

"Nothing is certain yet. I mean . . ." Conflicting emotions battled inside Marti. She wanted so badly to search through clothing racks and shelves for newborn boys. She wanted outfits, and despite everything she ever said or thought about it, she'd imagined playsuits, booties, burping pads, and onesies. She'd changed diapers, dangled rattles, and nursed her son time and time again.

Morgan had gotten up and was staring out the apartment window. "Okay, Runt, make up your mind because here comes the merchandise." She turned to her sister. "In or out?"

Marti chewed her bottom lip. The anticipation rose inside her and she decided. "In!" she declared.

For the next hour and a half, Marti had her pick of some of the finest baby clothes, toys, and equipment she'd ever seen. Kenyon had made a deal with the owner of American Baby Co. to close down a local store for the afternoon and load a truck full of merchandise to her apartment. Kathryn and Jacq directed traffic through the apartment, the employees of the store hauled in items, and Morgan helped her sister pick the things she wanted.

Marti was elated. As soon as Kenyon returned, she would thank him profusely. She wished there were other ways she could thank him, but under the circumstances, she would have to wait until after the baby was born.

She also wished that he could be there with her, so they could pick out things for the baby together. But she knew it was a guy thing. No matter how strongly he suffered from Couvade or read books on pregnancy, he was still Kenyon Williams, and she knew the last thing he would want would be to sit in a room with a bunch of women oohing and ahing over bibs and binkies.

"Breathe, pant, pant, pant. Breathe, pant, pant, pant. Push!" Kenyon pressed the green button on his stopwatch and timed an imaginary contraction. "And relax."

"Kenyon, can we take five? I need a break."

"You won't be able to take a break when you're in labor for real."

"I know, but I need one now. You've been punishing me."

"No, I haven't. I've been reading up on this stuff. They say it's best to simulate as close to the real thing as possible. Otherwise we're just wasting our time."

"Since when have you been reading up on anything?"

"What do you think I do when you're busy taking all those naps?"

Kenyon watched as a smile as bright as the sun lit up Marti's face. He knew instantly what it was for. "What?" he asked, teasing her.

"You know what."

"What?" he asked again.

She simply continued to smile.

"I, uh . . ."

"Yes?"

"I care about you."

Marti rose an unimpressed eyebrow.

"Okay. I care about you a lot."

Marti crossed her arms.

"All right, all right," he said. "I love you, Marti. You and the baby. I—"

Before he could finish, she threw her arms around him and gave him a bear hug.

"Careful! You're going to squeeze Kenny Jr. out."

She pulled back a little. "Kenny Jr.? We never said anything about—"

"Thank you," he said, running a finger down the side of her face.

"For what?"

"For waiting. For being patient. For believing I would come to my senses."

Marti grabbed his face and pulled it to hers. Their lips touched and parted for the kiss that would seal their love. Their tongues rolled eagerly over the other's, searching, confirming, validating. Kenyon drew her closer. Her enlarged breasts brushing lightly against his arm and chest. Only her swollen belly came between them.

Out of all the things he'd craved—grilled cheese sandwiches, bacon, apple juice, and cheesecake—this was what he craved most. This exchange with Marti, this mating dance and prelude to becoming one. This is what he'd been searching for since the night he'd stumbled drunk out of the bar at two in the morning. Since the afternoon he fell backward in his chair in the state room of his mansion. Nothing he'd done since then, not even his philanthropy as Saint Black had made him feel this whole.

Until now.

"Wow!" Marti said, pulling away and gasping for air. "That's some kinda kiss!"

Kenyon laughed. "You're some kinda woman."

She looked happier than he'd ever seen her, and that included her artist's reception.

"Say it again," she whispered.

He licked his lips. "I love you, Marti Allgood." He kissed her forehead, then he kissed her round belly. "I love you both."

She ran her fingers through his hair and grinned like a child with a wonderful new present. The sensation sent his blood racing through his veins.

"Too bad we have to wait until the baby is born," she said, stroking his earlobe, following the strong line of his jaw and chin with her finger.

He brought her hand to his mouth and kissed each finger. "Maybe we don't have to."

Her eyes grew wide. "What do you mean?"

"I mean, we need to be close now." He cupped a hand around her breast. "Real close."

"But what about—"

"I would never do anything to harm our child."

Marti shuddered. The way Kenyon said "our child" moved her to tears.

"Shh," he insisted. "Prenatal care isn't the only subject I've been reading up on."

Marti's mouth made the cutest little O he'd ever seen. He kissed it and laid her down on the bed.

First, he wanted to build the ambiance. Kenyon took a sheet of paper from Marti's small writing desk and painted DO NOT DISTURB in large black letters with some acrylic and one of her paintbrushes. He took some tape and walked carefully to the door of the apartment and taped it to the front.

"I know how your sisters and your friends like to just drop in on you from time to time." A mischievous smile crawled across his lips. "Not today."

He walked over to the phone and pushed a few buttons on the answering machine. At the beep, he recorded, "Hello there. This is Kenyon Williams. Marti can't answer the phone right now. She's busy getting the most erotic massage a man has ever given a woman. She will be deliriously content for the next several hours. So you probably shouldn't call back until sometime tomorrow."

"Kenyon!" she said, astonishment lacing her tone. But the look in her eyes told him she was pleased and waiting with anticipation.

"What if I . . . ?" She blinked innocently.

"I thought I told you to shush." He strode to the closet and pulled out a gift basket. "When you were having one of your power naps, I called Ashley and told her I wanted to do something special for you. I think the proper thing to say here is, she hooked me up."

Marti sat up a little and watched as Kenyon closed every window blind and pulled the curtains. He turned off all the lights and the television. He placed the basket on the bed beside her.

"Open it," he said.

She removed the bow and the clear plastic wrap. Carefully arranged inside were six multicolored candles. They looked like wax confetti arranged into round mosaic balls. Marti also found a baby bottle full of saffron oil. It smelled like lemon meringue pie. Next she pulled out a CD. She recognized it as one of Ashley's homemade meditation CD's. She could hear Ashley's ethereal voice chanting to cosmic melodies and new-age rhythms. Next, she removed a small sack of flower petals—lavender and lilac. Tucked into the very bottom of the basket was a bottle warmer.

When she was surrounded with all of the items that she now recognized as things her sister had made and gathered with her own hands, Kenyon took the basket and set it aside.

"Now," he said, spreading his arms out to his sides, "Open me."

Marti's pulse throbbed at pressure points all over her body. A warm shot of adrenaline moved across her nipples and between her legs. She reached up and undressed Kenyon as slowly as she possibly could. She wanted to savor each revealing moment. She removed his shirt and kissed his arms and hands. She removed his pants and boxer briefs and kissed his stomach, his navel, and the hair just above where his manhood hardened and throbbed. When he stood before her completely naked, he moaned as she tongued his thighs and the area leading to his most sensitive places.

He growled and stepped back. "That feels so good to me," he said.

He gathered the items from the basket. First he placed three candles around the bed and lit them. He placed the baby bottle into the bottle warmer and plugged it in.

"Just relax," he crooned, putting the CD into the player and turning it on.

In the bathroom, he ran warm bath water and tossed the flower petals in. He stopped in the linen closest, removed two large bath towels, and threw them into the clothes dryer.

"While your water is running, I'm going to undress you . . . with my mouth."

Marti gasped and almost came. The very thought of Kenyon lavishing such attention on her was enough the plunge her over the edge.

He knelt beside her and clasped his hands behind his back. Three ties kept Marti's blouse closed. With he teeth and lips, Kenyon pulled the end of each one in succession, until each fell free. He bit into the soft fabric and pulled it down. Marti wriggled one arm out. He did the same with the other side, then Marti arched her back as he clamped his lips around the edge of the blouse and pulled it out from under her.

He moaned at the sight of her bare breasts. They looked ripe and succulent. He couldn't help himself. He tasted one nipple and then the other. Remembering the sensitive condition of his own over the past few months, he made sure his licks and sucking were like mere whispers against her flesh. He rolled his head between her large, full breasts and licked from side to side. She tasted like a rainfall in his mouth.

Nibbling his way down to her shorts, he rested

awhile at the roundness of her stomach. Kissed acrossed the skin stretched accommodate their growing child. He inhaled and kissed more passionately down the dark line that had formed under her navel and into the triangle of hair at the seat of her desire. Marti breathed harder and louder. With one last lick, he hooked his teeth into her shorts and pulled them down. She helped him by lifting her legs up and out as he slid the bottom part of her pajamas down until they were off. Satisfied, he flung the shorts into the other room.

Slowing he scanned her body, committing every inch to memory. She looked like an angel. His angel, who was blessing him with a son. He knew of no greater miracle in the world.

"Have I told you how beautiful you are?"

Marti shook her head.

"Well, you are. I've never seen anything, anyone so . . . so . . ." Tears danced at the corners of his eyes. "So wondrous in all my life."

He bent down and before Marti could take a good breath, he plundered her mouth. Ravaging the edges of her lips, undulating his tongue against hers. With one hand, he stroked her hair. With the other, he massaged her feminine opening with featherlight touches. She gasped and whimpered. Marti slowly approached release and Kenyon stopped just in time.

"I think your bath water is ready."

As Marti and Kenyon walked naked toward her bathroom, she knew that at seven months pregnant, she could have easily thought of herself as fat and ugly. She knew that in fact many women at her stage did. But Kenyon had never once looked at her as if she was unattractive. On the contrary, he had given her the kind of looks that under normal circumstances would have caused her to immediately remove her clothes and prepare for some serious lovemaking. And for him to state, with tears in his eyes, that he thought she was desirable and beautiful affirmed her own belief that she was.

She took his arm and strode proudly into her bathroom.

Kenyon took his time washing her. Marti closed her eyes and let the man who possessed her heart cleanse her body. The flower petals permeated the small room and wafted into her nose from the heat rising from the water. Each time Kenyon touched her skin with the warm washcloth, her muscles relaxed just that much more. Within minutes, euphoria took her over and she purred with contentment.

The water cascaded down her skin like hot fingers dancing all of the tension from her muscles. Their lips met again and again, and Marti found herself fully aroused. Even the gentle sounds of the water splashing and lapping against her thighs coaxed her deeper into a sensually induced joy. She had found her paradise, and his name was Kenyon Williams.

She breathed carefully. Not wanting to disturb his enchantment with even her breathing. His washing of her body was reverent, sacred, and she felt blessed beyond her worth. She trembled. Her tears mixed with the water running down her body.

"Don't," he said. His well-deep voice moving deliberately through the steam in the room.

"It's me who doesn't deserve you. Remember that. No matter what happens." He rinsed the soap from her arms. "It's me who doesn't deserve you."

He kissed her face and swallowed her tears. "I'll be right back."

He stopped the dryer and took the towels out. When he went back to the bathroom, he placed them on the sink and helped Marti out of the tub. He took one of the towels, still warm from the dryer, and dried her off thoroughly. Placing that towel in the hamper, he wrapped her in the other towel, which also held heat from the dryer, and carried her back to her bed.

Kenyon wasted no time in furthering his luxurious treatment. A practiced lover, he created a map of her body with his mouth against her skin. Every inch charted and surveyed by his lips and tongue. Every lick like velvet. Every nip a satin pinch. Every suck a tender pulling. Her body felt lighter than it had since the beginning of her pregnancy. It would not have surprised her if she had levitated right off her bed.

Her body forgot the meaning of tension, stress, and worry. All she knew was tranquillity.

"You look so peaceful," he said.

"I am," she smiled.

He reached over to the nightstand where massage oil warmed in the bottle.

"I'm peaceful, too, Marti. You helped me to find a kind of peace I thought couldn't belong to me. It's a strange feeling. Sometimes I still try to shake it off. Then you look at me, and I know you love me."

He took the bottle from the holder. It was warm in his hand. "The crazy part is, I love myself. You know, despite everything, I'm not such a bad person."

Marti wanted to respond, but when his hands touched her shoulders, the heat radiated through her and all she could do was moan.

Her sister's serene vocals glided out of the speakers like a milky blue ocean. Kenyon kneaded her shoulders back and forth like a slow pulse. She was floating.

The vocal track faded softly into acoustic spirit music. Marti thought the sound was entering her body and sweeping her away.

Kenyon's hands slid over her skin. He worked her chest and rubbed oil tenderly into her breasts. On her arms, he pushed soft circles from her wrist up. He squeezed and rolled each finger between his own, paying special attention to the area between each finger by sliding his own fingers back and forth inside the delicate area.

The soft-hued citrus aroma from the candles filled the room. Marti breathed deeply while Kenyon's masterful hands worked their enchantment on her. Each delicate pass over her flesh bore the same rhythmic signature as their lovemaking. Gentle and attentive strokes over her stomach. Tender presses into her thighs and hips. Refined caressing of her calves and feet. They all mimicked the same intimate motions that created the life inside her. The ascension to her peak rose languidly.

When her body had been touched completely and was shining with oil, Kenyon's urges took over and he descended upon her breasts, sucking a nipple into his mouth and fingering another.

Marti moaned softly. He continued to suck and roll his tongue wetly over the ripened bud. Lying next to her on the bed, he licked and stroked while she whimpered and panted.

Kenyon rubbed his hardness against her side and moaned. She wiped her hands against her thighs, which were as soft as butter, and massaged him where his need was most urgent.

The oil she'd taken from her body made it easy to slide her hands up and down his love muscle. The room came alive with the sounds of their yearning.

Kenyon's easy mouth-play went on. Her nipples tightened even more in his mouth, and before she realized what was happening, a soft wave of pleasure broke open inside her. "Oh!" she cried, as she rode out the gentlest orgasm she'd ever had.

Only a few seconds later, Kenyon noticed her grip on him loosening and slowing. Then it stopped altogether. He smiled and almost laughed. Marti had fallen asleep.

Twenty-one

Eight Months

He said he was getting into practice for the baby,
but Marti knew he was getting into her. First, he had
started rubbing her all over with baby oil or baby lotion. He claimed he was also doing it as part of her
physical therapy. She just smiled and played along.
Next, he organized visits from her family and
friends, claiming that once the baby arrived, he
didn't want crowds of people getting germs on his
son, so it was best to start scheduling people's time
now. Marti believed him, but she also believed that
he had become protective of her and wanted to
make sure that she didn't get overly tired by having
constant guests. The gesture that elated her soul
came when Kenyon unexpectedly ordered in dinner from Pano's and Paul's, an exclusive restaurant
in the Buckhead area.

He had occasionally ordered dinner in before, but
this time he created a rich ambiance by lighting candles and fixing a special place setting on a bed tray
with linen cloth, linen napkins, and a small bouquet
of red and white roses. Then he proceeded to feed
her every morsel of the French onion soup, filet
mignon, asparagus tips, St. Claire whipped potatoes,
and tomato-garlic bread.

Marti sighed through every mouthwatering fork-ful of her dinner. She didn't have to lift a finger. Kenyon did all the work. And when she felt a small bit of juice trickle from the corner of her mouth, Kenyon promptly dabbed her lips with the corner of her napkin.

She was in heaven.

Just when she thought that it couldn't get any bet-ter, Kenyon lay in bed with her one night talking. She'd received flowers from her sister Roxanne that morning. After reading the card that said, "Always re-member I love you," Marti had burst into tears. She pulled herself together with Kenyon's help but had been quiet most of the day.

When Kenyon crawled in bed that evening and started massaging her stretch-marked stomach, she felt an overwhelming need to talk. She thought maybe her pregnancy had triggered it, but suddenly the need to talk about the rift between her and her sister was stronger than she'd ever felt it.

She pulled her finger across the smooth petal of a chrysanthemum. "I've always been small. So my brother and sisters always seemed like these giants to me. Giants who pushed and shoved me, stepped over me, and called me Runt all the time."

Marti swallowed hard. "When you're the youngest and the littlest, it's easy for you to be overlooked."

Kenyon saw the pain of remembrance forming in her eyes and ran his hand through the short tufts and curls of her hair.

"The only thing I knew for sure was that when I told on my siblings, I got a lot of attention from everybody. It was like I could magically grow big and capture everybody's attention for good or bad. Well . . . it took me a long time to grow out of that."

The dull ache in her heart that never completely

went away surfaced from the dark space where she had tried for years to ignore it. "I always thought that things would just automatically get better between us," she said, lowering her eyelashes.

Kenyon lifted her chin with the soft tip of his finger. "What happened between you and Roxanne?"

Marti's eye's fluttered with discomfort. "I must have been about twenty-three. Roxy was dating this guy named Haughton Storm. He was so nice. He never talked down to me because I was younger, and he always made time for me like he knew I sometimes felt neglected. Most of all, he was so in love with my sister he couldn't see straight. I'm pretty sure she loved him too, but at the time, I thought she loved to fly more."

Kenyon's eyebrows wrinkled. "I don't understand."

"Roxy had wanted to be an airline pilot since she was three years old. She graduated from high school when she was sixteen just so she could start flight training as soon as possible. Roxy is a great person now. But back then, she would have sold her soul to become a pilot."

Marti pulled a flower from the vase and lifted the bud to her nose. She inhaled the heady scent and hoped this was a sign that her sister had begun to forgive her.

"Well . . . one day Roxy was in Morgan's room making all this noise. I thought she was laughing so I started to go in. When I realized she was crying, almost hysterically, I hung back. Whenever I entered a room and something important was going on, people tended to shut up and stop talking until after I left. So I figured the best way for me to find out what was going on was to listen in."

Marti took a deep breath and released it.

"I found out that she was pregnant and scared to death that her pregnancy would ruin her career.

"After a few minutes, they got real quiet. But I could hear Roxy going on and on about how she couldn't have it and how she didn't want it. And what a rotten thing to happen to her now. She said that Haughton would probably want to marry her if he found out and that she didn't want that either. Then I heard the word abortion. It turned my blood to ice. Haughton was such a nice man. I loved him as if he and Roxy were already married. I knew she would put her career first and not tell him about the pregnancy.

"So I told him."

"Hmm," Kenyon said, fingers sliding pensively down his goatee.

"It's been ten years, and after all that time, part of me still thinks I did the right thing." Her eyes bore into Kenyon's. "She and Haughton broke up right after that. She's never fully forgiven me for it."

"She never had the baby. At the time, she claimed she had a miscarriage. No one believed her, especially not Haughton. But now, after everything that's happened to me, maybe she was telling the truth after all."

A solitary tear slid down the side of Marti's face. She wiped it away and placed the flower back in the vase.

"I'm tired," she said and lay down, covered herself with a bright white sheet, then closed her eyes.

Kenyon rushed into Marti's apartment, grabbed the remote control, and turned off the television.

"Hey!" she protested. "I was watching that!"

Kenyon paced in front of her with a stack of books and CDs gripped in one arm. When he had announced that he wanted to go shopping, Marti was grateful. Even spending long hours with the man she loved could get old after a while. She was hoping to spend the afternoon vegged out in front of the television. But Kenyon had come back too soon. And now he was acting all keyed up and excited.

"I've been reading."

"Oh, no," Marti sighed. The last time he made that pronouncement, he'd seen an article in *Gourmet* magazine that convinced him he could prepare fondue. They tried to eat the melted cheese concoction but eventually had to give up and settle on a fruit salad instead.

"The experts say that babies are affected by what they experience in the womb."

"That's what they say," Marti responded watching the wheels turning in her beloved's head. "Why?"

"Well, I want my son to have the best experience possible."

Her skin prickled with euphoria and amazement. "So, now he's your son."

Kenyon kept pacing, then stopped to give her the shrewd eye. "One of the experts said that expectant parents should provide as much positive stimulus for their baby as they possibly can and eliminate all negative influences like television, radio, newspapers, and certain people. Those things affect the mother's mood and the mother's disposition affects the development of the child."

"Kenyon, I'll be bored out of my mind if I can't watch TV or read. I'm already feeling kinda crazy now, and I have all those things."

"Well," he said, extending his arm. "That's why I got these."

Marti took the books and CDs from him and a warm feeling radiated from her soul out.

"Let's turn off those outside influences and start doing a little influencing ourselves."

Marti smiled brightly eyes twinkling like stars. "Okay," she said.

For days and days, they listened to the classic music from the CDs Kenyon had purchased. The genius of Scott Joplin, Count Basie, Louis Armstrong, among others, filled the space of her apartment during the day. In the evenings, Kenyon positioned himself next to her large stomach and read poetry to their child. Some of it came from writers she'd heard of, like Rita Dove and Robert Pinski. Other names weren't as familiar, but their words soothed her, reached out to her heart, and made her love Kenyon all the more.

One night, while the rolling base of his voice vibrated against her skin, she heard the poem she'd been waiting her entire life to hear.

That you could love me
brings a strange mending
summer's brilliant change to fall a skylark's promise
song to wind to song to heart you are beauty walking

Loving hearts
returned too soon from mourning days past
a sorted wound for a nightingale or a moon and a lover
my mouth is full with your name

That you could love me
these sad steps taken to measureless lessons in humility
worn like a garment
shook from the black rain of sin
a sadness sweet and broken
like the sea against rocks

Oh stop near beauty walking
and toss me like a leaf to your bosom

in a sunless sky you listen cheerfully
and make me forget

As if the poem was meant for them, Marti and Kenyon wept together and then fell asleep—Marti against her pillow, Kenyon against her stomach.

Kenyon was dreaming and he knew it. He sat at a banquet table laden with food. Smoked ham, steamed asparagus, artichoke salad, and tapioca pudding lay before him. The smell of the food overwhelmed him. He was starving.

He didn't want to wake up until he'd eaten his fill of the delicious feast. Until he'd savored each tender morsel on his tongue. His cooking was getting better, but he had to admit, the last decent meal he had was leftovers from the food Marti's sisters prepared and left in the freezer. He was just grateful he hadn't poisoned Marti or the baby with his attempts.

He took a roll from a basket. The top of it glistened with butter. He pulled it apart. Steam rose from its soft white center.

"Umm," he moaned, putting the fresh baked bread into his mouth. In a matter of seconds he devoured it and reached for another. But something was wrong. He didn't know where the food had come from and that worried him. His gut told him that it wasn't Roberta. She was someplace else. But if not her, who? Then the answer jolted him awake. Marti!

He yawned and stretched. Then he realized that the delicious aromas from his dream were right here in the room with him. Where is that heavenly smell coming from? And where was Marti?

"Breakfast will be ready in a minute," he heard her say.

"Marti!" he dashed into the kitchen. "What the hell are you doing?"

"Oh, I thought I would do cartwheels and calisthenics this morning." She laughed. "What does it look like I'm doing?"

Although his stomach rumbled out of control with hunger, he ignored it. He walked up beside her. "It looks like you're up and you're cooking."

"Wow! You're quick."

"Marti, if you don't get back in the bed right now, I'll throw your pregnant ass across my shoulder and carry you back there myself."

She turned off the eggs and onions with bacon. They were done. Right on time, two slices of toast popped out of the toaster. She touched his shoulder. "I just want to say thank you for . . . everything."

Kenyon placed his hands on her abdomen. "You already have."

Just then, the area beneath his hands hardened like quick-drying cement.

"Ow!" Marti screamed, and dropped to the floor.

She clutched at her stomach while Kenyon tried to help her up. "Can you stand?"

Heavy breathing, then another scream.

He lifted her into his arms and carried her to the bed. He laid her down and saw that his right arm was wet. Her water had broken.

"It's too soon!" she yelled. "I've got four more weeeeeks!" Another contraction gripped her and tears rolled down her cheeks.

She writhed in the bed. "Mama," she whispered.

"Marti, I'm going to get your clothes and your suitcase."

She grabbed his arm. "No! Don't leave me."

"You don't want to show up at the hospital in your

pajamas, do you?" He leaned over her and stroked her forehead.

"Something must be wrong. They said it wouldn't hurt bad at first. They said—" Another scream pierced the air, and Kenyon's pulse jackhammered in his veins.

"I'm calling Andreas," he said.

"No!" she hollered. She clutched at him like a small, terrified animal. Clinging and afraid of everything.

"I'm just going to the phone. It's on the nightstand. All I have to do is walk to the other side of the bed."

Marti closed her eyes and let go. She rolled and sobbed from one side of the bed to the other.

Kenyon snatched up the phone and dialed the numbers quickly. When the old man answered, Kenyon found himself shouting. "She's in labor!" he said.

"Sir," Andreas said, a strange quivering in his voice. "I was just about to call you. There's something you need to know."

"Not now! Just bring the car," he said and hung up.

He darted into Marti's bedroom where her going-to-the-hospital clothes were already laid out right next to her suitcase. He grabbed them both and ran back to the living room.

Marti sobbed and held herself. "Help me," she whispered.

He put the suitcase down and knelt beside her. Staring into her eyes, he could see the deep pain and fear running rampant there. "Breathe with me," he said.

After a few moments, he coaxed her to focus on his face and to breathe in and out with him they way they'd been taught in class. He timed her contractions at three minutes apart. The concentrated breathing calmed her down.

"I'm going to put your clothes on now," he said.

She nodded her consent.

He took off her pajama top, and helped her into a nursing bra and short-sleeve sweater. He pulled the wet pajama bottoms off and gasped.

"Honey, we're not going to make it to the hospital."

"What's wrong?" she screamed.

"Nothing," he said, setting the pajamas and skirt to the side. "I can see the baby's head."

"Oh, God, Kenyon! It's coming again! Please make it stop! I can't take . . . aaaaah!"

Together they breathed through her contraction. They were coming now at about one and a half minutes apart.

"I'm going to get some towels."

"Don't leave me, Kenyon!"

"I'll only be a second."

He made it to the linen closet and back again before the next contraction.

"I want to push," she said. "I have to push."

He'd read the numerous books Marti had stacked on the floor next to the bed. Ashley had given her one on midwifery. In his boredom one evening, he's skimmed its pages. He wished he'd paid better attention to it.

"I think it's too early to push, sweetheart."

"Why are you calling me sweetheart? You've never called me that before?"

Kenyon frowned. "It just came out."

"Well, it sounds patronizing. Don't patronize meeeeeee!" Another contraction. he held her hand and they panted. One minute apart now. She was getting close.

Sweat and amniotic fluid drenched the bed beneath her.

The doorbell rang.

"Andreas!" Kenyon called.

"Yes, sir."

"Call an ambulance."

"Yes, sir!"

He spread her legs and pushed them up. The baby was coming all right. A mound of slick black hair poked through her opening.

"The baby is . . ." What was the word he saw in the book? "Crowning," he remembered.

Marti had closed her eyes and sucked in her bottom lip. She looked as though she was about to calm down a little, but another contraction claimed her body.

He was so frightened, he was calm. The torture he saw on his beloved's face scared him more than anything he'd ever experienced. And heaven help him, just when he wished he could feel what she felt—and not only feel it but somehow take it from her—all his symptoms of Couvade disappeared. Fear was a strange sensation. Living the kind of life he led meant he didn't experience that emotion often. Being part of the society that owns and controls so much, you never had to fear anything, except someone coming in and taking all of that away.

"Oh, Kenyon! I have to push. I can't help it!"

His heart thudded like a kick drum on espresso. "Okay, Marti," he said, snatching the covers off of the bed. "I'm going to help you slide down to the end of the bed."

"What is this, a pap smear?" she snarled.

"Come on!" he said, pulling and guiding her down. "I can't guide the baby out if the bed is under you."

She maneuvered herself to the edge of the bed and bent her knees up. Kenyon placed a towel on the floor where blood and other fluids were already beginning to drip.

"I'm cold," she said.

He picked up one of the sheets on the floor and

wrapped it around her. Each of them braced for the next contraction. But it didn't come.

"Oh, God. Please don't let my labor stop now!"

Then another piece of information peeled itself away from the corners of Kenyon's mind.

"This is the second stage. Remember? The contractions come slower now because it's time to expel the baby."

"Expel?" You make it sound like he's in schoooool!"

"Okay, Marti. Breathe, breathe, breathe, push."

"Ah!"

"That's good! The head is coming!"

The sight of his child emerging from Marti's body let him know just how incredibly brave she was to go through this. To have been willing to go through this despite everything, including his rotten behavior. Despite him! Dear Lord. His heart was so full of love for this woman! It was as if he had been pregnant with his feelings. And all these months, they'd been growing. And now—now the love that had matured inside him was being fully born at the same time as his son, and the sensation overwhelmed him.

"Pant, pant, pant, push!" he coached.

"Kenyon!"

"What's wrong?" he looked up, alarmed.

"It feels so good to push."

Kenyon smiled for the first time since Marti went into labor. She smiled a little, too. He wiped the area around the birth canal with a towel.

When the next contraction came, they were both ready.

"Breathe and push, Marti. Keep going. Keep going."

Marti pushed as hard as she could. "Ah!"

"Good! It's coming. It's coming. It's . . . out! The head is out. Look."

Marti looked down, panting through her breaths, to see the head of her child emerging from her body.

There was a pounding at the door. "Paramedics!" a female voice called.

Marti's eyes widened.

"Don't worry. I'm not going anywhere. He turned toward the door. "Hold on!" he shouted.

Another contraction came and Marti pushed again. Kenyon held his son's head and gently guided one shoulder out.

"Oh!" Marti moaned.

"Don't stop now, sweetheart. He's almost here. You can do it."

As the end of the contraction faded, Marti pushed one more time and Kenyon pulled his newborn son out. He placed the baby on Marti's stomach and stared in awe. A child more perfect than he could ever imagine lay on the woman he loved.

And to top it off, all three of them were crying.

Kenyon opened the door for the paramedics. They came in with their dark blue uniforms and clanking and rattling gear.

"You got a woman in labor? Whoa!" the woman said. "I guess she's already delivered."

The two paramedics went to work cutting the umbilical cord and checking the vital signs of both Marti and the baby. Andreas hung back in the hallway.

"Come in, Andreas. Let me introduce you to my son," Kenyon said. As he motioned the elder gentleman in, Kenyon realized his pride has swollen so large it was barely confinable in the room. He was proud, actually proud to have a son. And he was proud of Marti for sticking to her principles and enduring the pain of labor and delivery to bring a new life into the world.

Andreas smiled and his whole face lit up with long

deep wrinkles. He nodded and Kenyon slapped him on the back. He looked on as the paramedics lifted Marti and the baby on to a stretcher. She looked fully content, gazing down at the child who had quieted down and drifted off to sleep.

"I'll follow you in the limo," he said, picking up her suitcase.

"Okay," she said, eyes still glued to the marvel in her arms. "Call my sisters and my brother."

One of the paramedics stared at him. Then he heard her say to the other, "That's him. That's the guy."

And then they were gone, and the strange comment with them.

"Come on, Andreas," he said, throwing an arm around his assistant and friend. "Let's go make sure they're all right."

The Atlanta Medical Center was a bustle of activity. There was even more activity in Marti's room. Her family arrived only minutes behind Kenyon. The rapture and joy on their faces when they finally got to see mother and child astounded Kenyon. For a moment, he considered calling his family. His mother, father, and brother would no doubt want to begin legal proceedings to guard against Marti extorting money for having a Williams child. They didn't know her like he did, and because their priorities had always been money first, people second, he knew what to expect. No, he would wait a while before telling them. He wasn't ready to squelch his happiness just yet.

Kenyon, who had just changed into fresh clothes, watched from afar as the Allgood family oohed and cooed over his son. He felt guilty about the way he'd treated Marti almost from the very beginning, so he believed it best to stay out of her family's way—or else he'd run the risk of incurring their wrath once more.

Just as that thought left his mind, the man he'd seen perform in concert strolled over to him, a veil of seriousness replacing his smile.

"When I first heard about you, I thought for sure I'd be in the tabloids for assault and battery."

"Look, I—"

"Then I heard my sisters beat me to the punch. No pun intended."

Kenyon was in for another scolding. He deserved it. He took a deep breath, and let the man continue.

"I heard you took care of Runt. Got her the best doctors on the planet, and stayed with her while she was on bed rest." Xavier sized him up. "Runt says you delivered the baby."

Kenyon nodded.

"I guess that makes you all right, for now. But if you mess up, ever, I don't care if I'm singing falsetto in Nepal, it won't be my sisters whom you deal with next time. You know what I mean, man?"

There it was again—the strong love of a strong family. Kenyon admired it. Wanted to emulate it. "I love your sister. And I will do right by her."

The two men looked eye to eye then Xavier extended his hand. Kenyon took it, and they shook briefly.

"Now that that's over," Xavier said, "What are you going to do about this Saint Black situation?"

A blast of pain hit Kenyon's stomach as if he'd been punched. "What?"

"Your philanthropy. You're going to have the press hounding you for days. I don't want my sister dogged by all those reporters. What are you doing about it?"

Kenyon backed away, confusion racing in his mind. *Why is he talking about it as if it's common knowledge? Did*

Marti tell him? Could she have found out? And why would the press be involved? Had someone tipped them off?

"Here he is!" a woman shouted from the entryway. She burst in with a cameraman, microphone in hand.

"Mr. Williams, will you continue to give away millions of dollars? And how do you respond to the allegations that your family's fortune stems from slave-holding?"

Marti and her family looked on, surprise and unease running rampant on their faces.

"You've got some nerve coming in here. My sister just had a baby!" Xavier shouted.

"Kenyon?" Marti's eyes were wide and pleading. "What's going on?"

"I'll tell you as soon as I get these people out of here."

Anger bubbled inside him as he said, "You can either leave quietly or not." He stepped closer to the woman and the man with the camera. "Which will it be?"

The woman blinked. "I guess we'll leave," she said.

"I'll just make sure," Kenyon said and followed them out.

Twenty-two

SAINT BLACK UNMASKED
by
Selena Graves

Wealthy entrepreneur and owner of the famous Soul Goddess painting by Biko is doing more than investing in art these days—he's investing in the African American community in a big way. Williams is none other than the philanthropist nicknamed Saint Black. The generous benefactor has been secretly leaving briefcases containing one million dollars on the doorsteps and entryways of homes in cities like Detroit, San Diego, Las Vegas, and Little Rock for the past ten years.

The recipients of Williams's million-dollar gifts were not chosen at random, but share one common characteristic. Genealogical research shows they all have a common ancestry as slaves that served on the same plantation—the Williams plantation owned by Kenyon Williams's great, great, great-grandfather.

In 1850s South Carolina, the Williams Brothers, Zachary and Turner, made a name for themselves as freed slaves who became tailors. As their business grew, so did their need for workers. They acquired their workers in the form of slaves.

Over a fifteen-year period, the Williams Brothers came to amass a considerable number of slaves for breeding, cotton picking, and tailoring work. While the average slaveholder

*in the South owned five or fewer slaves, the Williams plan-
tation boasted over one hundred, placing the Williams family
in the echelons of slave magistrates who were owners of fifty
slaves or more.*

*"At first, I thought it was fake," Chance Williby said. Her
investments over the past four years have brought her net
worth to just under two million dollars. Similarly, with recipients Michael Willms and LaTivia Willhem have chosen
to save more than they've spent and consequently are worth
more today than the day they received their gifts.*

*Williams may have used the Internet and other genealog-
ical research avenues to investigate the descendants of the
slaves. During the time of slave emancipation, it was common practice for newly freed slaves to take on the last names
of their former masters. This may explain the reason for the
similarity in the last names of the recipients.*

*Although Williams had a reputation for being a ladies'
man and had several run-ins with tabloids as recently as five
years ago, this attempt at reparations may go a long way to
changing his image.*

*Today, Williams Brothers Enterprises—run by CEO Rey-
nard Williams—consists of several clothing lines including
Williams Brothers Suits; boasts of Magic Johnson, Steve Harvey, and Donald Trump as clientele; and has assets
estimated at nearly one billion dollars.*

*To date, Kenyon Williams, who currently makes his home
in Atlanta, Georgia, has given gifts of approximately fifteen
million dollars. The entrepreneur, known in recent years for
reclusion and most recently for being the financial catalyst
for up-and-coming artist Marti Allgood, was unavailable for
comment at the time this article was being written.*

Twenty-three

When Kenyon escorted the reporters out of her hospital room, Marti waited for his return. And she waited. And waited.

Her sisters told her to forget about him for good and concentrate on her son. Ashley told her to light a long-stemmed candle and chant a return prayer until it burned halfway down. Xavier left to find him. But Marti was tired. She'd held on to the notion that he would find his way to love her, and just when she believed he had, he'd gone again. And the funny thing was, she had no compulsion to paint, sculpt, or immerse herself in any other art form. Through her experience with Kenyon, she'd learned how to channel all her emotions through her art, not just her pain. More importantly, she'd learned how to do it on her own terms. Gazing down into her son's bright young eyes, she realized that she'd already created a masterpiece.

At home with the baby two weeks now, her mind whirred with anxiety. While she was still in the hospital, her sisters had shown her the newspaper exposé by a reporter named Selena Graves. The article chronicled her investigation into the mysterious one-million-dollar donations by an anonymous philanthropist and how the trail led to the Williams family, specifically Kenyon Williams.

"Why didn't you call me?" Marti had asked.

"We did. Your answering machine didn't seem to be working. By the time we got to your apartment, you were already headed for the hospital," Morgan had replied.

The article went on to describe the multibillion-dollar clothing company and its history, which she'd discovered was steeped in the unforgivable owning of slaves.

Since that article, Marti divided her life between taking care of her child and fending off reporters. She was seriously considering taking up her brother's offer of staying at his place. His rising musical career prompted the recent addition of surveillance equipment and twenty-four-hour guards around his home. To keep her mind off of the travesty that had quickly become local scandal, she turned off the television, where Reverend Al Sharpton was calling for a full investigation and reparations for all of the Williams family's misdeeds.

Maybe it wouldn't have been so bad if Kenyon had made some kind of public statement or gesture. But he hadn't. He'd disappeared. No one seemed to know where he was. Even Andreas, who had to know but wasn't talking. Kenyon's parents had taken on the burden of dealing with the media. Reynard had been very little help, especially when it came out that the woman he'd been dating was the reporter who broke the story. Since then, he'd been scarce as well.

Marti stared down at the bundle in her arms. "Maybe your father and uncle are together. What do you think, little Kenyon?" She kissed his brown puck nose. He yawned but kept his eyes closed.

Her sisters had a conniption when she named the baby after his father. But she wouldn't have it any other way. Her child—her beautiful, beautiful child with thick raven hair and skin a combination of every wondrous color on her palette—would know his father and his heritage. Even a tarnished one. And he would know that he was born of love. She would tell him stories of how his father, who had never done a day's work in his life, stayed with her for four months cooking, cleaning, washing clothes, and seeing to her every need. How he summoned the most prestigious doctors in the country to see to her care. And when it was time for him to be born, his father was right there to deliver him with tears in his eyes. She would tell him what she knew—that his father loved him.

Three months. It had been three months since the birth of his son. That day would mark a change in Kenyon Williams's life forever.

When the story broke about him, he was almost relieved. He felt like he'd been carrying an enormous secret on his back for years and now the whole world knew. But it was the part about his family's shame that paralyzed him. He wanted to walk away from the entire scandal and take Marti and his son with him. He wanted to go somewhere where they could be a family without the stigma of his ancestors' tragic past to plague them. The thing he'd feared most in life had happened.

Even with all his money, he could not erase history.

He'd spent the first month angry and resentful. He figured, maybe if he disappeared, the frenzy would die down, the media would turn to the next big societal wrinkle, and Marti and the baby would be left alone. He spent the second month berating himself for the first month. He should have never left her side. Leaving her side had probably caused more damage than if he'd just told the reporters to kiss off they way he'd wanted to.

By the third month, he'd stewed in his own anger long enough. He decided to resurface and take whatever consequences life dealt him.

First, he moved out of the mansion. With the money he got for selling most of the artwork he'd collected, he had enough funds to buy himself a reasonable home and furnishings. Then one by one, he answered the correspondence that had come in from the people who'd received money from him. The overwhelming majority of people wanted to thank him for attempting to set right a wrong. One older gentleman sent the money back untouched. He said his life was just fine without it and was glad to be able to send it back to the rightful owner. What started to create hope in Kenyon's troubled life was the mass of e-mail and letters he'd received asking him how he'd done it—how he'd found the descendants of the slaves his family owned.

At first he'd sent the same e-mail and letter to hundreds of people. When he started receiving similar questions from genealogists, he realized what he could do that might heal the wound in his heart and help someone in the process. It finally dawned on him that he was a man plagued by his past, and until he could come to terms with that, he wouldn't do anyone any good—not Marti, not his child, not even himself. So, he called a family friend who was on the Board of Directors for the Smithsonian Institution and took the first step in his own healing process.

A week before her son's four-month birthday, Marti Allgood went for a walk. She pushed Kenyon Williams, Junior in his stroller and squinted into the sun. It was a beautiful July day. Not too hot. Just perfect for a mother and infant son to enjoy.

Kenyon liked the sun. The warm rays always put him to sleep no matter how fussy he'd been. She could tell already that he would be the outdoors type. Fresh air was always good for a coo or two. In her mind, she could see her son at three, four, and five, running willy-nilly in his father's majestic gardens, getting lost among the green, being a boy, being happy. But each time that dream crossed her mind, it had faded a little from the last time, until now, all she was left with was a lackluster memory of something wonderful that might have been.

Each day Kenyon didn't call and each week Kenyon didn't call destroyed just a little bit of her hope.

And she'd been so sure.

She would have staked her very life on her belief that there was a good man inside him. A good and honorable man that wanted to do right by her and by their offspring. In fact, she'd staked the nuclear family life of her child on it. As she turned a corner and headed toward the park, a terrifying thought gripped her. She'd been wrong.

Determined not to allow her sinking mood to interfere with their outing, Marti stayed the entire time she'd planned, allowing little Kenyon to soak up as much sun and good weather as his tiny heart desired, and then headed back.

On many occasions, when she'd taken her son for a walk, she had imagined a dark man with long, flowing, ink-black hair leaning against a limousine, waiting in front of her apartment building for them. As she approached her building, she knew that image would never become real.

Marti heard the ringing phone and hurried inside.

She picked up Kenyon from his stroller and grabbed the receiver.

"Hello?" she said slightly out of breath.

"Hey, Mama Bear. What you know?"

"Hey, Miss Jackson. We just stepped in the door. What's up?"

"Nada," Jacq said. "I just wanted to check on you to see how you were doing."

Marti sat down and rocked her baby. "I'm good."

"How do you feel about going back to work?"

"Sad. I just want to take him with me."

"Girl, you better be glad you can get away and get some rest!"

"The only time I really rest is when he's right next to me. As long as I know he's all right, I'm all right."

"What did you decide on for day care?"

Marti smiled. She was so fortunate that her family was willing to step in and help her. Her twenty-year-old niece had agreed to watch Kenyon during the day. "Amara. She's taking night classes and she'll let me pay her half of what it would cost to put him in day care."

"I thought Big Baller was sending you money."

"He is, but who knows how long that will last? It's not as if it's court ordered."

"Well, maybe it's time it was."

Marti closed her eyes, wishing her soul was as peaceful as the one sleeping in her arms. Of course it was time. It was time for a lot of things, first and foremost moving on with her life, with her child's life. She'd been in denial for way too long. "I guess you're right."

"You guess?"

"Okay, okay. You're right."

"You know Davis knows just about every high-powered lawyer in town. I'm sure he could hook you up."

Marti surveyed her tiny apartment. The once maroon and rum-red accent colors had been eclipsed by pastels and heavy doses of powder blue. Her sisters had helped her clean out her art supplies and turn her spare room into the baby's room, complete with crib, changing table, rocking chair, and Blue's Clues wallpaper. How had her little world become cluttered with such enormous problems?

"Have him call me tomorrow, Jacq."

"Done, girlfriend. Now all you need to do is—"

"Hold on. Someone's at the door." Marti got up from the couch to answer the doorbell. She hoped it wasn't one of her well-meaning family members. She wasn't in the mood for their exuberance right now.

"Who is it?" she called.

"It's me," a deeper than deep voice answered.

The cavern-deep voice halted her. "It's Kenyon, Marti."

Marti backed away from the door, pulse pounding. She picked up the phone with an unsteady hand.

"Jacq . . ."

"I heard that baritone, girl. Don't let him in!"

"Jacq, I have to go." She hung up the phone half in a trance. She wondered what would happen if she opened the door. Would her newly formed resolve melt away like warm butter as soon as she saw him? Or would the sight of Kenyon anger her beyond reason?

Marti kissed her sleeping son's tiny forehead and placed him in his bassinet. The small chocolate-brown baby squirmed and fussed for a moment and then drifted back into a careless sleep.

That's the way Marti wanted to be—careless about this whole situation. But she wasn't. And it was time she reconciled her feelings once and for all. She and Kenyon needed to talk. They needed closure, and they needed an understanding of what their responsibilities were as parents. They needed . . .

Marti swung open the door. The man standing there with his dark skin, ponytail, and expensive clothing looked relieved. As if someone had just saved his life.

"Come in, Kenyon," she said.

He stepped inside. His eyes swept the apartment and immediately found the bassinet.

The Couvade hadn't ended when Marti delivered, as the doctors had predicted. It continued. Everyday he'd felt his child's heartbeat, could smell his skin, heard him cry. Kenyon's emotions had been drawn, pulled, and stretched in every direction. Once when he was helping to drywall the bathroom, he became overwhelmingly sad for no reason. Another time he was installing a window, and a vision of his son smiling came as clear to his mind as if Kenyon Junior had been in his arms. No, his bond with his son and Marti hadn't ended in their time apart. It had grown stronger.

His heart pounded. "Can I see him?"

"After all this time," she said, closing the door, "I should think you would want to."

He walked to the bassinet and peered inside. He took a startled breath. "He's so big. It's like he's doubled in size."

Marti leaned against the door to keep from falling. Where was her anger, her resentment? Her rage that her baby's father was missing in action for months? It seemed her frustration had built nicely when he was gone, but now that he was here, it deflated like a popped balloon. "He weighs nine pounds now."

What Kenyon wouldn't do to hold that nine pounds in his arms right now. If he had to beg Marti for her permission, he would do it.

"Pick him up. See for yourself."

Relief washed over him. He bent down and picked up the child that already looked like him.

He was warm and soft and precious. The most perfect creature he'd ever seen. His love weakened him. His regret for his actions made him hold on tighter, determined to never let go.

"I have a house," he said, staring into his son's just opening eyes. "It's just outside of the city, but far away from the mansion. It has three bedrooms. One of them was just a regular old bedroom until I painted it sky blue and hung mobiles and put up handprint wallpaper."

He looked up at Marti. "I got a job. I work for the African American Genealogical Research Institute. I'm going to help others to research their past like I've done. I won't make millions, but I won't be relying on blood money to maintain my living."

Marti wrapped her arms around herself and kept her distance.

"I'm trying to tell you I'm ready."

"You're ready!" His comment brought out the rage that she didn't realize had been simmering inside her. "So now that you're ready, everything's okay?" She gnashed her teeth. He looked away.

"Look at me. Do you think I was ready to get pregnant? Ready to be a mother? No! But I got ready."

"Marti—"

"No! This whole thing has been so convenient for you. Sex when you were ready. Come to see me when you got ready. Accept my pregnancy when you got ready. Accept the baby when you got ready. Have us in your life *when you got ready!*"

Kenyon placed their son back into the bassinet.

Marti stared at him incredulously. "Give me one good reason why I shouldn't throw a pot of hot grits on you right now."

He moved closer, the strain of worry deepening lines in his forehead. "Because for the past twenty years, my world has been a dark place. I've spent my entire adult life searching for light, for color, for beauty, for goodness." He stepped closer. "I found it in you."

The closer he got, the more Marti trembled. Finally, he reached out and took her hand. "And I know I'll never become the man I was meant to be without you."

She moved away.

"Let me make you happy, Marti. I know how important family is to you." Kenyon stood in front of her. "We're family now."

He stroked the area beneath her chin. "I know you love me. You have to know that I love you, too."

Tears welled up inside her eyes, but they did not fall. The pain in her chest was too great. "I think you should go now."

Kenyon's stomach twisted into knots. "I can't."

"Please go," she choked the words out.

"I made a promise to myself that I would never leave you again."

"Please . . ."

He pulled her into his arms and held her tight against his chest. "I can't. I can't. I can't. I can't."

Marti broke into sobs and, cradled in each other's embrace, they both let go of the past and forgave.

Dear Readers,

I hope this letter finds you well and happy. Thank you for reading Marti and Kenyon's story. I've always been fascinated by history, and this novel allowed me to explore one of history's best kept secrets. Many of you have been with me since *Destiny's Song*, when Marti and her sisters were first introduced. *True Devotion* is the first in a series of stories I hope to bring you about the Allgood women. Look for Roxanne Allgood's story, *Glory of Love*, in August of 2003. Until then, stay positive, keep your head up, and with hope you will find—or keep—your true devotion.

Peace and blessings!

Kim Louise

MsKimLouise@aol.com
http://www.kimlouise.com

More Sizzling Romance from
Candice Poarch

More Arabesque Romances by
Monica Jackson